# DEATH FALL

H. E Joyce

**Death Fall**

# *Chapter 1*

'YOUR FATHER AND I are going away for a few days. Emily, you're the eldest; you'll have to look after your brother and sister while we're gone,' said Rhona Thorne in the usual brusque manner she adopted towards her children. Emily was fourteen, slight, with shoulder-length brown hair, so dark, it could have been black, and very dark eyes to match. She nodded resignedly, knowing better than to question her mother. Rhona's word was law and inexorably final.

Rhona's second husband, Peter, a thin man who always looked malnourished, was forty-five and five years Rhona's junior. He was not a bad man, merely weak and rather fearful of his strong-willed wife. He would also never dare to question her. He was fond of the children, particularly Emily, none were his own, but fathered by Rhona's former husband, Roger Thorne, who had not been around since Emily was very young. He gave a furtively ironic smile to the children as if to say he was on their side.

If only, he thought, he had the strength to stand up to his wife, just once. He knew it was quite wrong to leave them to fend for themselves for weeks on end while Rhona went in search of her dream in America. And yes, it was nothing but a dream that could never come true, Peter knew it, even if Rhona didn't.

As a singer, her talent was barely enough to perform in the small, seedy clubs in London, yet her ego was such that she felt she could make the big time, and America seemed the obvious choice to fulfil her ambition. Taking her children along would only be an unnecessary burden that she would rather do without. She believed they would not be good for her projected image.

It was true that Rhona always dressed lavishly and had an air of sophistication in her manner. She would also put on her grand accent for people, a far cry from the East London inflexion that was her true accent, at all times addressing friends and just about everyone as "Darling," everyone that is, except her children. For them, there was no such affection shown. She was a narcissist by nature in which everything in her insular world revolved around her, her husband, Peter and her three children had no real place in her life. Rhona would stop at nothing to achieve her ambition of becoming famous. She was deluded, at fifty years old, and of limited talent; her chance, if ever there had been one, of becoming a star had long since passed.

Emily looked down at the floor as she asked, 'How long will you be away mother?'

'I don't know yet, as long as we need to be. that's all *you* need to know,' replied Rhona.

'Where are you going?' asked Emily, looking up from the floor.

'That doesn't concern you either, does it? Anyway, we'll be leaving early tomorrow morning. I'll leave you a little money for food. Now run along and make me a cup of tea and don't ask so many questions.'

Emily turned to her brother and sister. 'Come on, let's go to the kitchen to make mother her tea.' They eagerly followed their elder sister. Simon was a sturdy lad, he was ten years old, the youngest of them, Bridget, was eight and a rather anxious child. The house was a large three-storey Victorian building, in Surbiton, dark and miserable, but with a generous rear garden, tall hedging virtually surrounded the property. Roger

Thorne had inherited the house from his parents some twenty years earlier in 1965.

Emily filled the kettle while her siblings looked on with sullen faces. 'Don't worry, we'll be alright as long as we have each other. I'll look after you,' she said, forcing a smile. The sad truth was that even when their parents were around, she was always the one to take care of the younger ones. Rhona had no time for such things and their stepfather was quite inadequate in standing up to her, and therefore allowed the wanton neglect of the children.

Friends were not permitted to visit the children at home; indeed, they were discouraged from making friends with anyone, not even at their respective schools, which led to a lonely, insular existence for them. Only certain friends of Rhona's were ever allowed at their home, and even then, only when specifically invited.

Emily poured the boiling water into the teapot and put three teaspoons of sugar into a china cup, poured the tea and added the milk and watched the tea change colour, Rhona insisted on the milk going in last. 'I'll take this through to mother. Why don't you two go up to my room, I'll be up in a minute,' said Emily.

'Alright,' replied Simon.

'Don't be long,' said Bridget quietly.

'I won't, don't worry,' said Emily, patting her younger sister's head. They scurried upstairs as Emily placed the teapot, sugar bowl and milk jug on a tray and took it through to the living room where her mother waited. Emily placed the tray down next to her mother and turned to leave.

'Emily, come here.'

Emily returned to where her mother sat. 'Yes mother?'

'I don't want to hear that you've invited anyone around here while I'm away. I won't be happy if you do, you do know that don't you?'

'Yes mother,' said Emily obediently.

'Just keep yourself to yourself, school has broken up for the Christmas holidays, there should be plenty of food in the house, so there's no real need for you to go anywhere. Do you understand?' asked Rhona.

'Yes, I understand mother.'

'Good, I'm glad we understand each other. Alright, you can run along now.'

Emily turned on her heels and went upstairs to her room with Simon and Bridget. She found them, not playing like other children of their age, but solemnly staring out of the bedroom window as if prisoners, unwanted, unloved.

Emily could sense how they were feeling; she felt the same way. Yet she knew she had to remain strong for them. Being the eldest, she had little choice but to play the part of their mother as well as older sister. Besides which, she loved them dearly and would do anything to protect them.

She held back tears as she watched them from the doorway. Composing herself, she entered her room with a forced smile, then sat on her bed. 'What do you want to do kids?' she asked cheerfully.

'Can we play hide and seek?' asked Simon, jumping excitedly on the bed.

'You know mother doesn't like us playing that, Simon. Maybe tomorrow after they've gone,' replied Emily, 'how about snakes and ladders?'

'Oh, alright then,' said Simon, reluctantly.

Bridget was still staring out of the window in a world of her own it seemed. 'Come on Bridget,' said Emily, 'come and play snakes and ladders, you like that game.'

Half-heartedly, Bridget pulled herself away from the window and joined them on the bed. 'Why does mummy hate us so much?' she asked, as Emily set up the board game. Emily hesitated momentarily. 'Of course she doesn't hate us sweetheart, I'm sure she loves us very much. She just – anyway, let's play, shall we? Come on, cheer up, let's see a smile.' In truth, Emily knew her little sister's perception of their mother was correct, Rhona couldn't have cared less about them, or anyone else for that matter; she only cared about herself. But at fourteen years old, what could Emily do, she was powerless. All she could do was to do her best for her siblings and count the days, months and years until she could leave home.

Despite her bleak home life, Emily was doing well at school, excelling in most of her subjects. She desperately wanted to succeed and hopefully go on to complete her education at university. More than anything, she wanted to become a journalist. The question was, when, and if that time came, would her mother allow her to fulfil her dream, or would she keep her a virtual prisoner as she had always done? Only time would tell, and for Emily, that time seemed to be an eternity away.

# *Chapter 2*

IT WAS 7.30AM WHEN Emily woke the next day.

The house seemed eerily quiet. Somehow, much quieter than usual. Emily instinctively went into Bridget's room, she was sleeping peacefully. Emily then peered through Simon's bedroom door, he was also soundly asleep.

Emily and the children slept on the top floor of the house, but normally she could hear her mother's voice or some kind of movement on the ground floor. Today there was not a sound to be heard. She went downstairs, first to the living room, then to the kitchen and dining room, but nobody was there. Returning to the kitchen to make herself a cup of tea, she found a hastily scribbled note on the kitchen surface, there was a twenty-pound note with it. "Left early. Use money only if you have to, Mother."

It came as no surprise that there was no affection shown in the note, Emily was used to that, but Emily thought she could have at least said Goodbye before leaving.  'I wonder where they've gone this time?' she said to herself. She sighed and went about making her tea. There was little point that she could see in waking the others just yet, it was early and the day would seem long enough in any case. And yet, Emily could not help feeling a degree of relief that her mother was not there to order her around. For a while at least, Emily, Simon and Bridget could put aside the lack of love shown by their mother.

Emily sat at the large table in the middle of the kitchen sipping her tea as she stared, deep in thought, out of the window. It was dark, gloomy, and misty. She wondered how long her mother and Peter would be away and where they had gone. Her thoughts wandered to her birth father. She hardly knew him; she was very young when he left. What was he like? And what would he have thought about Rhona's treatment of his children?

She remembered very little about him, yet she seemed to recall he was a kind and gentle man. Emily often thought about him and where he might be. He had never tried to make contact with them after leaving, which she found strange. Maybe when she was older, she would try to find him, she thought.

She continued to daydream as she sipped her tea, thinking about what life held in store for her. Would she fulfil her ambition to attend university? Would she become a journalist, her greatest wish? She longed to be older and have her freedom; it could not come soon enough for her.

After some time, she went upstairs to dress. It was around 9am, after which she woke her brother and sister and returned downstairs to prepare breakfast for them. They joined her in the kitchen soon after.

'Where's Mummy?' asked Bridget.

'Mother and Peter have already gone,' replied Emily. 'So we've got the house all to ourselves, haven't we? It'll be fun,' she said, trying to sound brave.

'Well, if they're not going to be here, can I ask one of my friends around?' asked Simon.

'I don't know, Simon, you know what Mother's like. Let's leave it for now,' said Emily. She empathised with him; they all craved the company of other children. 'If only I knew how long they were going to be away, but if she found out I'd allowed other people here, she'd go mad. I'd rather not think about what she'd do to punish me.'

'Alright,' said a stoic Simon. He knew deep down that Emily was right.

'Would Mummy really punish you?' enquired Bridget timidly. Being such a young age, Bridget was naively loyal to her mother, even though she had been shown no love.

'Don't worry yourself Bridget. Now, come on, eat your breakfast, there's a good girl. We'll have some fun today, you'll see.'

'I hope they never come back,' said Simon with fervour.

'You mustn't say that Simon, especially in front of...' Emily gave a sideways glance towards Bridget.

'Well, I mean it anyway,' said Simon.

'Just eat your breakfast Simon,' said Emily. After a few moments, she said, 'Well, what shall we do today?' in an effort to change the subject.

'I still don't know why I can't ask some of my friends around,' said Simon.

'You know perfectly well, why not,' replied Emily, curtly.

'But mother will never find out,' he said.

'She'd find out somehow, Simon, believe me,' said Emily.

Leaving his breakfast unfinished, Simon stormed out of the kitchen, cursing his mother as he did so and ran upstairs to his room. Emily thought about going after him, but thought that she would give him some time on his own to calm down. Bridget picked at her breakfast, Emily looked at her thoughtfully, she felt for her younger sister intensely. Despite her loyalty to Rhona, it was plain to see that the lack of love or any kind of affection returned was making Bridget an extremely sad little girl. Emily's love for her was clear, but it did not compensate for the absence of a mother's love. Emily worried about her constantly.

This was not the first time that their mother had left them alone, she and Peter had gone away on other occasions for a few days and Emily was only too aware that it amounted to child neglect, but apart from letting someone know what was happening, there seemed little she could do about it. Informing the authorities might mean that she and the children would be taken into care and worse still, split up. She would not allow that to happen.

Her ambition to go to university was fierce. She desperately wanted to make something of her life and escape her mother's clutches. If it ever happened, that was a few years away in any case, but what would happen to Simon and Bridget if she did go away concerned her deeply. They would, of course, be a few years older and maybe better equipped to cope, yet it still worried her.

'What would you like to do today, Bridget?' she asked in a gentle voice.

'I'm going to my room to read.' Bridget was solemn.

'Oh, okay, if that's what you want to do, that's fine,' Emily said, 'I'll probably do the same. Do you want me to bring your lunch up to you later?'

'No thanks.'

'You've got to eat something; you've hardly touched your breakfast.'

'I'll have something later,' said Bridget.

'Okay, fair enough,' said Emily, 'I'll see you later then.' With that, Bridget pushed away her cereal bowl and sloped off to her room.

Emily rose from the breakfast table and tipped away the contents of Bridget's untouched breakfast bowl and washed up. At that moment, she felt extremely lonely and tired of everything. Tired of the insular existence her mother had imposed upon her and her brother and sister. She looked out of the window onto the rear garden, the gloom and mist persisted, which only heightened her sense of sadness and despondency.

She took the two flights of stairs to her room, first of all though, she looked in on Simon. He was stood peering through his window which faced the street below. Being on the top floor, he could see beyond the high hedges that surrounded the house, people, other children walking by. He, like Emily, longed for his freedom and to be able to see his friends whenever he wanted to.

'Are you okay?' asked Emily, as she stood in his doorway.

'No! I'm bored,' he said.

'I know, Simon, I know,' sympathised Emily. 'Do you want to play in the garden?'

'Not really. I want to go out, that's what I want to do.'

'I know you do. Don't you think I want to as well?' said Emily.

'Well why don't we? She won't find out,' he exclaimed with enthusiasm.

'She might, and then what will happen?'

'She won't, I promise. Please Emily, just for a little while?'

'I don't know, I'll think about it. I'm going to my room for a while,' said Emily.

Emily tried to immerse herself in her books on English grammar as she so often did at home, such was her desire to do well at school. However, Simon's plea for a taste of freedom haunted her, she could not concentrate fully and eventually, an hour or so later, she gave up. Suddenly, an air of excitement arose within at the thought of venturing outside the confines of the house. Maybe Simon was right, maybe it was time.

## *Chapter 3*

IT WAS 3PM BEFORE EMILY decided to take the plunge and tell Simon she was prepared to leave the house and take a walk down the street. She knew he would be thrilled at the prospect, as was she. Her body tingled with excitement. Bridget, on the other hand, she thought, might not be so easily persuaded to leave the house, such was her conditioning. She was a nervous child due to the virtual incarceration and lack of love given by her mother.

Simon's bedroom door was closed, Emily knocked gently and after a moment, he shouted, 'Come in.' Emily found him still looking out of his window, she wondered just how long he had been there, staring longingly at the outside world.

Simon turned his head to Emily for a moment as she entered his room, then continued looking out. 'I've been thinking about what you said, Simon,' said Emily.

His head turned quickly this time, 'Have you changed your mind?' he said with excitement.

'Yes, we can go out for a while, not too long mind you, just for a short while, alright?'

Simon rushed to Emily and threw his arms around her. 'Thanks Emily.'

'But when I say it's time to come home, I don't want any argument, do you understand?'

'Yes, I promise,' he replied, excitedly bounding around the room.

'It'll be cold outside, so put a coat on. I'm going to see Bridget,' said Emily.

Emily found Bridget laying on her bed. She had fallen asleep, her book still resting in her hands. 'Bridget, wake up sweetheart,' she said softly. Bridget stirred and opened her eyes. 'Is Mummy back?' she asked, in a half-asleep state.

'No, Bridget, not yet. She said a few days – remember?' said Emily. 'Try to wake up, we're all going for a little walk, that'll be nice, won't it?'

'A walk?' asked Bridget, rubbing her eyes.

'Yes, just a short walk.'

'I'll stay here,' said Bridget.

'Come on sweetheart, it'll be nice to get out of the house for a short while, besides, I promised Simon we would, and I'm not leaving you here alone. Come on, put your shoes and coat on, I promise we won't be out for long, it'll do you good, it'll do us all good,' said Emily.

'But Mummy will be cross if she finds out,' said Bridget.

'She won't find out sweetheart, but even if she did, she wouldn't be cross with you; it's me she would be cross with, so don't worry.'

Although reluctant, Bridget finally agreed, 'Alright, I'll come.'

'Good, I'll see you downstairs in a few minutes then.'

Simon had already put on his coat by the time Emily got downstairs, he was eager to go. 'Where's Bridget?' he asked.

'She'll be down in a minute,' said Emily.

'Hurry up, Bridget!' Simon shouted impatiently up the stairwell.

'There's plenty of time, Simon, don't be in such a hurry,' said Emily.

After a few minutes, Bridget's slow footsteps could finally be heard coming downstairs, eventually arriving in the dark hallway where Emily and Simon waited.

'Okay, Bridget, let's get your hat and coat on, then we'll go,' said Emily, 'better wear some gloves as well, it's going to be cold out there.'

'Where are we going anyway?' asked Bridget.

'I don't know, we'll just walk for a while and see where it takes us. Come on then, let's go,' said Emily.

Although it was an extremely dull day, and already quite dark, Emily was glad she allowed Simon to talk her into venturing out. It felt good to be away from the oppressive atmosphere of the house and seeing her breath in the cold air. It was also an act of defiance against their uncaring mother, it was a good feeling and highly satisfying, she thought.

Walking down the avenue where they lived, they passed other people; it made a pleasant change to see different faces, yet as Emily observed, some gave them rather strange looks as they passed by. It was disquieting, she wondered what it meant. They continued walking until they eventually reached a children's playground. Although the light was fading fast, there were a number of children playing on swings and a slide.

'Do you want to go in?' asked Emily.

'Can we?' said Simon, 'I think I can see my friend from school in there.'

'Well, yes, for a little while then,' Emily said.

Tom spotted Simon as they approached the play area and came over to see him. 'What are you doing here? I've never seen you here before. Do you want to come and join in with the others?'

Simon turned to Emily for approval. She simply nodded with a smile.

Simon wasted no time, he ran off with his friend, heading straight for the slide. It pleased Emily to see him happy, even if for a brief time.

'How about you, Bridget, do you want to play? I see there are some little girls over there about your age,' said Emily.

'No,' was the brief response.

'Why not? Are they from your school? Do you know them?' asked Emily with curiosity.

'Some of them go to my school, they'll just poke fun at me. I'm not playing,' Bridget insisted.

'Okay sweetheart, you don't have to. But why do they poke fun at you?'

'I don't know, they just do,' said Bridget.

'I see,' said Emily. 'Well, look, there's nobody playing on the roundabout, let's just you and I go on it. Come on, Bridget, don't be scared, I'll protect you.'

Bridget reluctantly followed Emily to the roundabout and got on, gripping tightly to the bars as Emily pushed it slowly around. Not used to such things, Bridget looked nervous and held on tightly, not really enjoying the experience. Emily could see the fear, and the tears in her sister's eyes and stopped pushing. As soon as it came to a complete halt, Bridget ran to Emily and flung her arms around her waist.

At that moment, they heard Bridget's contemporaries taunting her, shouting, "Scaredy cat, scaredy cat! Weirdos!"

'Just ignore them sweetheart, they're just being silly.'

That was not the end of it. At almost exactly the same time, a group of slightly older boys started pushing and shoving Simon and his only friend where they played by the slide. Emily rushed over to them, keeping Bridget close to her.

'What's going on here?' barked Emily.

'We know all about you,' said the leader, 'you're the weirdo that lives at, 124 Main Street, aren't you?'

'I don't know what you're talking about, and most likely, neither do you, you silly little boy,' said Emily, angrily.

'Look at you, even your clothes are weird,' said the boy.

Emily did not respond to the taunt. 'Come on kids, we're leaving,' she said. 'We'll be back though, I can promise you that,' she said to the group of bullies. It was twilight as they left the park and walked home. Bridget clutched Emily's hand tightly, as Simon walked in silence just ahead of them. Perhaps, Emily thought, it was not such a good idea for them to have ventured out after all.

On their return, they took off their coats. Emily, as she caught a glimpse of herself in the full-length mirror in the hallway, thought about the words of the boy in the playground regarding their clothes. Much as she hated to admit it, she knew that the cruel words were true. The clothes provided by their mother were old-fashioned, dull and dowdy, not the type of clothes other kids of their age wore in 1984. Emily was never given the opportunity to choose her own clothes like other teenagers. Perhaps that was what the grownups in the street were staring at as well, she thought.

'Why are people so horrible to us?' asked Bridget sombrely.

'Some people are just foolish, Bridget, they're no better than us, so don't worry about it, okay,' said Emily with sympathy. 'I'll get us some dinner; you run along and stop worrying. I'll call you when dinner's ready.'

When they were alone, Emily turned her attention to Simon. 'Are you alright Simon?'

'I suppose so,' he said.

'Do you and Bridget get bullied at your school too?' she asked.

'All the time,' said Simon. 'Tom is the only one who doesn't, he's the only friend I've got. He's always asking if I can go to his house to play or if he can come here, I have to make excuses every time, it's not fair.'

'Well, maybe we can do something about that; at least while Mother's away,' said Emily.

'Really?'

'Yes, really.'

'Thanks Emily. When?'

'It'll have to be soon; we don't know when Mother will be back. She could be back any day,' said Emily. 'Okay, I'll call you when dinner's ready.'

'Have you got any friends at your school, Emily?' asked Simon.

'Yes,' said Emily, with a faint smile, 'like you, just one. She's a swot the same as me.'

'What's a swot?'

'Someone who likes to read a lot and learn things,' said Emily.

'Well, why don't you ask her around as well?' asked Simon.

'It's a thought, Simon, who knows, I might just do that.'

# Chapter 4

IT WAS SUNDAY MORNING. Emily woke late at 9am to find Bridget fast asleep next to her. She had crept into her bed at some point during the night. Emily was blissfully unaware. She did not disturb her young sister as she got out of bed. It was when Bridget slept that she looked most peaceful. It was hardly surprising to Emily that during her waking hours, she seemed like a troubled soul.

The room was cold. Emily put on her dressing gown and slippers and quietly made her way down the stairs to the kitchen. Looking out of the window, she could see that there was a heavy frost. The grass, hedge and trees in the substantial garden were thick with frost and looked quite beautiful, she thought. There was little heating in the house, so Emily lit two gas hob rings to warm the kitchen. She filled the kettle and placed it on one of the gas rings in order to make herself some tea.

As she sat waiting for the kettle to boil, she wondered just how long her mother and Peter would be away this time and whether it would be safe to keep her promise to Simon about inviting a friend to the house. It was only the second day, though, and they were usually longer than that when they went away, she thought. The kettle began to whistle, snapping her out of her contemplative state.

She poured her tea and returned to the kitchen table to think. Emily was confident Simon and his friend could amuse themselves somehow, and as for her own friend, well, they would probably end up revising their schoolwork. There was no television to watch; the only one in the house was in their mother's room, and that was strictly out of bounds to the children.

The sound of footsteps coming down the stairs was instantly recognisable as Simon's; he entered the kitchen bleary-eyed and, in a half-asleep state, sat down opposite Emily.

'Would you like a cup of tea?' asked Emily. Simon shook his head with a wide yawn.

'Did you sleep okay?' she asked.

He did not answer; instead, he asked, 'So when can Tom come around then?'

Emily hesitated for a moment. 'Well, I suppose today might be the safest day – if his parents let him,' she said.

With that, he suddenly woke up. 'Today? Thanks, Emily, I'll phone him now.'

'Well, leave it for a little while. It's Sunday, and his parents might still be in bed, phone him at 10 o'clock, okay.'

'Oh, alright,' said Simon, a little deflated.

'Come on, cheer up; it's only a short while to wait,' said Emily reassuringly. "I'm going to phone my friend later as well. The only thing that worries me is that we might have our friends, but what about Bridget? I'm worried she'll feel left out.'

'She can play with me and Tom if she wants to,' said Simon.

'That's nice of you, Simon, but you know how she is—she may not want to. Anyway, it wouldn't be the same as having her own friend. Now, you'd better get dressed, and I'll get you some breakfast, and after that, you can phone Tom.'

Simon did as Emily suggested and ran up the stairs. Emily finished her tea and followed soon after, getting washed and dressed as quickly as she could. The bathroom was as cold as the ice outside.

It was around mid-day when Emily's friend, Patricia, arrived at the doorstep, accompanied by her mother. Tom, Simon's friend, had arrived an hour earlier and was upstairs with Simon.

'Hello, Emily,' said Patricia's mother cheerfully. She was a pleasant lady in her late forties with blonde hair and a kind face.

'Hello, Mrs Parker,' said Emily. 'Hello, Patricia.'

'Hi Emily,' replied Patricia.

Mrs Parker peered into the grey, drab hallway. 'Is your mum home?' she said with a smile.

'Uh, no, not at the moment. She just popped out for a little while,' said Emily nervously.

'Oh, okay, well tell her I'll come and collect Patricia at about 5 o'clock if that's alright?' said Mrs Parker.

'Oh, yes, I'll tell her. Thank you,' said Emily.

'Okay. Well, I'll leave you to it then, have fun.'

Emily closed the door, and the two girls smiled at each other and hugged. 'I'm really glad you could come,' said Emily.

'Me too,' said Patricia. I've never been to your house before. Maybe you'll be able to come to mine sometime.'

'I'd like that Pat, but I'm not sure if mother would allow it,' said Emily.

'Well, if she's finally allowing friends to come here, then why wouldn't she allow you to come to my house?'

'I'm afraid I wasn't honest with your mum,' said Emily, 'the truth is, mother is away at the moment. I don't know for how long, but she must never find out you were here, you must promise not to tell your mum about this. If my mother ever found out – '

'Don't worry, Emily, I won't say a word. Where is she anyway?'

'I don't know. She didn't tell me where she was going or for how long.'

'Has she done this before?' asked Patricia.

'Yes, but it's only a few days here and there. I manage.'

'But you shouldn't have to. It's not right, Emily.'

'There's nothing I can do about it, Pat. Come on, let's forget about it. Here, I'll take your coat.'

Patricia shivered. 'It's freezing in here, Emily; don't you have any heating?'

'She must have turned the heating off when she left,' said Emily, 'I suppose we're used to it. Come on, let's go up to my room.'

Simon and Tom rushed past them on the stairs, almost knocking Emily over. 'We're going out in the garden to play, alright, Emily?' said Simon excitedly.

'Alright, but put your coats on,' said Emily.

'So, Simon has a friend around as well,' said Patricia.

It was he who persuaded me I felt sorry for him. And I thought, if he can have a friend around, why not me as well. 'In for a penny" and all that,' said Emily.

'What about Bridget?' asked Patricia.

'Poor little thing, she doesn't have any friends at all. We'll look in on her.'

Emily peered through Bridget's bedroom door. She was lying on her bed reading. 'Are you alright, sweetheart?' asked Emily.

Bridget nodded but said nothing. 'Can I come in for a minute?' asked Emily.

'If you want to.'

'This is Patricia, a friend of mine,' said Emily.

'Hello, Bridget,' said Patricia.

'Hello,' said Bridget timidly.

'Would you like to come with us to my room?' asked Emily.

'No, I'm reading my book,' Bridget replied.

'Oh, okay, that's fine. But join us later if you want to,' Emily said gently.

The two girls went to Emily's room. It was spacious like all the rooms in the old house, but the wallpaper was old and faded, the carpet threadbare and the furnishings, such as they were, old-fashioned. There was a bookshelf which had seen much better days, crammed with books of all descriptions, they had all been read at least twice by Emily.

'Emily, I hope you don't mind me saying this, but the life you're all leading isn't normal. I know you've hinted at it before, but I didn't realise how bad it really was – it's not right,' said Patricia.

'I know Pat.'

'You're only fourteen yourself; you shouldn't be left alone for days on end and be expected to look after your brother and sister.'

'I know you're right, ofcourse I do. But what can I do?'

'There *are* people you can contact, you know,' said Patricia.

'I can't risk it. I can't risk us three being split up. Promise me you won't mention any of this to anyone, not even your parents. Promise me!' said Emily.

'Yes, I suppose,' said Patricia.

'Say it! Say you promise.'

'I promise.'

It was almost dark by 3pm. Emily and Patricia joined the two boys out in the rear garden. The frost had not dissipated all day.

'What are you two up to?' said Emily. They appeared to be staring at an area of the garden with interest. 'What is it? What are you looking at?'

'Look!' said Simon, 'There's a strange sort of outline in the frost,' he said.

Emily and Patricia leaned over to examine the area. 'Yes,' said Emily, 'you're right, but it's nothing, probably just where the earth has been dug at some point. Or I suppose it could be where our grandparents buried their dog, I know they had one.'

The time arrived too soon for Emily when Patricia's mother would be coming back. The two girls spent their last minutes talking about how they both looked forward to the time when they would go to university together. This was especially true for Emily, and yet, for the moment, it was pure fantasy. The doorbell rang. Emily's heart sank as she opened the door to find Patricia's mother standing there. The time had gone all too quickly. 'Hello, Emily. Is Patricia ready to come home?'

'Yes, I think so. I'll get her -she's in the kitchen,' said Emily reluctantly.

'Can I come in while you get her? It's very cold out here,' said Mrs Parker.

'Uh, yes, okay.'

'Where's your mum? I've never met her before.'

'Um, she's not back yet, but I'm sure she won't be long now,' said Emily.

'Oh, really?' said Mrs Parker curiously.

As Emily went into the kitchen, Patricia's mother shivered in the hallway. It was barely any warmer than outside. Out of curiosity, she made her way to the kitchen, peering in the living room as she went.

'It's a shame your mum and dad aren't here, Emily; I would like to have met them. They won't be long, you said.'

'No, they shouldn't be,' replied Emily cautiously. Patricia looked awkwardly at Emily for a moment.

'And this must be your brother?'

'Yes, Simon.'

'Hello Simon,' said Mrs Parker, 'and Patricia tells me you have a younger sister as well.'

'Yes, she's upstairs,' said Emily.

'Well, we'd better be going. You must come to our house sometime, Emily,' said Mrs Parker.

'Thank you, I'd like that very much.'

'Okay then. Come on then, Patricia, let's get you home. Are you sure you're alright, Emily and that your parents will soon be home?' asked Mrs Parker.

'Oh yes, they'll be back soon, I'm sure of it,' said Emily.

'Well, you have our telephone number. Call if you need anything – anything at all,' said Mrs Parker. 'Well, bye for now, Emily, take care.'

'I'll phone you tomorrow,' said Patricia as she and her mother left the house.

'Okay, bye, thanks for coming round,' said Emily. She closed the door, sad that her friend had gone yet relieved that the questions from Patricia's mother had ended. She had seemed suspicious that all was not as it should be – and, as Emily knew, it wasn't.

## *Chapter 5*

One week later

THERE HAD BEEN NO form of contact from Emily's mother since she and Peter had gone away, which, according to Rhona, would only be for a few days. A week had passed, and there was no sign of them returning. Christmas was just a week or so away. Not that it would make a great deal of difference to Emily and her siblings. Rhona didn't like Christmas; it was never celebrated in their house; she did not give presents to any of her children.

In that respect, Rhona would not be missed if she was still away by that time. In fact, Emily secretly hoped they would not be home by Christmas, she thought she could at least then try to make Christmas something a little special for the kids. It was not much, yet Emily was already making plans on how to best use the twenty pounds her mother had left for, as Rhona put it, essential use only.

As Emily lay on her bed reading, she wondered where her mother was. She also felt an uncharacteristic anger that she should be left in charge of the house and children for so long that a great sadness came over her. How dare Rhona think she could leave them for so long and get away with it,  she thought. She considered reporting Rhona to the authorities, but that would only mean facing the very thing she wished to avoid – the children being split up.

It was only 11am, and it looked like it was yet another long, boring day. Emily rose from her bed wearily, went downstairs to the kitchen and looked in the refrigerator, the food supply was dwindling fast; she knew she would have to do something about it that day and made the decision to go shopping. She shouted for Simon and Bridget to come downstairs. After calling a second time, they duly arrived in the kitchen.

'First of all, would you like some hot chocolate?' asked Emily. They both answered positively. 'Secondly,' said Emily, beginning to prepare their drinks, 'I think we should take a little walk down to the supermarket to get some food. Would you like that?'

The answer, of course, was a resounding "Yes" from Simon and the usual silence from Bridget. She was always more content staying in her room.

'That's settled then; we'll go as soon as we've finished our drinks,' said Emily. It was half a mile to the supermarket and a few other shops, well away from the residential area, and it was cold and misty. They walked at a brisk pace, their breath visible with every step. For Emily and Simon, it was an unheard-of treat, not so for Bridget, who would have much instead stayed at home.

The supermarket entrance had a highly decorated Christmas tree welcoming shoppers, lively Christmas music played, and the shop was crowded with people buying gifts and festive food for the big day itself. Emily and Simon smiled at one another with excitement at seeing so much life outside their dull existence. Emily looked at the twenty pound note she had. She would have to spend it wisely, she thought.

The first priority was food, hopefully, with enough spare money to buy something special for Christmas day. They headed for the food section, where Emily searched for a small turkey or, if she could not afford it, a small chicken instead. After some searching, she managed to find a tiny frozen turkey crown that was affordable, followed by some vegetables and stuffing. She also bought some cheap tinned food to see them through for a while. Emily had carefully totted up how much she had spent so far and found she would still have a few pounds left. She escorted Simon and Bridget to the section that had sweets.

'Will you stay here both of you and choose yourself some sweets? I won't be far away and I won't be long. Don't wander off, will you?' said Emily.

'Can we really have some sweets?' asked Simon.

'Only if you stay here while I'm gone, okay?'

'We will,' said Simon eagerly.

Emily wandered through the store until she found a small section that sold toys, books and wrapping paper. She eventually decided on a small teddy bear for Bridget and a plastic space gun for Simon, which lit up when the trigger was pulled. It wasn't much, but it was better than they had been used to. At least, she hoped so. She calculated there would be just seventy-five pence left, just enough to buy the kids a few sweets as she had promised. She made her way back to them through the crowds of people. It made her quite sad seeing complete families out together and all the smiling faces.

Her sadness turned to panic and not without a degree of embarrassment as she approached the children. Patricia's mother was talking to them, she had a look of concern about her. Emily, with her shopping basket, got closer. Patricia's mother looked at her and smiled, which made Emily slightly less nervous.

'Hello Emily,' said Mrs Parker, 'doing some shopping?'

'Uh, yes,' said Emily.

Mrs Parker stealthily peered into the shopping basket. 'Doesn't your mum usually do the shopping?' she said.

'Yes, usually,' said Emily.

'I see,' she said suspiciously, 'look, why don't you come to our house tomorrow? I know Patricia is eager for you to come. You can bring Simon and Bridget with you. They can play with Steven. He's about their age.'

'Well, I… I don't want to be any trouble, Mrs Parker.'

'You won't be. Come at lunchtime, say about 12.30. Better still, I'll get my husband and Patricia to come and pick you up in the car.'

'Well – if you're sure, Mrs Parker, that would be really nice, thank you,' said Emily.

'Of course I'm sure, it'll be lovely to have you, and by the way, please, call me Gwen.'

'Oh, alright.'

'Okay, Emily, we'll see you tomorrow then. Patricia *will* be pleased. She was going to invite you around anyway. Bye for now, then.'

'Bye, and thank you – Gwen,' said Emily.

Gwen Parker began to leave the children, but stopped and turned to Emily once again. 'Oh, have you finished your shopping, Emily?'

'Yes, almost, I just need to buy some sweets,' said Emily.

'Well, would you like a lift home after you've done that? It's quite a long walk home for you,' said Gwen.

'Oh, no, that's alright, we'll enjoy the walk, but thank you.'

'Well, if you're sure?' said Gwen.

'Oh yes, we'll be fine, thanks.'

'Okay, well, take care, and we'll see you tomorrow then.'

'Yes, I'll look forward to it,' said Emily.

*Chapter 6*

SUNDAY MORNING ARRIVED. Emily was excited to at last be visiting Patricia in her own home, yet also, deep down, she had a feeling of dread that Patricia's mother might ask her awkward questions. If that was the case, how would she deal with it, she wondered? Nevertheless, she was looking forward to seeing her friend very much.

There was also lunch to look forward to – a rare treat. Christmas was only four days away now, and this year was looking like the best one that she, Simon and Bridget had ever had. She was glad her mother was away. Emily could cook; she'd had to learn fast, and at least this year, they could have a turkey dinner, and she would be able to give some small presents to her siblings, something they'd never experienced before.

There was, however, a problem that suddenly hit Emily. She had spent all of the twenty pounds her mother had given her, all except for a few pence. What would they do when the food ran out, she wondered? It was a concern, but she was determined not to allow it to ruin her day – not for one moment.

'Come on, kids, Patricia and her dad will soon be here,' shouted Emily from her bedroom.

'I don't want to go,' Bridget shouted back. Emily went to Bridget's room to find her lying on her bed.

'Come on Bridget, you'll have a nice time while we're there, you'll see. Now come here and let me brush your hair. You can't stay in your room forever. It'll do you good to get out,' insisted Emily.

'We went out yesterday,' protested Bridget.

'I know, but that doesn't mean we can't go out again today, now, does it?'

Bridget fidgeted while Emily gently brushed her hair. 'When's mummy coming home?' she asked.

'I'm sorry, Bridget, I don't know the answer to that,' said Emily, 'but I'm sure it won't be too long,' she added sympathetically.

'Okay, that's your hair done. Now let's go downstairs; Patricia will be here soon.'

Begrudgingly, Bridget slid off the bed and followed Emily downstairs, quickly followed by Simon.

Ten minutes later, Patricia knocked on the front door. It was beginning to hail, and the cold was bitter. She did not have to wait long before Emily opened the door. The girls greeted each other warmly.

'Glad you could come, Emily. I'm guessing your mother isn't back yet?' said Patricia.

'No, she isn't,' replied Emily.

'You've got to do something, Emily. You can't go on like this, it isn't right.'

'Oh, she'll turn up eventually. She always does,' said Emily.

'Anyway, shall we go? Dad's waiting in the car,' said Patricia.

'Sure, come on, kids,' instructed Emily. Bridget looked suitably unimpressed, whereas Simon was excited at the thought of making a new friend.

'Come on, Bridget, cheer up; you never know, you might just enjoy yourself; anyway, it'll do you good to get out for a while,' said Emily as they left the house. Bridget looked up at her sceptically.

Alan Parker was leaning against the roof of his Vauxhall Cavalier, looking along the path towards the house. Other than that small gap, the house was barely visible from the road with the high hedges that surrounded it. 'You must be Emily?' he chirped.

'Yes, hello, Mr Parker.'

'And your brother and sister?'

'Yes, Simon and Bridget,' said Emily.

'Well, I'm pleased to meet you all. Hope you're hungry, Gwen's cooked a lovely roast for lunch.'

'Mum does a great roast,' said Patricia.

'Oh lovely, yes, I'm starving,' Emily said.

'Hop in then,' said Mr Parker.

They drove the short distance to Patricia's home; it was the first time she had been in a car for as long as she could remember. Moreover, she could not remember ever having visited anyone else's home before. It filled her with excitement. Yet still, she dreaded awkward questions about her mother and her home life.

As they drew up the driveway to Patricia's home, Emily marvelled at the Christmas lights adorning the outside of the house and also the neighbouring properties. They exuded love and joy; it was a far cry from the lifelessness of her own home.

'Here we are then,' said Mr Parker.

'I love your decorations,' said Emily.

'Oh, thank you, Emily. We do this every Christmas, don't we, Patricia?'

'Yes, Dad,' Patricia replied, she could not help noticing a hint of sadness in Emily's eyes.

'Come on, Emily, let's go in.'

As they entered the brightly lit entrance hall, the wonderful smell of a special lunch emanated from the kitchen. Emily and Simon glanced at one another and smiled.

'Come on, Emily, let's go and see if lunch is ready,' said Patricia as they hung up their coats.

'Okay, said Emily.' Bridget stuck to Emily like glue as they entered the very modern kitchen.

'Hello Emily, hello Bridget, hello Simon, it's nice to see you. Lunch is almost ready. Are you hungry, Bridget?' Gwen Parker asked, sensing the girl was not at ease. Bridget simply looked around, not answering.

'I'm sorry, Mrs Parker, she's very shy,' said Emily.

'Oh, that's quite alright, Emily. We don't stand on ceremony in this house,' said Gwen, 'Why don't you take everyone through to the dining room, Patricia? I'll be serving lunch in just a few minutes. Oh, and call Steven down, will you? He's in his room.'

Emily found the atmosphere relaxed and easygoing - such a difference from what she and her siblings were used to. The dining room was highly decorated. A small Christmas tree sat in one corner of the room, and their dog, a golden retriever, lay by the fire.

'You and Bridget sit next to me; Simon can sit next to Steven,' said Patricia. They took their seats at the table. Then Steven came in and stared at Simon for a moment before speaking.

'I've seen you at school, haven't I?'

'Yes, probably,' said Simon.

'I'm Steven, what's your name?'

'Simon.'

'Is she your sister?' Steven said, pointing to Bridget, 'I've seen her too, I think. Do you want to play after lunch?'

'Yes, okay,' Simon replied eagerly.

At that moment, Gwen Parker entered the room carrying a joint of roast beef; she set it on the table and returned to the kitchen to bring dishes of vegetables with the assistance of her husband. 'Are you all getting along?' she asked rhetorically, taking her seat.

Alan Parker began to carve the meat into thick slices. Emily and Simon looked on in awe as the juices flowed from the succulent beef. He asked Patricia to pass the plates along one by one and placed a generous serving on each.

'Help yourselves to vegetables,' he said, directing his speech to Emily, Simon and Bridget in particular.

'It looks delicious,' said Emily.

'Well, tuck in, there's plenty of it,' said Gwen.

As the meal progressed, the atmosphere was one of joy and laughter until the moment that Emily dreaded came, the questions about her mother.

'How is your mum? Is she well?' asked Gwen.

'Uh, yes, she's okay,' said Emily hesitantly.

'Patricia tells me she's a singer.'

Emily, feeling a degree of embarrassment, simply replied, 'Yes.'

'That must be interesting work. Where does the singer sing?' asked Gwen.

'Um, I'm not really sure.'

'Oh, okay. It doesn't matter anyway,' said Gwen. She sensed Emily was ill at ease with the questions and quickly changed the subject. 'Aren't you hungry, Bridget?' she asked.

She shook her head; her food had hardly been touched.

'Come on, Bridget, eat something,' Emily whispered.

'I don't want to,' Bridget exclaimed loudly, putting down her knife and fork.

'I'm really sorry,' said Emily, 'I can never get her to eat much.'

'*You* can never get her to eat much? What about your mum?'

'Well, I – '

'Anyway, don't worry about it. Maybe she'll have a bite to eat later,' said Gwen.

'Yes, maybe,' Emily said, relieved that the line of conversation had ended.

Gwen was growing more and more concerned about the children. There was something, she thought that was not quite right. She began to clear away the plates after lunch, ready for washing up.

'Can I help?' said Emily.

'No, dear, you go with Patricia and do whatever you want to do. Oh, before that, maybe you'd like to phone your mum and ask her if you can stay for tea. Would you like that?'

'Are you sure? We don't want to be in any trouble,' said Emily.

'I'm quite sure Patricia will be glad of your company, and so will I. Go on, phone her, the phone is in the hall.'

'Well, if you're sure. Thank you, Mrs Parker.'

'Now, what did I say? Call me Gwen. I'll leave you to it then.'

Emily waited until the coast was clear before picking up the receiver, pressing some numbers and speaking so that Gwen could hear in the kitchen.

'Yes, she said it was okay,' Emily said, entering the kitchen again.

'Oh good,' said Gwen.

'What do you want to do?' asked Patricia.

'Anything you say.'

'Well, I'll show you my room, I've got a telly in there if you want to watch something?'

'That sounds good,' said Emily.

Once they had gone upstairs, Gwen dried her hands and went into the hallway. Picking up the receiver, she pressed the redial button. It rang a few times before someone answered. Gwen immediately recognised the voice as being that of a friend she had called earlier that day. 'Is that you, Kate?'

'Yes, is that you, Gwen?'

'Yes, I'm sorry, Kate, I think I must have pressed the redial by mistake.'

'That's okay. Are we still on for lunch after Christmas?'

'Of course, we're looking forward to it. Anyway, I'll let you go. See you soon, bye.'

Gwen hung up; she was stunned. There seemed little doubt in her mind that Emily had not called her mother; something was not right. She returned to the washing-up.

'There's something very wrong about that family, Alan,' she said.

'What do you mean? What family?'

'Emily's!' she didn't call her mother; she must have pretended to phone her.'

'Well, you know what kids are like, I'm sure it's nothing,' said Alan.

'I'm afraid I don't agree, and I intend to find out what's going on.'

*Chapter 7*

AFTER TEA, GWEN WENT up to Patricia's room. A film was just finishing on the television, and Bridget was with them too. She was not familiar with television and had been engrossed in the film, lying on her stomach on the floor, her face resting in her hands as she looked up at the screen.

They all looked round to Gwen as she poked her head through the doorway. 'I'm sorry to break things up,' she said, 'but it's getting late. Perhaps Emily needs to go home.'

'Does she have to mum?' asked Patricia.

'I'm sure her mum will be wondering where she's got to. Isn't that right, Emily?' Gwen said.

'Uh, yes, I suppose we ought to go really.'

'Well, come down when you're ready,' said Gwen. She closed the bedroom door and left.

'I wish you'd let me tell Mum what's going on,' said Patricia. 'Why don't you stay the night? You've got nothing to go home for, and Mum won't mind.'

'I'd really like to Pat, you know I would, but I really should go home, just in case my mother comes home herself. I'm taking a risk being here at all. I've told you what she's like. And please promise me you won't say anything to your mum and dad?'

'I promised once before, Emily, but I'm not sure how much longer I can keep that promise,' said Patricia.

'Please try Pat, for mine and the children's sake.'

'Okay,' said Patricia, sombrely.

Emily hugged her tightly. 'Thank you, Pat, you're a great friend,' she said.

'Am I? I'm not so sure, Emily.'

'Don't be silly, of course you are. Well, I suppose I'd better be going.'

Simon was already downstairs with Steven; he was unenthusiastically putting on his coat in the hallway along with Patricia's parents.

'I'm coming along as well,' said Gwen.

Emily felt a tinge of panic. Did Gwen suspect something? She wondered.

Emily and the other children all squeezed into the back seat of the car. Gwen Parker, in the front passenger seat, turned to Emily. 'I hope you've all had a nice time today, Emily. You must come again soon.'

'Yes, we had a great time. Thank you for having us,' said Emily.

'It was an absolute pleasure,' said Gwen. 'What are you doing on Christmas day? I suppose it'll be just you and your parents, will it?'

'Uh, yes, I suppose so,' Emily replied. Was Gwen attempting to catch Emily off-guard?

'Well, that'll be nice, won't it?'

'Mum!' Patricia interjected.

'Yes, dear?'

'Oh, nothing, it doesn't matter.' Gwen looked at her daughter curiously.

The first thing that struck Gwen as they pulled up outside Emily's house was that it was in complete darkness. There was not a light to be seen. 'I'll walk Emily and the children to the house,' said Gwen, 'You and Steven stay in the car with Dad. I'll only be a moment.'

As Gwen walked with Emily, Simon and Bridget along the path that led to the front door, she felt a chill down her spine and a sense of great apprehension.

As they reached the front door, Emily took out her door key. 'Well, thank you again for having us. We'll be alright from here,' she said almost dismissively.

'I think I'll come in with you until you've turned on some lights,' said Gwen.

'There's no need, really,' said Emily, inserting the key in the lock.

'Nevertheless, I'd feel much better if I came in with you,' said Gwen insistently.

Emily hesitated but unwillingly turned the key and entered the darkened hallway.

'Why is it so dark in here? Where are your parents?' asked Gwen.

Saying the first thing that entered her head, Emily replied, 'Uh, I suppose they're in bed.'

'In bed? But it's not even 7 o'clock,' said Gwen.

'Um.'

Gwen took it upon herself to make her way slowly down the gloomy passageway, she fumbled for a light switch in the living room, then the kitchen, then the landing. She made her way up the stairs, which creaked heavily underfoot until she reached the landing. She tried each bedroom door in turn. The house was freezing and she felt the same chill up her spine again as she tried the final door. Turning the light on, it was clearly her mother's room, yet she was not there. The children were clearly at home alone.

She rushed downstairs, glad to get away, she found the atmosphere of the whole house unnerving and eerie.

'Your parents aren't here, are they, Emily? How long have you been living alone like this? I suspected something wasn't right when I bumped into you shopping for groceries. How long, Emily? The truth now.'

'It's not what it looks like, Mrs Parker,' said Emily.

'I know exactly what it looks like. Why are you protecting them? This is child neglect, Emily. How long?'

'A week or so, but – '

'Do you know where they are?'

'No, not exactly.'

'Well, have you heard from them?'

The silence from Emily told Gwen all she needed to know. 'You poor children,' she said, placing her arm around Emily, with tears forming. 'I'm not going to leave you here alone. You're coming home with us,' she said.

'We can't,' said Emily, 'what if she comes home and we're not here?'

'Why? What would happen? Would they punish you? Anyway, we'll cross that bridge when we come to it. Now, grab your toothbrushes and anything else you want to bring; we're leaving right now.'

'What's going on?' asked Alan Parker as they all returned to the car.

'I'll explain everything later,' said Gwen, clearly upset. 'Emily and the children are coming to stay with us for a while.'

'That's great,' said Patricia excitably. 'Oh, I take it, you know?' she said more soberly.

'Yes, I think I do,' said Gwen.

There was no such excitement from Emily, however. She was, for the time being, distraught at what would become of her and the young ones. She particularly worried about Bridget being split from her, Emily had become something of a mother figure to her. She was a timid and nervous child; Emily could not bear to think of what it would do to her if the worst should happen.

Gwen and her husband were kind-hearted people who meant well, Emily knew that, and yet, she could not help feeling anxious about the unfamiliar future that might lay ahead.

As they drove back, Emily whispered, 'You didn't tell your mum anything, did you?'

'I promised I wouldn't, and I didn't,' whispered Patricia. 'She must have guessed somehow. The clues were there. Cheer up, Emily, my mum and dad wouldn't let anything bad happen to you.'

They shortly arrived back at Patricia's home. Emily looked apprehensive, and Simon and Bridget were slightly bewildered at what was happening.

'Okay, Patricia,' said Alan Parker, 'can you all go upstairs for a while? Your mum and I need to talk.'

Gwen and Alan went into the kitchen. Alan poured two glasses of wine and handed one to Gwen. 'So, what's going on, Gwen?' he asked.

'Those poor kids have been living alone for over a week. They don't even know where their mother and stepfather are or how long they're going to be away. I couldn't leave them on their own, Alan. I just couldn't.'

'Good God, no, of course you couldn't. But we'll have to report it to the authorities. You do know that, don't you?'

'I know, but not just yet, okay. You don't mind them staying here for a while, do you?'

'No, of course not, but – '

Gwen took a large sip of her wine. 'I couldn't bear to see them placed into a care home over the Christmas period. Let's leave reporting it for now, if that's okay with you?'

'I suppose so,' he said, 'immediately after Christmas, though, otherwise we might find ourselves in trouble.'

'Agreed. But I really want to find out more about what on earth has been going on. How could she just leave them on their own like that? The house was freezing cold. The woman should be locked up, said Gwen furiously.'

'I agree, but we don't want to end up being locked up ourselves for kidnapping.'

'I understand what you're saying. After Christmas, then, as agreed,' said Gwen. 'I'd better go up and make some sleeping arrangements,' she said, draining the last drop of wine from her glass.

'Okay darling, I'm going to pour myself another glass – I think I need it,' said Alan. 'Shall I pour you another?'

'Oh, yes, please, I think I need it too. That house gave me the creeps.'

# Chapter 8

THE NEXT DAY, Gwen rose early following a restless night. She poked her head into Patricia's room; all three girls were sleeping soundly. Emily shared Patricia's bed while Bridget slept on a fold-away bed that Alan had got down from the attic room.

She crept over to Patricia and gave her a gentle shake of her arm. Patricia stirred and slowly opened her eyes. Gwen gestured with a finger to her lips so Patricia would not disturb Emily. 'Come downstairs, I need to speak to you,' whispered Gwen. Patricia rubbed her eyes and, in a half-asleep state, nodded.

Gwen went to the kitchen to make some coffee and waited for the arrival of Patricia. She came downstairs almost immediately, but she knew what was coming her way.

'Sorry to disturb you, love. You can go back to bed in a minute if you want to. I just need to talk to you about Emily and the children. You don't mind, do you?'

'No, mum, I suppose not.'

'I'm not going to be angry or anything, but I need to ask; did you have any idea what was going on with Emily?'

'Well, yes, but she made me promise not to tell anyone, not even you and Dad. You've always told me not to make promises if you couldn't keep them. I'm sorry, mum.'

'I know I have, love, but there are certain times when – Anyway, I'm not cross with you. Just tell me now everything you know.'

'All I can tell you, mum, is that Emily's mum often leaves them on their own, but never as long as she has this time.'

'Is that everything?' asked Gwen. 'What I mean is, why is it that we have never seen her out before? I mean, she's never been around here before, and you've never been to her house either. Not until this past week anyway.'

'No, her mother won't let them out except to go to school.'

'So they've been virtual prisoners in their own home,' said Gwen.

Patricia nodded.

'This just gets worse and worse.'

'I'm sorry I didn't tell you this before, Mum. It's just that Emily's terrified of them all being split up and going into different homes. I did try to tell her to let someone know what was happening, but she just wouldn't.'

'It's alright, darling,' said Gwen, giving Patricia a hug, 'none of this is your fault.'

'What's going to happen to them?' asked Patricia solemnly.

'I don't know. Dad says we have to report it to the authorities – I don't want to, but I suppose he's right. We have to do something.'

'Why can't they stay with us?' said Patricia.

'I'd like them to, believe me, but I'm afraid it's not that simple, Patricia.'

'It's not fair, poor Emily,' said Patricia.

'Well, just enjoy the time we have with them. Your dad and I have already agreed that they'll stay with us over Christmas,' said Gwen.

'I suppose that's something.'

'I tell you what, I'll go to the shops today and get them some Christmas presents. Poor kids have got to have something to unwrap,' said Gwen, lightening the mood.

'Now, you'd better go back up to your room. If she's awake, she'll wonder where you are.'

'Okay, mum.'

Patricia ran upstairs, passing her father, who was going down. 'Morning, sweetheart, you're up early. It's only 7.30.'

'Mum wanted to talk to me, but I'm going back to bed now.'

Alan would generally have been on his way to work in his office in the city by now, but. He had booked some days off in the lead-up to Christmas. 'Morning, Darling,' he said to Gwen as he entered the kitchen, 'I heard you get up. Couldn't you sleep?'

'No, not really; in fact, I hardly slept a wink all night,' said Gwen, 'Coffee?'

'Oh, yes, please,' he said. 'Why couldn't you sleep? Worrying about the kids, I suppose.'

'Yes. In fact, I've just been talking to Patricia about them. Apparently, she has always known about their mother leaving them on their own, and it's not the first time it's happened either.'

'Well, it's a clear case of child neglect, isn't it? And all the more reason why the authorities need to be informed.'

'Yes, I know, I know. But Patricia said that Emily is terrified of them all being parted.'

'Well, let's hope that doesn't happen, but at the end of the day, there isn't much we can do about it, is there?' said Alan with his usual logic.

'Isn't there?' said Gwen, handing him a mug of coffee.

'Nothing that I can see,' said Alan, 'hold on, are you suggesting - ?'

'We can afford it, Alan, and it would be good for Patricia. She's always said how much she'd love to have a sister. It'd be good for Steven as well to have a brother.'

'Yes, that might be the case, but if you're suggesting adoption? That's a big step,' said Alan.

'At least think about it, Alan; that's all I ask.'

'I think you're getting a little ahead of yourself. We haven't even reported this yet.'

'I know I may be jumping the gun a little, but just consider the possibility for now, preferably without your logical hat on,' said Gwen.

'Yes, alright darling, I promise I'll think about it,' said Alan reluctantly.

'Thank you, darling,' said Gwen, giving him a kiss on the cheek. 'Oh, I'm going out today to do some last-minute shopping. Is that okay?'

'Yes, of course, I'll look after the kids.'

Around 11 o'clock, Gwen set off on her shopping trip. But before that, she drove to Emily's house to drop the note she had hastily scribbled to Emily's mother. As a matter of course, she knocked on the door, there was no answer, so she dropped the note through the letterbox and continued her journey to the shops.

She wondered to herself where Emily's mother had gone and why?

*Chapter 9*

IT WAS CHRISTMAS EVE. Rhona Thorne was singing to a small audience in a seedy bar in Phoenix, Arizona. She had not secured any bookings anywhere in Las Vegas, as was her dream. She blamed her husband for that, of course, not the limited talent she had shown during various auditions.

The truth was, she was not as glamorous as she thought she was, nor did her repertoire appeal to an American audience. She could just about get by in the small clubs and venues in London, but not here. She was never going to make it as big as she had hoped. Tonight was the last straw for her; the audience was less than impressed, and they made their feelings very clear.

'They don't appreciate talent here,' she said to her husband as she got changed in her dressing room. 'We're going home on the first available flight tomorrow. At least my audience in London loves me.'

'Yes dear, whatever you say,' said Peter.

'Let's get back to the hotel and pack, I don't want to stay here a minute longer than I have to,' she growled.

'Alright, dear, don't upset yourself. It'll be good to get back home. I wonder how the children are?' he said timidly.

'Huh! Come on, take my bag and let's get out of here.'

At that moment, the bar owner knocked on the dressing room door and entered. 'Just to say we won't be needing you anymore, lady, here's your fifty bucks.'

Rhona snatched the cash from his hand and pushed past him. 'I quit your cheap joint anyway,' she said.

'Who are you calling cheap, lady? Go on, get the hell outa here,' shouted the owner as they left.

Rhona and Peter caught the earliest flight they could get to New York the following afternoon. From there, the next stop would be England.


On Christmas morning, as was their tradition, the Parker family rose early to open their presents. Yet Emily held back from immediately joining the others downstairs. She felt awkward and embarrassed at intruding into the family's festivities.

Patricia shouted up the stairs for her to come down and join them, Emily called back to her that she and the children wouldn't be a moment. She took the small teddy bear which she had wrapped from her bag and gave it to Bridget.

'I'm sorry, it's not much Bridget, it's all I could afford. But I hope you like it.'

Bridget smiled uncharacteristically and pulled the fluffy toy to her face. She simply said, 'Thank you.' Emily kissed her gently and said, 'Merry Christmas, Bridget.' The two of them went to Steven's room in search of Simon, but he was not there. Emily assumed he had already joined the others downstairs; he was not so easily embarrassed. She and Bridget followed suit and slowly went down the stairs; they could hear laughter and joy, something they had never experienced at Christmas before.

They approached the living room with its enormous Christmas tree and lavish decorations. 'Come on,' said Patricia, 'we've been waiting for you to open our presents.'

'Oh, sorry,' said Emily, 'I didn't realise.'

'Well, you're here now,' said Gwen, 'Come and join in, let's start opening these presents, shall we? I've put the presents in piles for you, so start digging in.'

Emily felt decidedly uncomfortable again. 'You really shouldn't have got us presents, Mrs Parker. I've got nothing to give to you and Patricia.'

'Don't be silly, I didn't expect you to. Now dig in!' said Gwen, 'And a Happy Christmas to you all, she added.'

'Happy Christmas,' said Emily. She sat on the floor next to Patricia and the other children. Alan Parker sat back in his armchair, looking on cheerfully, with a glass of sherry in his hand.

Patricia began to open her presents while Emily looked on awkwardly. 'Well, come on,' said Patricia, 'open your presents.'

Emily reluctantly began unwrapping one of the presents from her pile, a bright and modern pullover, the next a blouse, a dress, and a selection of toiletries. With a tear in her eye, she thanked Gwen and Alan and rose to kiss them.

'It's our pleasure, sweetheart,' said Gwen.

Simon and Bridget had also opened their gifts, a variety of toys and clothes. It was clear that the children, including Emily, had only old-fashioned clothes that had seen better days. Simon had only a pair of short trousers, so Gwen had bought him a pair of long trousers. After all, it was the middle of winter.

'Say thank you to Gwen and Alan, kids,' said Emily.

Simon was enthusiastic in thanking them, while Bridget was still very timid and shy in her approach. She still clutched the teddy bear given to her by Emily.

'Oh, here's my present to you, Simon,' said Emily, handing him the wrapped space gun.

'That's a lovely teddy bear you have there,' said Gwen, 'did your mum give you that?'

Bridget shook her head.

'It's just something I bought for her,' said Emily.

Gwen suddenly felt very emotional, fighting back the tears; she made an excuse to go to the kitchen. Once she was alone, the tears flowed. Alan had noticed a change in her mood and, after a few moments, followed her. She turned away as he entered the kitchen and hastily wiped away the tears.

'Are you alright, darling?' he said, approaching her.

'Yes, fine,' she said.

'No, you're not. It's Emily and the children, isn't it?' He took her in his arms and embraced her. Gwen dropped her head on his chest and, unable to keep up the pretence, allowed the tears to flow.

'Those poor children, Alan,' she sobbed, 'we must help them.'

'We will, don't worry,' he said, gently stroking her hair.

'But what if we can't? What will happen to them, Alan?'

'Try not to think about it, not today. Here, have a drink. It'll make you feel better. Don't worry, we'll think of something.'

'I hope so,' Gwen said.

Alan poured her a glass of sherry. 'Let's go back in, shall we?' he said. 'Come on, let's join them and make it a Christmas for them to remember. We'll work something out, darling.' Deep down, he knew they were just words of comfort. The reality of the situation could be much more problematic.

# Chapter 10

IT HAD BEEN A wonderful day, particularly for Emily and the children, almost magical, the family atmosphere, the joy and laughter, the party games, the roaring fire, and a marvellous Christmas lunch that even Bridget could not resist. Patricia eventually lost the battle to stay awake, as did the other children, yet Emily fought hard not to. She wanted the day to go on for as long as possible.

Gwen and Alan were also succumbing to tiredness. Gwen left the sofa and went over to the one opposite to wake Patricia. 'I hope you've enjoyed today, Emily,' said Gwen with a hushed voice.

'It's been wonderful, the best Christmas we've ever had. Thank you, Gwen, for everything.'

'It's been my pleasure, sweetheart, it really has. Emily - ?'

'Yes?'

'Oh, nothing. Now, I think it's time for bed for all of us, don't you?'

'I am tired,' said Emily, attempting to stifle a yawn.

Gwen woke Patricia and the younger children; they went upstairs without protest while Gwen went about tidying the living room and taking plates and glasses out to the kitchen. Alan woke up with a jerk. 'What are you doing, love? Leave that till the morning. It can wait.'

'I suppose you're right,' she said wearily.

'I see the kids have gone up. Let's do the same, shall we?'

'Yes, let's,' said Gwen.

It was in the early hours of the morning that Alan woke up. Gwen was tossing and turning and could not sleep at all.

Alan wearily rolled over to face Gwen. 'What's wrong love? Are you okay?' he said.

'I'm sorry if I woke you, but I can't seem to get to sleep. I just have this feeling that something bad is going to happen. I can't shake it off,' said Gwen.

'You're probably just overtired; nothing bad is going to happen, love.'

'I've never felt like this before, Alan. The feeling is so strong.'

'You're imagining things that aren't there,' said Alan, 'Try to get some sleep. Things will seem different in the morning, you'll see.'

'I wish I could believe that I really do, Alan. I'm sorry, go back to sleep, I'll be alright,' Gwen said.

'Alright, but try to get some sleep yourself. Don't forget, your parents are coming for the day tomorrow.'

'I'll try, goodnight darling.'

Alan rolled over again. 'Okay, goodnight love.'

Gwen laid on her back, wakeful and feeling no better, yet she avoided disturbing Alan further. It was not until 6 o'clock in the morning that she finally succumbed to exhaustion. She drifted into a light, uneasy sleep. A couple of hours later, she stirred briefly as she heard Alan getting up, then dozed off again. A short while later, Alan entered the bedroom with a cup of tea.

'Morning love,' he said. 'Did you manage to get some sleep after all?'

'Morning darling, yes, a little,' she said, propping herself up to drink her tea. 'What time is it?' she asked.

'About eight-thirty.'

'I'd better get up; mum and dad will be here in a few hours. I've got a lot to do.'

'Don't panic,' said Alan calmly, 'we've got plenty of time.'

His words fell on deaf ears as she hurriedly rose from the bed and slid into her slippers. 'There's all the things from yesterday to clear up, apart from anything else,' she said.

'Stop panicking, I've already loaded the dishwasher,' said Alan, trying to calm her.

'Are the kids up yet?' she asked, still in a flustered manner.

'Yes, they're all downstairs, and they're fine,' said Alan. 'Now drink your tea and calm down.'

'Okay, I'll be down in a minute,' said Gwen.

'Take your time, there's no rush,' said Alan, firmly.

While getting ready, Gwen suddenly realised she had the beginnings of a headache. She caught a glimpse of herself in the bathroom mirror. And said, 'Oh God, you look awful' to herself. She still couldn't shake off the feeling of dread she had endured throughout the night, feeling somehow responsible for Emily and her siblings.

Three hours later, Gwen's headache persisted, and she started preparing things in the kitchen for her parents' arrival. Lunch today would be cold turkey and all the usual trimmings. Alan did what he could to help while simultaneously sipping at a glass of sherry. Gwen declined the offer of a glass.

The doorbell rang. To Gwen it seemed louder than usual, more insistent. 'Who's that?' she said to Alan, deeply on edge.

'Relax, it'll just be your parents,' said Alan. 'Come on, love, don't be so jittery.'

'I'm sorry, I can't help it at the moment,' said Gwen. He went to the front door and let them in. She relaxed a little when she heard their voices. It was an extremely welcome sound. She went to greet them and ushered them into the living room. They were both in their late sixties and kind, gentle people, like their daughter.

Patricia and Steven rushed over to them, excitedly hugging them. They did not live in the area, so they were not seen as often as Gwen and the children would have liked. Their grandfather carried a bag full of presents for them. 'It's lovely to see you all. Did you have a nice Christmas day?' he said, 'Oh, and what do we have here? Friends of yours?'

'Yes,' said Patricia, 'this is my friend, Emily and her brother and sister, Bridget and Simon.'

'Very pleased to meet you,' said their grandfather.

'Pleased to meet you,' said Emily.

'Yes, they're staying with us for a while,' interjected Gwen.

'Oh, that's nice,' said Gwen's mother.

'Let me take your coats,' said Alan, then you can sit down and get comfortable.

'I'll give Gwen a hand in the kitchen. Is that alright, Gwen?' said her mother.

'You don't have to. You've had a long journey,' said Gwen.

'I'm fine anyway I'd like to.'

Once they were alone in the kitchen, Gwen's mother said, 'Are you alright, dear? You look a little peaky?'

'Yes, I'm fine. Just a slight headache that's all,' replied Gwen, 'it'll pass.'

'I do hope so dear.'

'Would you like a glass of something, mum? Or maybe you'd prefer tea,' asked Gwen just as the doorbell rang again. Gwen's face drained of colour.

'What's the matter, dear? You've gone as white as a ghost. Is there something wrong?'

'I'll explain later, Mum,' she said, making her way slowly out of the kitchen. Somehow, she knew what was coming as she opened the door.

'Where are they?' shouted Rhona.

'And you are?' said Gwen. Alan joined them at the front door.

'What's going on?' he said.

'You've got my kids. They're coming home – Now!'

Rhona was intimidating; she scared Gwen. 'You can't take them home now. They're having a nice time,' said Gwen.

'We'll see about that,' Rhona barked as she pushed past Gwen and Alan and made her way to the living room.

'Hold on, who do you think you are? You can't just barge into our home like this,' said Alan, in a rage, as he followed after her.

'What on earth is going on?' asked Gwen's mother, coming out of the kitchen.

Gwen couldn't reply, it seemed her feeling of foreboding was coming true.

'Mother!' said Emily, jumping to her feet.

'You're all coming home, and what's that you're wearing?'

'It was a present.'

'Well, take it off and put on your own clothes right now.'

'Now look,' said Gwen angrily, 'you can't be so cruel. I gave her that dress as a Christmas gift, which is more than you've done for her and the children by the looks of things. You abandon them for over a week and then bluster your way in here and demand they come home. Well, I won't have it, do you hear?'

'Oh really? They're my kids and are coming home with me, and if you try to stop me, I'll have the law on you. Do I make myself clear?' yelled Rhona.

'Look here, I don't know who you are, but you don't seem to me to be a very nice woman,' said Gwen's father, jumping to his feet.

'I'm afraid we have to do as she says, Gwen. She is their mother and legal guardian,' said Alan.

'Oh, you and your logical mind, Alan!' said Gwen angrily.

'I know how you feel, love, I feel the same way, but I don't see that we have any choice,' he retorted.

Gwen knew he was right. She looked at Emily, biting her lower lip and with tears in her eyes. Emily went to Gwen and hugged her. 'I'm sorry, don't blame yourself, we've had a wonderful time. She ran upstairs to change back into her old clothing and neatly folded the dress Gwen had given her, leaving it on the bed.

'I'll see you in hell,' shouted Gwen, but before that, I'll see you in court. Why do you want them back so much anyway, to wait on your hand and foot? So you can keep them prisoners? Why?'

'As I said, they're my kids, not yours,' Rhona growled. 'Come on, we're leaving,' she said once Emily had rejoined them in the living room in her old clothes.

'Don't worry, Emily, I'm not going to let this rest,' said Gwen.

'I wouldn't get any bright ideas if I were you,' said Rhona, pushing her face into Gwen's.

'You haven't heard the last of this, I promise you that,' shouted Gwen as they left.

# *Chapter 11*

RHONA SENT BRIDGET AND SIMON to their rooms, but not Emily; as the eldest and left in charge, she was to be punished in a manner that would ensure she would never venture out again and would be obedient to her mother at all times in future.

Yet before the punishment, Rhona questioned Emily about the Parker family and how it came about that they stayed at their home. 'Didn't I make myself clear? You never leave the house – never! How did you meet this woman?' she growled.

'She's my friend's mother,' said Emily.

'Friend, you don't have any friends.'

'I have *one*, a school friend.'

'Not anymore, you don't,' said Rhona, 'I'm going to keep you off school.'

'You can't, please don't do that,' pleaded Emily.

Rhona slapped her. 'How dare you question me! I'll be keeping you away from school, and that's the end of the matter, do you understand?'

Emily sobbed uncontrollably.

'You need to take a while and have a long hard think about what you've done, young lady.' Rhona grabbed Emily roughly and dragged her to the understairs cupboard. 'Get in!' she barked.

'No! I won't,' said Emily, defiantly.

'What did you say?' Rhona shoved her inside and locked the door. 'Maybe after this, you'll think twice about your actions,'

Peter looked on, horrified, but said nothing.

The day passed slowly for Emily. She had no concept of time, no food or drink, and no light in the cramped cupboard. She wondered how long she would be left there; it seemed like forever. She eventually fell asleep.

It was not until the early hours of the following day that she heard the key being turned in the lock. She could just make out her stepfather in the dim light outside the cupboard. He had crept downstairs while Rhona slept. 'I can't let you out, Emily, but here's some food and drink,' he said. 'I'm so sorry, Emily, I am really.'

'If you're so sorry, why don't you do something about her?' Emily said crossly.

'Shh, she might hear. Just eat your food. I'm sorry, I must go back upstairs now before she wakes up. If she catches me too.'

'You're a coward,' said Emily as the door closed and the key turned again. Peter knew she was right; he *was* a coward, and scared to death of Rhona. He sometimes wondered why he stayed with her, in fact, why he had married her in the first place. Not that it had been his idea to get married; he remembered how she had suggested it, not him. Perhaps, he thought, even then he had been too scared to say no. Now, he hated her, yet through the hate, he stood by her for some reason. He was certainly not dependent on Rhona for money, he had inherited a considerable amount from his parents, of which Rhona had always taken full advantage.

Emily's words of truth resonated in his mind as he crept back into bed. He held his breath for a moment as Rhona stirred, but she quickly went back to sleep, snoring heavily. She had never explained why her first husband left her so many years ago when Emily was very little. Maybe he was scared of her too, he thought. Peter had never met him. The divorce was granted on the grounds of desertion a few years after he had left. Peter did not sleep well that night.

Neither did any of the Parkers. Gwen was distraught after the events of the morning, so was Alan. Patricia was distraught by what had happened to her friend and lay awake, occasionally weeping, wondering what would have happened once her mother took her home. She could not have imagined, though, the level of torture Emily was actually going through. The next day, Friday, was not a holiday but a typical working day. Gwen and Alan had discussed the matter of Emily while they lay sleepless, and agreed that something must be done – and urgently.

Gwen planned to make an appointment with Social Services that very day if possible and was determined not to be fobbed off. The crisis was real, she knew it, Alan knew it, and so did Patricia, and Gwen was going to make it very clear she wanted immediate action taken against Emily's parents, particularly her mother.

The morning came, Rhona went downstairs and unlocked the cupboard where Emily had been all night. 'Alright, you can come out,' said Rhona. Emily pulled herself out stiffly.

'Now go and make the tea. Hold on - what's this?' she said, picking up the small plate and cup from inside the cupboard. 'Who's responsible for this? Wait till I get my hands on those kids,' she growled.

'It wasn't them,' Emily remonstrated, 'it was Peter.'

'You're lying,' said Rhona.

'No, I'm not, ask him.'

Rhona went upstairs at a gallop and burst into the bedroom where Peter was getting dressed. She still held the plate and cup in her hands. 'Are you responsible for this?'

'Well, I – '

'So you are? How dare you interfere with my punishment.'

'I thought – ' he said timidly.

'You pathetic excuse for a man. Well, you've done it now, haven't you? From now on, stay out of my sight.'

For once, he stood up for himself. She was cold and hungry. I thought it best to give her something. You shouldn't have locked her up like that.'

'What's this? You've never argued with me before, Peter. Well, maybe you're no longer useful to me,' she said menacingly.

'Yes, maybe you're right. Maybe it would be best if I leave.'

She gave him an uncharacteristic smile. 'Let's not be hasty, Darling, I didn't mean what I said.'

'It's too late, Rhona, I *am* leaving, and what's more, I'll be reporting you to the authorities for child abuse.'

'If I go down, you'll go down with me as well,' said Rhona.

'I don't care. Maybe I deserve to,' he said.

He cowered a little as Rhona approached him slowly and menacingly. She had shown displays of violence towards him before, and he was terrified of her. 'Let's talk about this, Rhona. Don't do anything hasty.'

'You're becoming a liability to me,' she said.

She took the heavy water jug from the dressing table and raised it. As he tried to back away, she smashed it into his skull with a dull thud, the jug smashing into several pieces. He fell silently onto the bed, blood pouring from his head and nose. She checked for a pulse in his neck. He was dead.

# *Chapter 12*

IT WAS 9 O'CLOCK EXACTLY when Gwen dialled the number for the social service department. A receptionist answered the call almost immediately. 'I wish to report a case of child abuse, and I would like to make an appointment to see someone,' said Gwen to the receptionist.

'I'll put you through to someone. Can I ask your name? You don't have to tell me if you'd prefer to remain anonymous.'

'I don't mind at all giving you my name. It's Mrs Gwen Parker.'

'Thank you, I'll put you through now.' The line went silent for a moment until someone answered.

'Mrs Parker? You're through to Jan; how can I help you?'

'Good morning, I would like to see someone about a case of child abuse and neglect, please,' said Gwen.

'I see. Do you mind if I take a few details?'

'No, not at all.'

The officer took a few brief details of the allegation. 'I could come to your home to discuss this further if you'd prefer Mrs Parker?'

'Yes, that would be fine. As soon as possible, please,' said Gwen.

'Well, in view of the seriousness of the allegation, how about today? I could make it at mid-day if that's alright with you?'

'Yes, that would be great, thank you, said Gwen.'

'Good, I'll see you later then. Thank you for calling us about this.'

'How did you get on?' asked Alan.

'Someone is coming here to see us at mid-day. I'm so worried as to what that evil woman is putting those poor kids through right now, Alan.'

'Yes, I know what you mean; she certainly is a piece of work. But let me just say this, don't get your hopes up that they'll allow them to stay with us; it isn't that simple,' said Alan gravely.

'I know, Alan, I know.'

A little after mid-day, Jan turned up with another officer. Gwen welcomed them in from the cold and took them into the comfortable living room. Alan asked if they would like tea or coffee. They both accepted a cup of coffee and sat down.

'Can I call you Gwen?' asked Jan.

'Yes, of course,' she replied amiably.

'So, Gwen, this is a serious allegation that you've made against Mr and Mrs Thorne, the latter, in particular it seems.'

'Yes, I realise that, but I can assure you, it's well-founded,' said Gwen. 'And what's more, I'm really worried that the woman will be punishing them for staying with us for a couple of days. She's totally evil, in my opinion. This isn't the first time she's left them on their own by all accounts. My daughter will tell you the same. It's become clear over the past few days that they're not allowed out of the house; their clothes are like rags; it's just appalling abuse.'

'I can see you feel very passionately about this, Gwen,' said Jan.

'Yes, I do.'

'Well, we are going to pay Mrs Thorne a visit after we leave here. We'll investigate this thoroughly, I promise you that,' said the other officer.

Alan entered with a tray with four cups of coffee and placed it on the large coffee table. 'What do you think can be done about this?' he asked.

'I take it you met Mrs Thorne as well, Mr Parker?'

'She's an absolute brute of a woman; the way she treated Emily and the children was appalling. She even made her change back into her old clothes. My wife had bought all the children new clothes for Christmas you see.'

'I see,' said Jan.

'What are you going to do about it?' asked Alan forcefully.

'As I just explained to your wife, we'll be investigating it thoroughly. We'll be going to see her as soon as we leave here. Gwen, would it be possible to have a few words with your daughter?'

'Yes, of course, but she's agitated,' said Gwen. I'll get her, she's upstairs.'

Gwen went to the hallway to call Patricia. She found her sitting at the bottom of the stairs, she had been listening intently to the conversation taking place in the living room. Gwen smiled. 'Are you okay, sweetheart? The lady would like to speak with you for a moment. Is that okay with you?'

Patricia nodded and rose from the stairs where she sat. She followed Gwen into the living room.

'This is Patricia,' said Gwen.

'Hello Patricia, I'm Jan, do you mind if we ask a couple of questions about your friend?'

'Are you going to help her?' asked Patricia solemnly.

'We're going to try,' said Jan.

'We all want them to come and live with us, don't we, mum?'

'Well, we'll have to see,' said Jan.

'What can you tell me about your friend and her brother and sister's home life, Patricia?'

'Her mother's cruel to them; she keeps them prisoner. The only time I see her is at school. She never lets them out other than that.'

'Does her mother hit them; do you know?'

'I – I don't know.'

'Isn't it enough that she keeps them inside all the time and abandons them whenever she feels like it?' interjected Gwen.

'I know how strongly you feel about this, but we have to establish the facts,' said Jan.

'By what I've heard from Emily herself, she's treated as nothing more than a servant to her mother. She has to cook the younger children their meals, the list goes on,' remonstrated Gwen.

'Alright, we'll leave it there for now, and we'll go around and see Mrs Thorne. Let's see what she has to say, shall we?' said Jan.

'Are you going to ask to see the children while you're there?' asked Alan.

'Yes, we'll do that too. Well, thank you for your time, we'll be in touch,' said Jan.

'Will you call me later today, please?' said Gwen.

'I can't promise that,' said Jan dismissively.

'But the weekend's coming up — how will we know what's happening?' asked Gwen.

'I'll endeavour to call you, but as I said, I can't promise anything,' Jan said.

After they had left, Gwen, Alan and Patricia could not help feeling that nothing would get done and that Emily and her siblings suffering would continue.

'If I don't hear anything by this afternoon, I'm going there myself,' said Gwen angrily.

'You can't do that love,' said Alan.

'Can't I? Just watch me.'

AFTER A FEW DAYS, when no phone call came from the Department of Social Services, Gwen was set to pay a visit to Rhona Thorne's house. She could not bear to think of Emily and the children enduring another minute of her cruelty. It was only the calm logic of Alan that persuaded her to postpone the visit until at least the next day and in daylight. She did not like it but knew it made some kind of sense.

Earlier that day, Rhona Thorne had not finished with the punishment of the children and in particular, Emily, for having disobeyed her orders never to leave the house. To make matters worse, she'd had an unexpected visit from social services. She regarded that as Emily's fault, not hers, and Emily would have to pay the price.

When the officers called at her house and asked to see the children, Rhona explained that they were playing in the nearby park, in reality, they were all confined to their rooms without food or water for the rest of the day and night. Jan and the other officer were unconvinced by her lies, but without a warrant and police presence, they could do nothing at that stage. Awkward questions were asked, however, regarding the accusation that she had left her children alone for over a week. She denied it, and again, her body language made it evident to the officers she was lying. Yet, such was her arrogance, she felt convinced her story was accepted and she would not be bothered by them again.

Nevertheless, it was a problem she could have done without, and she knew very well who had made the complaint.

If she ever saw Gwen Parker again, she would make her pay, she thought. Much later that night, she checked that Emily and the children were soundly asleep and went to her bedroom. She opened her wardrobe, and Peter's body that she had hidden there fell onto the bedroom floor. His eyes were staring lifelessly at her. She felt no emotion.

She dragged him down the stairs, through the hallway and into the rear garden. The ground was wet and easy enough to dig a shallow grave. After dumping his body inside the makeshift grave, patting down the earth, and replacing the turf, she went back inside, poured herself a large whiskey, and slumped breathlessly into a kitchen chair. After another large whiskey, she fell asleep in the chair, her arms splayed, wellington boots and coat still on. Early that morning, Emily got out of bed; she was hungry and thirsty, and believing her mother to be still in bed, she made her way downstairs to the kitchen in search of anything that she and the children could eat.

She was shocked to see her mother asleep; she noticed her muddy boots and hands as she made her way quietly to the cupboard. Rhona stirred a little, snorting as she did so. Emily froze. Yet hunger drove her forward; she opened the cupboard door, and it creaked; she had never noticed it do that before. Rhona snorted again and woke up with a start.

'And what the hell do you think you're doing?' she barked.

'I'm hungry,' said Emily.

'Oh, are you now? Well, you'll eat when I tell you, now get back up those stairs.'

'*Where's Peter?*' asked Emily curiously.

'Not that it's any of your business, but he's gone. I threw him out, satisfied?'

'Oh.'

'Now go back to your room, and don't come down until I say so.'

Emily did as she was ordered and returned to her room empty-handed. The hunger was beginning to make her stomach hurt severely. She curled up in her bed in a vain attempt to sleep, but apart from the hunger pains she was feeling, she was also finding it strange at Peter's abrupt departure. And why was her mother in muddy boots with equally muddy hands? Emily became suspicious. Had her mother been up all night? And if so, what had she been doing?

As Emily lay awake a short time later, she heard the footsteps of her mother traipsing up the stairs and then her bedroom door being closed. Perhaps she had been up all night and was now going to bed. At least if she went to sleep, there would be a chance of creeping downstairs and finding some food, Emily thought.

Gwen had not found restful sleep since the awful day that Emily's mother had come to their home and taken Emily and the children away. She had sat in the kitchen drinking coffee since 8 o'clock that morning, thinking of nothing else. She also wondered what action the social services officers would take—if any. It troubled her deeply. Alan joined her a short while later; the events of that day had upset him too—more than he cared to admit.

'How long have you been up, love?' asked Alan.

'Oh, a while. Coffee?'

'Oh, yes, please, darling. I gather you didn't sleep well again?'

'No. How about you?' asked Gwen.

'Not great, I'm afraid.'

Gwen knew he was as worried as she was, even if he would not admit it openly. She knew him too well for him to disguise the fact. 'I'm going to that house today to check on Emily and the children,' she said with determination in her voice.

'Gwen, you can't just turn up there; what are you going to say?'

'I'll think of something.'

'Have you thought that it might mess up the investigation, you going there?'

'I don't see how,' said Gwen, 'I have to know they're alright, Alan.'

'Well, if you're that determined, I'm going with you. I'm not having you face that dreadful woman alone.'

'You'd do that for me?'

'Of course, love, that goes without saying,' said Alan.

'Thank you, darling, that means a lot to me. Drink your coffee. I'm going to get dressed. The sooner we go, the better I'll feel,' said Gwen, her spirits raised.

'Don't get too excited, love, we're just going to see them, that's all, and that's if their mother allows it, and to be perfectly honest, I can't realistically see that happening,' said Alan.

'There you go again with your logical hat on. I don't care, I have to try,' shouted Gwen as she ran up the stairs.

An hour later, Gwen gathered up Patricia and Steven. 'We're going to see Emily and the kids to see if they're alright. You can come too, but stay in the car, okay.'

'Can't I see her? Asked Patricia.

'We'll have to see what happens, sweetheart,' said Alan, 'it may not be possible.'

A short while later, arriving outside the house, it was shrouded in mist, as was the entire area. Gwen and Alan got out of the car, their hearts pounding with trepidation. 'Stay here, kids,' said Alan.

Alan knocked firmly on the door. At first, there was no answer, but then the door opened slightly ajar. They saw

Emily's face poking out from the gloomy hallway. On seeing them, Emily opened the door wider and gestured to them to be quiet. 'Gwen? What are you doing here?' Emily asked in a hushed voice.

'We just had to come to see if you were alright,' said Gwen, 'where's your mother and stepfather?'

'Mother is in bed, and Peter has gone. I don't know where to.'

'Are you alright, dear?' asked Gwen, 'I've been so worried about you. Where's Simon and Bridget?'

'They're upstairs. Yes, I'm alright,' Emily said stoically. 'You should go. If she catches me talking to you, she'll…'

'She'll what? Did she punish you before?' asked Gwen.

'Well – '

'What did she do to you?'

Emily opened the front door a little wider and gestured to the understairs cupboard.

'Are you telling me she locked you in there, Emily? How long for?'

'All night. But don't say anything, it'll only make things worse,' said Emily.

'How on earth could it be worse,' said Gwen, glancing at Alan. 'Did your mother have a visit from social services yesterday?'

'I don't know, we were kept in our rooms all day.'

'That's it, Alan, we're taking them back to our place right now,' said Gwen.

'We can't do that, love, she'll only call the police. We wouldn't have a leg to stand on. We'll just have to wait for social services to do their job. I'm sorry, but there it is,' said Alan.

Once again, Gwen knew deep down that he was correct. 'We'll get you out of here as soon as we can, I promise you.

Would you like to come and say hello to Patricia? She's in the car.'

'I'd like to, but better not. Tell her not to worry, though—I'll be alright,' said Emily.

'What's going on down there?' Rhona shouted. Emily's eyes widened.

'You'd better go,' Emily whispered, then quickly closed the door.

'Come on, Gwen, let's get out of here—we don't want to make it worse for those kids,' said Alan. Gwen saw sense, and they hurried back to their car, and they drove away.

'Who was that you were talking to? It was them, wasn't it?' growled Rhona.

'It wasn't my fault, I didn't ask them to come,' said Emily.

'I told you never to answer the door. Maybe you need a little more persuasion to do as you're told in future,' Rhona said menacingly.

'I will, I promise,' said Emily, her courage now failing her.

'I don't quite know what I'm going to do with you. The truth is girl, you're becoming a serious problem to me.'

IT WAS 10AM ON NEW YEAR'S EVE that the social services officers and police attended Rhona's house with a view to speaking to the children and seeing for themselves the living conditions of the household they were living under. Jan knocked on the door.

'Mrs Thorne, you may remember me from last Friday, I'm from the social services department, children's section. As I explained to you, there has been a serious allegation against you, and I would like to come in and see your children.'

'Well, you can't,' said Rhona.

'I'm afraid I can under the Children's Act, Mrs Thorne,' said Jan, showing her the warrant.

Rhona scowled at her and the two police officers; one of them was a female constable.

Jan was not prepared to stand on the doorstep arguing—she pushed past Rhona along with her colleague and the two police officers and entered the hallway.

'You can't just barge your way into my home. You have no right!' exclaimed Rhona.

'I have every right,' said Jan, 'now where are your children?' Rhona did not answer. Jan made her way systematically through the ground-floor rooms, then the first-floor rooms, until finally proceeding up the final flight of stairs to the top floor. She entered Bridget's room first and found her huddled in her bed for warmth. The stranger startled her. 'Don't be frightened; Is your name Bridget?' she asked gently. Bridget simply nodded. 'You stay there; I'll be back in a moment.'

'This door's locked,' said her colleague, trying the handle of Emily's door.

Jan turned to Rhona, who had been shadowing them. 'Key, please,' said Jan.

Rhona knew, at that moment, the game was up and fumbled through her cardigan pocket for the key. She reluctantly gave it to Jan.

Jan unlocked the door to find Emily standing close by; she had heard everything but looked shocked at the stranger standing before her along with the female police officer.

'What's happening? Emily asked Jan.

'You must be Emily. Don't be alarmed, my name is Jan. I'm from social services. How long have you been locked up in here?'

Emily looked at her mother momentarily.

'Don't worry, Emily, you're quite safe. You can speak freely now.'

'Since yesterday, I think,' said Emily.

At that moment, Simon came running into the room. 'What's going on?' he asked Emily.

'Don't worry, Simon, I believe these people are here to help us. You are, aren't you? She asked Jan.

'Yes, Emily, we are,' said Jan. She turned to Rhona. 'Mrs Thorne, false imprisonment of a child is very serious, and we *will* be bringing charges against you. In the meantime, we are taking your children into our care with immediate effect. Do you understand?'

'Take them. They're more trouble than they're worth, especially that one,' she said, gesturing to Emily.

'Well, your words speak volumes, don't they?' said Jan, with contempt in her voice. 'Come on, kids, let's get a few things packed.'

'Where will you take us?' asked Emily.

'Somewhere safe and warm, with other kids your ages; you'll be fine,' said Jan.

'Can't we stay at my friend's house, it's nice there, we stayed there on Christmas day.'

'Do you mean the Parker's house, Emily?'

'Yes, that's right, my friend's mum is so lovely. But how did you know?'

'It was Mrs Parker who reported your situation, Emily, but I'm afraid we can't do that right now; we have to go through certain procedures, you see,' said Jan sympathetically.

'Oh, I see. Well, can I phone Gwen and my friend?' asked Emily.

'Of course you can, but a little later, alright, once we've got you settled. You're very fond of Mrs Parker, aren't you?' said Jan.

'Yes, I am. She's been so kind to us.'

'Well, we'll have to wait and see what happens, but I'm sure everything will work out fine,' said Jan.

Later that afternoon, Jan dialled out the number for Gwen's house. 'Mrs Parker?'

'Yes, speaking.'

'Oh, hello, it's Jan from social services, I came to your house the other day about – '

'Yes, what's happened? Did you pay that woman a visit?' asked `Gwen.

'We did, and we've been back there today with the police. I have to say, you were absolutely correct in contacting us. Anyway, I thought I should let you know that the children are now in our care, such was the seriousness of the case.'

'Oh! Well, I suppose that's kind of good news, but I was rather hoping that you were going to say they could come and stay with us.'

'Not that simple, I'm afraid; it'll have to go before a judge.'

'Oh, I see,' said Gwen, downheartedly.

'But don't worry too much; if that's really what you and your husband want, the judge will have to listen to my recommendations, also the wishes of the children, and I know that's what they would like to happen too.'

'Could I speak to Emily?'

'Of course, I'll get her for you.'

After a few moments, Emily picked up the phone. 'Gwen?'

'Yes, are you alright? Are you being treated well?'

'Yes, we're fine. I'm just glad to be away from that house and my mother. And they haven't split us up, that's the main thing.'

'Emily, I don't want to raise your hopes too much, but I have to ask; would you like to live with us, permanently, I mean?'

'It's what I'd like more than anything,' said Emily, becoming emotional.

'Stop it, you'll make me cry. Look, we'll come and see you very soon. Would you like to speak to Patricia?'

'Oh, yes, please,'

'Alright, dear, I'll hand you over to her. And don't worry, I'm sure things will be fine. Goodbye, Emily. See you soon, dear.

'Hello Em, are you okay?' asked Patricia.

'Yes, don't worry about me, I'm fine.'

'What's it like where you're staying?'

'Oh, it's nice. At least it's warm and we get fed properly.'

'I'm certain you'll be living with us soon, Em, so don't worry.'

'That'd be so good. I hope you're right,' said Emily.

'I know I am,' said Patricia.

# Chapter 15



*One month later*

AFTER A SHORT COURT HEARING, the judge, having listened to the case made by Jan and her colleagues, Gwen and Alan Parker, and also taking into account the wishes of Emily and Simon, ruled that as an interim measure, they should stay with Gwen and her family. Bridget had been too traumatised to offer any opinion; she had a naïve loyalty to her mother and had been seeing a child psychologist since being taken into care.

Rhona had absconded soon after the day her children had been taken from her and had been told she would face charges of child neglect and abuse. Nobody knew where she was. Gwen and Alan had been in attendance at the hearing; Gwen could not hide her feelings of joy at the judges' decision but was quickly, yet sensitively reminded by him that, at this stage, it was merely an interim measure.

After the paperwork and formalities were completed, Gwen thanked Jan for her support and told her she wanted to file for the adoption of all three children as soon as possible. Then, the moment arrived when they all left together and drove to Parker's home for what would, at least for the time being, be Emily and her siblings' home. Gwen had arranged for her parents to come and take care of Patricia and Steven while they were in court. They had formed a welcome home party in the hope that the hearing was favourable.

Patricia was anxiously and frequently looking out of the window, awaiting, she hoped, the arrival of Emily along with her parents. Finally, after what seemed like an eternity, the car pulled up on the driveway, and she could see them all quite clearly. She jumped with excitement and told the others to get ready to welcome them. They all gathered in the spacious entrance hall and waited for the door to open.

When the door opened and they all entered, Patricia, Steven and their grandparents all shouted 'Welcome Home' in unison. Patricia ran to Emily and hugged her. 'You're home now,' she said.

'This calls for a celebration,' said Alan, 'I'll get the champagne.' They had all gathered in the comfortable living room with a welcoming, roaring fire by the time he returned with a tray of drinks. 'Soft drinks for you, I'm afraid kids – well, here's to us, cheers everyone.'

There had been a heavy snowfall the night before, which made the warmth and cosiness of the house seem even more welcoming. For the rest of the day, the house was filled with happiness and laughter, even Bridget showed slight signs that she may be coming out of her shell.

Gwen had decided it would be a good idea to have a second bed put in Patricia's room so that she and Emily could share. Patricia was more than glad about the decision, as was Emily. When it came time for bed, Gwen said, 'We're going clothes shopping tomorrow, girls. We'll get you a set of nice new things to wear.' Gwen kissed them goodnight. 'See you in the morning,' she said and then returned downstairs.

'All settled?' asked Alan.

'Yes, it's good to see them so happy at last,' said Gwen, settling back on the sofa next to him. 'I'm still concerned about Bridget, but although she's still very quiet, I think she's making some progress.'

'Hardly surprising that she's the quiet, poor kid. She's been through a lot for a child of her age,' said Gwen's mum, 'she'll come around to the idea of her new home soon, I'm sure.'

'Yes, I'm sure you're right, mum, it's just a matter of time.'

'But I will say this, Gwen, don't get your hopes up too much about adoption. I'd hate to see you disappointed,' her mum added.

'I know, but Jan thinks our case looks very favourable.'

'Not to mention that even if you are successful, it's a huge responsibility,' interjected Gwen's dad.

'Alan and I have discussed it at length, and we're both in agreement that it's what we want, it's what Patricia wants, too. We've always wanted a large family anyway,' she laughed.

'Well, I'm sure you both know what you're doing,' said her mum, 'but have you thought of the cost of it all?'

'Yes, of course, we can afford it easily. I'll be starting the adoption process straight away. Jan warned me it could take up to eighteen months. We'll just have to take one step at a time and hope for the best, that's all we can do.,' said Gwen.

'It's also a huge responsibility,' interjected Gwen's dad.

'We know, Dad, but I can assure you we've considered everything, and we can handle it,' said Gwen.

Six months later

Nothing had been heard of Rhona since she had absconded. There was no knowledge of her whereabouts. It was as if she had simply disappeared. The only thing the authorities and police knew for sure was that she had emptied her husband's bank account. There was, of course, no knowledge of his whereabouts either. Emily had informed them of what her mother said, that he had gone, she had thrown him out. Yet there was no trace of him to be found.

The police had also attempted to track down her first husband and the father of Emily and the children. Again, their efforts had revealed nothing. In light of this and the circumstances that led to the children being taken into care, then placed in the care of Gwen and Alan Parker, the judge found in favour of the adoption taking place without further delay. The relief on Gwen's face was clear. A week later, the legal documents were signed. Emily, Simon and Bridget finally became their adopted children.

Patricia was overcome with happiness at having Emily as her sister. The same could be said of Emily, but she was mostly grateful and joyous to be part of a loving family at last. Yet despite this, she still wondered about her mother from time to time, where she might be, and whether or not she felt any remorse for the way she treated her and the younger children.

She confided with Patricia and vowed that one day she would track her mother down and confront her – but not yet. For now, she was content with her life and simply wanted to concentrate on doing well in her studies and eventually going to university. With a stable and happy family that she was now a part of, achieving that ambition seemed ever more likely as the weeks and months passed.

# *Chapter 16*

*Four Years Later*

IN 1988, HAVING ACHIEVED top grades in her A Levels, Emily applied for a place at Oxford University and was accepted. Given her past home life, it was against all odds; it was down to nothing less than pure determination and the will to succeed. The stable life she had experienced since her adoption had also made a significant difference.

Patricia had, although not by any means terrible, not received quite so impressive results. She had hoped to attend the same University as Emily, but it was not to be, she was eventually accepted for a place at Bristol University to study medicine. By the last week in August, a few weeks before her course was to begin, Emily moved into her student accommodation, in order to orientate herself, settle in her new environment and meet other students. It would be a three-year-long course to obtain her degree in journalism.

It was difficult to adjust to her new life away from home at first, she missed Patricia, Gwen and the family, yet Emily soon made new friends and was enjoying her course very much. She and Patricia kept in touch by telephone at least once every week, as she also did with Gwen and her siblings. Bridget was now twelve years old, and Simon, fourteen, and during the last four years they had seemed to settle down very well with their new family.

Six months into her course, Emily received a phone call from Gwen. One of the students in her accommodation block had answered the phone in the hall and knocked on the door of her room. 'Emily, there's a phone call for you.'

'Oh, okay, thanks.' She rushed out and picked up the receiver that hung down from the payphone. 'Hello.'

'Hi sweetheart, it's mum. How are you doing?' said Gwen.

'Hi mum, yes, I'm fine. Is everything alright at home?'

'Yes, we're all fine. We're missing you, of course, but as long as you're enjoying yourself, that's all that matters.'

'Oh yes, the course is going well. I miss all of you, though.'

'Listen, I've got some exciting news for you, Emily,' said Gwen.

'Really? What is it?' asked Emily curiously.

Rhona had not been mentioned for a very long time and Gwen was reticent in saying her name, but she knew she had to. 'It's to do with Rhona's house,' said Gwen.

'What about it?'

'Well, I've been contacted by a solicitor. It would seem that because the authorities have been unable to trace Rhona or your biological father, the house is to become legally yours.'

There was a prolonged silence from Emily.

'Are you there, Emily?' asked Gwen.

'I don't want it. I never want to see that house again,' said Emily.

'But you don't have to love. You can sell it without setting foot in the place. Alan and I can make all the arrangements for you. It's what's rightfully yours; it's the least you deserve,' said Gwen persuasively.

'I suppose you're right. As long as I don't have to go in there.'

'You won't, I promise.'

'Okay, thanks for letting me know, mum,' said Emily.

'And Alan can advise you how best to invest the money once it's sold,' added Gwen.

'That would be great. Of course, I would want to share the money with Simon and Bridget.'

'Naturally, it would, of course, need to be put in trust for them, but it should still leave you all with a nice sum of money. Anyway, how would you like to come home for the weekend and we can talk about it? Patricia's coming.'

'Yes, I'd like that,' said Emily.

'Oh, excellent. I miss you both so much. It'll be wonderful to see you. Let me know which train you'll be getting, and I'll let Patricia know to catch the same train from Bristol.'

'Okay, I'll let you know. Looking forward to seeing you all. Anyway, I'd better go, I've got a supervision soon.'

'Alright dear, speak soon, bye,' said Gwen, blowing a kiss down the phone.

Her tutor, Doctor David Robinson, was a forty-one-year-old man with slightly greying hair at the sides, sporting a neatly trimmed beard and of average build. He was also a stickler for good time-keeping. Emily was five minutes late for their private tutorial at his on-site accommodation.

'You're late, Miss Parker!' he said sternly as he answered the door.

'Yes, I'm very sorry, I got held up,' said Emily

'I do have other students to see, you know. Anyway, you'd better come in.'

'Thank you,' said Emily, 'it won't happen again, I'm sorry.'

'Make sure it doesn't,' he said, ushering her into his study. Emily took a seat facing his large paper-strewn desk. 'I've read the essay I asked you to write for me, and on the whole, it's good enough, although I think you missed out on some salient points which I would have liked to see you raise,' he said, leaning back in his chair.

'Oh, really?' said Emily, disappointedly.

Doctor Robinson raised himself from his chair, moved slowly from behind his desk and stood behind Emily. 'I wouldn't worry too much about it. I'm sure there's nothing we can't iron out with a little more work,' he said, placing both hands on her shoulders. Emily began to feel decidedly uncomfortable. She stood up abruptly.

'What do you suggest?' she asked nervously.

'I've made some comments on your essay, write it again and bring it back to me before our next tutorial,' he said.

'Okay, is that all?' she asked.

'For now,' he said, moving back to his desk and flicking through his diary. 'I'll see you at the same time next Wednesday, but be sure to let me have your new essay before that,' he said.

'Yes, I'll do that,' she said, moving towards the door of his study.

'Maybe next time, we could have a little drink,' he said, opening the door for her.

'I don't think so,' said Emily, 'besides, I don't drink.'

'Pity,' he said brusquely, 'next Wednesday then.'

As she left, she felt Ill at ease about seeing him again. She had heard rumours about him from other female students but had never experienced anything first-hand before. Although she had always got the feeling he didn't like females very much, at least not in a professional sense. Having been at Oxford for only six months, Emily did not want to make trouble, and would avoid it at almost any cost to achieve her goal of becoming a journalist. Nevertheless, she could not help feeling that he was a misogynist who did not want her to succeed. But what *did* he want? She wondered.

# Chapter 17

IT WAS A TWENTY-MINUTE WALK to the railway station from her college and it was raining steadily enough to soak Emily to the skin despite her having an umbrella. The train eventually arrived, albeit a little late; Emily boarded and went in search of Patricia, who had said she would try to get a seat in the first carriage.

It was early Friday evening, and the carriage was crowded, but Patricia spotted Emily and waved to her over the seats. Emily made her way through the standing passengers and joined her, and they greeted one another warmly. They chatted about their work, life at their respective universities, and how much they were both looking forward to being at home for the weekend. An hour and a half later, they reached Paddington station.

'Let's find Dad,' said Patricia as they stepped off the train.

Alan stood on the platform amongst the crowds of people coming and going, yet he managed to catch the girl's eyes as he waved to them.

'Lovely to see you both,' he said, 'come on, the car's parked outside.'

'Is mum with you?' asked Patricia.

'No, sweetheart, she's at home getting the dinner ready.'

They reached his Volvo estate, and Emily and Patricia got in the back seat.

'By the way, Emily, it's good news about the house, isn't it?' said Alan.

'Oh, yes, I suppose it is,' said Emily, unenthusiastically.

'What's this about?' asked Patricia.

'Sorry Pat, I forgot to tell you. Apparently, I'm inheriting the house I used to live in.'

'Really? That's great – *isn't it?*'

'Yes, I suppose so.'

'Well, of course, it is. Emily, you'll be quite a well-off young woman,' Alan interjected. 'I assume you *will* want to sell it?' he added.

'Definitely!' said Emily, emphatically.

'Well, I think it's marvellous that you'll finally get something for the years of misery you went through,' said Patricia.

Emily smiled at her pensively.

The next day was another bleak February day. The rain continued to pour. It didn't matter—just a couple of lazy days in the comfort of their home had been planned.

'The solicitor believes the house will fetch a good price, maybe as much as one hundred and twenty thousand pounds,' Gwen said to Emily over breakfast.

'I don't really mind how much it sells for. I'll just be pleased not to have it in my life anymore,' replied Emily.

'That's completely understandable,' said Gwen, 'but the money will be useful to have.'

'Yes, I see that now.'

'There'll be papers for you to sign, of course, but other than that, you won't need to be involved in the sale at all— unless you want to be. Alan and I can take care of everything for you.'

'That'd be good if you're sure,' said Emily.

'No problem at all, love,' said Alan, taking a bite of his toast. Of course, it might take some time to sell; it needs modernising quite a lot from what Gwen told me.'

'Oh yes, it certainly does,' said Emily.

'Well, there's no hurry, is there,' said Gwen cheerily. 'Now, has everyone had enough to eat?'

'Yes, thanks,' everyone said in agreement.

'In that case, I'll clear the things away, you all go and relax.'

'Are you sure?' asked Patricia.

'Quite sure, love, after all, it's not every weekend you both come home.'

It was a couple of hours later, after watching some TV and talking about their different lives at university, that Emily became restless. The matter of her mother's house had begun to play on her mind, and despite having made it clear that she wanted little involvement in the selling of it, suddenly, she felt a strong urge to lay her past life to rest once and for all.

'I think I might go for a walk,' Emily said.

'Okay,' said Patricia, 'I'll come with you.'

'I'd rather go alone if that's alright, Pat? You don't mind, do you?'

'No, not if that's what you want,' said Patricia, a little perplexed.

'I won't be long,' said Emily as she left the living room and made her way upstairs to her room.

'Don't be offended, I think I have a clue where she's going. She probably needs to be alone,' Gwen said to Patricia.

Emily searched through her bedside drawers and eventually found her key to the old house, put on her coat and left. It was a twenty-five-minute walk, but luckily, the rain had stopped. When she finally reached her old home, she hesitated before entering the gate. It was the first time she had been to the house since being taken into care four years previously. She steeled herself and made her way up the path to the front door. The high hedge was out of hand, and the grass was completely overgrown.

She took the key out of her pocket and placed it in the door; she hesitated a little before turning it, but turn it she did, then entered the dark hallway. A chill like she had never known travelled through her entire body as the understairs cupboard where she had been punished came into view. She opened the cupboard door. Eerily, the cup in which her stepfather had taken pity on her and brought her a drink still lay on the floor. The bad memories flooded back in an instant.

'I wonder where you are now?' she said aloud to no one but herself. She speculated for a moment whether her mother was alive or dead. Rhona was not exactly an old woman, so the chances were high that she was still alive and well somewhere, she thought. Emily imagined what it might be like if she were ever to see her again. There would certainly be questions as to why she had been so cruel to them as children, and as an adult, Emily would be better prepared to ask those questions and to seek an apology for her actions.

Emily was lucky. She was resilient. Bridget, on the other hand, had been badly affected by her mother's cruelty and lack of love and still was, as far as Emily could make out. Yes, she had come out of her shell a little, yet she was still a relatively subdued child and Emily and the others could see the pain she was still going through. There was no doubt she had been damaged by the unreciprocated love from Rhona, and perhaps that damage would be with her for the rest of her life. Emily could never forgive Rhona for that.

Having made her way through all the rooms in the house, Emily decided she had seen enough to remind her how fortunate she and the children had been that Gwen and Alan Parker had been so kind and had taken them on as their own. She locked the door and walked home, vowing never to set foot in the house ever again.

The weekend went by all too quickly. It was early Sunday afternoon that Gwen and Alan dropped off Emily and Patricia at the railway station to return to their respective universities. They hopped aboard and found a seat. Emily had not spoken about the visit she had made to her old home, and neither had Patricia until now.

The carriage was virtually empty as they waited to get underway. 'I didn't say anything before, but yesterday when you went for a walk, you went to the house, didn't you?'

Emily smiled. 'Yes, yes, I did, and I'm sorry I excluded you, Pat. It was just something I had to do on my own. Did Mum and Dad know where I was going?'

'They guessed. Are you okay?'

'Yes, I'm fine. I'm not sorry I went, I realised it was something I needed to get out of my system, and it worked. I'll never go back there again; I don't need to.'

Patricia nodded thoughtfully and took Emily's hand. 'I understand.'

A few minutes later, the carriage began to fill with other passengers, and soon after that, the train began its journey. They wished one another a fond farewell as the train pulled into the railway station in Oxford exactly an hour later.


Doctor Robinson sat behind his desk, silently scrutinising Emily's rewritten essay even though he had already marked it. This was purely for effect. He enjoyed making his students feel ill at ease, it seemed, especially the female students. Emily sat back in a chair facing him across his desk, watching intensely and listening to his occasional murmurs as he read. It was not clear if they were sounds of approval or not.

'Hmm, it's better, but I still think there's room for improvement,' he finally said, looking over his glasses.

'In what way?' Emily asked.

'Tell me, why do you want to become a journalist?' he asked, reaching down to one of his desk drawers. He pulled out a bottle of whiskey and two glasses, placing them on his desk.

'To report the truth,' she replied, 'and as I told you before, I don't drink.'

'Oh yes, of course, I forgot; you don't mind if I do?'

'Not at all,' she said.

'So you want to report the truth?' he said, leaning back in his chair.

'Yes, I believe in the truth.'

'That's all well and good,' he said, 'but your writing needs to be compelling as well.'

'Well, that's what I'm here to learn, and I've only been here a few months.'

He topped up his whiskey. 'Are you sure you won't join me' You should learn to loosen up a little, you know.'

'I'm perfectly fine, thank you, Doctor Robinson.'

He moved from behind his desk and drew his study curtains closed. As he had before, he stood behind her and began massaging her shoulders as she sat. 'Yes, the muscles in your shoulders feel very tight,' he said intimidatingly.

'Please don't do that, Doctor Robinson!' she said, her voice raised. She stood bolt upright and began to make her way to the door. He grabbed her arm tightly.

'Oh, come on, you little tease,' he said, moving closer.

'I'm warning you, Doctor, now please let go of my arm.'

He pulled her closer still and moved in for a kiss, but Emily drew up her knee to his groin, causing him to double up in pain. As she left him nursing his pain, she stood in the doorway for a moment, paused enough for him to regain composure. 'Don't ever try anything like that again; otherwise, I'll report you. I believe in the truth, remember?'

On that note, she left. He did not trouble her or any of the other female students again.

## *Chapter 18*



*Three Years Later – 1991*

EMILY'S PAST LIFE HAD SPURRED her on to succeed, and so had the initial problem she had faced with her tutor, in fact, having asserted herself, he had applied himself to assist her in achieving her aims and to eventually gain her degree. She had, in effect, changed his attitude towards the female sex, and it showed by his actions towards Emily and others. Indeed, over the coming months, they became firm friends, he was an asset to the university and extremely proud when, having completed her post-graduate course, Emily finally succeeded in obtaining her first-class degree.

The day of the award ceremony arrived; it was a bright, sunny day in June. Gwen, Patricia and Emily arrived at The Sheldonian Theatre on Broad Street in good time. It was a grand, historic building where graduations had taken place since 1670. Only two guest tickets were available, so therefore, Alan and Emily's siblings were unable to attend. They were eventually spotted in the crowd and greeted by Doctor Robinson.

'Emily, I hardly recognised you,' he said.

'Hi, yes, I thought a change of hairstyle was in order,' she said, sporting her new shorter, rather stylish haircut.

'And you must be Emily's mum and sister, Emily tells me you're studying medicine, and I'm very pleased to meet you both. You must be very proud of both of them, Mrs Parker.'

'How do you do? I've heard so much about you. Yes, we're extremely proud, and thank you for all you've done for Emily.'

'I can assure you; her achievement is wholly down to her intelligence and sheer determination. She's been an exceptional student.'

'She's an exceptional young woman all together,' said Gwen.

The compliments embarrassed Emily. 'I'd better go and get my robe on,' she said.

'Alright, dear,' said Gwen, 'Good luck with the ceremony.' The good wishes were echoed by Patricia and Doctor Robinson as Emily made her way to the changing rooms behind the stage.

An hour or so later, after the award ceremony had taken place, all the recipients and their families gathered in a side room for informal refreshments. These days, Emily now enjoyed the occasional glass of wine, and this day was for celebration, so she joined her parents in a glass of white wine. David Robinson joined them for a moment and congratulated Emily once again. He did not linger.

'Anyway, I suppose I'd better mingle, it was lovely to meet you,' he said to the Parkers. He smiled at Emily, 'Good luck in whatever you do, Emily, I'll miss you.' On that note, he melted into the crowd.

'Something tells me he has a soft spot for you,' said Patricia knowingly.

Emily smiled coyly.

Once the official photographs had been taken in her gown and proudly holding her rolled-up degree, and some more informal photographs were taken by Gwen and Patricia, Emily found her friends who had also graduated. She said her goodbyes, each promising to stay in touch. She then departed with Gwen and Patricia for the journey home.

Once they had arrived home, Gwen opened a bottle of champagne to keep the celebration going. 'Well, congratulations, dear, and in about a year, it'll be your turn, Patricia. I'm so proud of you both.'

'I couldn't have done it without all of you,' said Emily, 'thank you so much – for everything.'

'Hopefully, Alan will be back soon to join in the celebrations; he promised he'd try to finish work early,' said Gwen.

Forty-five minutes later, Alan's car pulled up on the driveway. 'Hi everyone, sorry I'm a bit late; the traffic was appalling. How did the ceremony go?'

'It was marvellous,' Gwen said enthusiastically, 'here, I saved you some champagne,' she said, handing him a glass.

'Well, Emily, many congratulations, well done indeed,' he said, lifting his glass.

'Oh, thank you, Alan.'

'Tell you what, who fancies going out to a restaurant tonight?' he said.

'Great idea!' said Patricia, how about you mum?'

'Yes, why not,' she replied.

'Good, that's settled then. I'll phone and book a table,' he said, going to the phone. 'Oh, looks like there's a message on the answering machine.' He pressed the play button. The estate agent acting for Emily stated they had finally had an offer on the house. It had taken a long time because of the dire need for modernisation of the property, but at last a property developer had viewed the house and planned to convert it into apartments, and furthermore, had offered a very realistic price.

'What do you think I should do?' asked Emily.

'If I were you, I think you would accept the offer,' said Alan, 'I don't think you'll get a better one.'

'That's good enough for me,' she said, 'As far as I'm concerned, it'll be good to get rid of that place.'

'Okay, I'll phone them tomorrow and let them know you accept,' said Alan.

'A double celebration then,' said Gwen.

'Yes indeed,' said Alan, 'and being a property developer, the deal will probably go ahead quite quickly. You'll have your money before you know it.'

'I'll need your advice on how best to invest the money, Alan,' Emily said.

'Of course,' he said.

'But I would like to buy myself and Patricia a small car, each with some of it,' she said eagerly.

'You don't have to do that,' said Patricia.

'I want to, Pat.'

'Well, in that case, you had better make sure you book some driving lessons so you can pass your tests,' said Gwen.

'Yes, as soon as possible,' said Emily, 'I'll need to be able to drive when I eventually find myself a job.'

'Well, there's plenty of time to find a job, but there are, remember, a couple of local newspapers around here, I'm sure with your qualifications, one of them will jump at the chance of taking you on as a trainee,' said Gwen, encouragingly. 'One small step at a time, Emily, one small step at a time,' she added, knowing very well that Emily had her sights firmly set on working for a national newspaper.

'You're right, one small step at a time.'

*Chapter 19*

ALMOST TWO WEEKS PASSED, Patricia had returned to Bristol, and Emily was decidedly bored. She had spent her days sifting through the local newspapers for openings as a local reporter without any luck. The only thing that broke the boredom was the driving lessons she had with Alan when he could fit them in. She had taken to driving like a duck to water, and Alan felt she would have no problem passing her test when the time came.

It was not enough, though, for her busy mind.

'I think I'm going to pop out for a while, Mum,' Emily said.

'Oh, okay, where are you going?' asked Gwen.

'Well, I thought I might pay a visit to the local newspapers to put the feelers out in person.'

'You *are* in a hurry, aren't you. I'll give you a lift if you like, as I'm not doing much,' said Gwen.

'Are you sure? I can easily catch the bus.'

'Quite sure. Be good to get away from the housework for a while.'

'Okay, great! I'll get changed,' said Emily.

'Before you do, I'm just wondering; wouldn't it be better to phone and make an appointment?'

'Possibly,' said Emily, 'I just think it's easier to fob people off over the phone.'

'Okay, if that's what you want to do –'

'I won't be long,' Emily said as she went to her room to change into a suit.

The first stop was at the offices of The Echo. Gwen waited in the car while Emily entered the reception area. A middle-aged woman smiled and asked how she could help.

'I was wondering if it would be possible to see someone regarding employment,' Emily replied.

'Can I ask what sort of position you're looking for?' asked the woman.

'Well, I'm looking for a position as a reporter.'

'Well, you'd need to see the editor; you may need to make an appointment, but I'll ask him if he can see you. Please, take a seat, and I'll try his office.'

'Thank you,' said Emily.

The receptionist spoke quietly on the phone; Emily could not make out what she was saying, and after a few moments, she hung up. 'I'm afraid the editor said he's not taking anyone on at the moment, but please feel free to try again in the future. I'm sorry.'

'Oh well, never mind. Thank you anyway. Could I leave a copy of my CV with you, just in case a vacancy occurs at some point?' said Emily as she raised herself and left.

'Yes, of course, I'll pass it on to the editor.'

'Any luck?' asked Gwen as Emily got in the car.

'No, they're not recruiting at the moment. The editor wouldn't even see me.'

'Well, don't be downhearted. You can't expect success on your first attempt,' said Gwen.

'Yes, I suppose you're right.'

'Look, it's almost lunchtime; how about we grab a spot of lunch before moving on to the other newspaper? After all, they'll probably be at lunch themselves soon anyway.'

'That sounds nice,' said Emily.

They found themselves at a pleasant pub and ordered sandwiches. Each of them drank lime and soda. It was fairly crowded with office workers on their lunch breaks, and the place had a good atmosphere. As they ate, Gwen paused for a moment. 'Emily, I've been meaning to ask you this, but it never seemed quite the right time.' Emily took on a look of puzzlement and concern. 'Oh' don't look so worried, it's just that – well, you've always called me mum, or at least you have for a long time. But your dad, you only call him Alan. I just wondered why? Do you feel uncomfortable calling him dad?'

Emily felt a little embarrassed. 'I'm sorry. I hope I haven't upset him. It's just that – I think it's just that I don't have any real information on my biological dad. I sometimes wonder where he might be or even if he's still alive. You see, although I didn't know him for very long before he left, I seem to remember he was a kind, gentle man – I hope you understand what I'm saying.'

'Yes, I think so.'

'It's stupid, I know, and I will call him dad from now on. The last thing I want to do is to hurt his feelings after all he's done for me.'

'Good, I'm glad we got that out of the way,' said Gwen, a little relieved.

'Me too, it wasn't a conscious decision, but it was selfish of me.'

'Not at all, I understand completely. So, The Surbiton News next stop, eh?' Gwen said, changing the subject.

'Hmm, I must say, I'm not too hopeful. Still, nothing ventured –'

'Exactly,' said Gwen.

The offices of The Surbiton News, a relatively impressive modern building for a local newspaper, were busy and bustling, with people coming and going. She assumed they were members of staff, perhaps even reporters. Emily took a deep breath before entering. This time though, Emily informed the receptionist of her qualification, hoping she would pass the information on to whoever it concerned.

Again, she was asked to take a seat while the receptionist called the editor.

'You're in luck, Miss Parker, the editor will see you. He'll be down in a moment to meet you.'

'Oh, thank you very much,' said Emily, her heart in her mouth.

A few minutes later, a rather stout man in his fifties appeared in a doorway. 'Miss Parker?'

'Yes,' Emily said, getting to her feet.

He gestured to her to follow him up the two flights of stairs to his office. 'Take a seat,' he said gruffly. A typical newspaper editor, Emily thought.

'So, you recently graduated from Oxford, I understand?'

'Yes, that's right, sir.'

'Did you write for the Oxford University Press or the Student Magazine?'

'Oh, frequently, yes.'

'Well, we don't have any vacancies for journalists at the moment.'

'Oh, I see, well thank you for seeing me anyway. Perhaps you could keep me in mind if any vacancies occur in the future.'

'Hold on, not so fast. I said, not at the moment. We do, however, have one of our reporters who will be retiring quite soon.'

'Oh, right.'

'How would you feel about working alongside him as a trainee to gain some experience? We'll need to fill his position when he goes. Anyway, it makes perfect sense for you to learn the ropes with him.'

'I'd love it,' said Emily, with obvious enthusiasm.

'I wouldn't be able to pay you much, and it'll be long hours,' he said.

'I'd do it for nothing to get the experience,' she said.

'Well, that's very commendable, but I'm not a slavedriver. When could you start?'

'As soon as possible, tomorrow, today!'

'Well, you'll have to wait a bit longer than that. We'll start you next Monday. Let's see how you get on from there.'

'Thank you so much for the opportunity, I won't let you down,' said Emily excitably.

With a hint of a smile, he said, 'Alright, Miss Parker, you can go home and relax now. Report to me on Monday at eight-thirty sharp.'

'Yes, sir, and thank you again. I'll see you on Monday.'

'Just one more thing before you go, stop calling me sir, it's Mr Mortimer, Bill, when we get to know each other better, alright?'

'Yes, Mr Mortimer,' she said with a smile.

'You were a long time,' said Gwen as Emily got into the car. 'How did you get on?'

Emily hesitated for effect. 'I've got a job as a trainee,' she finally blurted out.

'No, really? That's really marvellous, Emily. Your strategy paid off then.'

'I can't quite believe it. Of course, the pay isn't very much to start, but I don't mind that, I've got my first reporting job!'

# *Chapter 20*

## *Four Months Later*

EMILY HAD VIRTUALLY BEEN Ron Clarke's shadow for the first two months of her on the job training. She was then allowed to go out on small assignments on her own, covering minor local stories. But now, as the editor, Bill Mortimer had promised, the time came for Ron's retirement. Ron and Bill had been impressed by Emily's work and dedication, working long and sometimes unsociable hours for low pay without complaint.

The staff all met one lunchtime in the Red Lion pub for Ron's farewell. He had worked on various papers for thirty years, so his training had been invaluable to Emily. He had unbeknown to Emily, spoken highly of her to Bill Mortimer, who now took her to one side at the party to speak to her alone.

'Well, Emily, it's Ron's last day tomorrow, and from what he says and what I have seen, I'm satisfied to offer you a staff reporter position with immediate effect. How do you feel about that?' he said.

'How do I feel? Absolutely over the moon. Thank you so much, Bill; it means the world to me.'

'Excellent! And I hope you'll stay with us for a while at least. I know you're ambitious, and you'll want to move on to bigger and better things eventually, but not too soon, I hope; you can still gain a lot more experience with our little paper.'

'After the chance you've given me, it's the least I can do. I'm in no hurry to move on. Besides, I've still got a lot to learn.'

'Yes, I'm still learning, and I've been in the business twenty-five years,' he said. 'Oh, and by the way, don't forget, your salary will be increasing too.'

'Well, that'll be nice as well,' said Emily with a smile.

'Come on, let's join the others,' he said.

'Congratulations on your retirement, Ron,' said Emily, 'and thank you so much for all you've taught me.'

'Not at all. It was a pleasure working with you, young lady.'

'What will you do with yourself?' Emily asked.

'I haven't quite decided, but to start with, I'll probably be taking to the golf course.'

'Well, the best of luck and happy retirement,' she said.

'And the best of luck to you too, Emily.'

A month earlier, Emily had passed her driving test, and at the same time, the sale of the house had been completed and she received her money. She had bought a small second-hand car, a Ford Fiesta, which suited her perfectly. With her new position as a staff reporter, she needed it now more than ever. Simon and Bridget's share of the proceeds was put in trust funds by Alan until they reached the age of twenty-one.

Emily arrived home at 6.30pm that day. She went indoors, beaming.

'You look extremely pleased with yourself, like a cat that got the cream. What's happened? Asked Gwen, deeply curious.

'I still can't believe it. Do you remember me telling you that Ron, who I've been training under, was retiring? Well, I've been promoted to staff reporter in his place,' said Emily.'

'

'Oh, that's fantastic news, sweetheart. Who would have thought it in such a short space of time? Congratulations!' said Gwen, giving her a warm hug. 'I'm so proud of you.'

'I think I was just lucky. Where is everyone?' Emily asked.

'Your dad isn't home yet, Steven and Simon are in the garden, and Bridget is in her room.'

'Again?' Emily asked rhetorically.

'Yes, I'm afraid so. In fact, I was going to have a word with you about her, she seems to be withdrawing into her shell again. I thought she was doing better until recently; I'm wondering if it has anything to do with the sale of the house, maybe it's stirred up memories,' said Gwen.

'I suppose it's possible.'

'Anyway, I wanted your opinion. Do you think we should get her to see the psychologist again, or should we leave it a little longer? I *am* worried about her.'

'How about if I try talking to her first?' Emily asked.

'Well, you could only try, I suppose.'

'I'll go up and see her now.'

'Alright, dear, good luck, and congratulations again,' Gwen said.

Emily knocked on Bridget's door. There was no answer, so she opened the door and peered into the room. Bridget was laying on her bed, her eyes closed, and with the headphones of her Walkman covering her ears.

Emily gave a loud, exaggerated cough.

Bridget opened her eyes, startled by Emily's presence. She pulled down the earphones so they dropped around her neck.

'What are you listening to?' asked Emily.

'Nothing much,' came the sullen reply.

Emily sat on Bridget's bed. 'Do you mind if we have a little chat?' she asked.

'What about?'

'I don't know, just a chat; we are sisters after all.'

Bridget shrugged.

'How are you doing? Are you happy? We don't get many chances to talk these days, with my job and everything.'

'I'm okay.'

'How are things at school?'

'Fine.'

'Do you have friends at school? It's just that you never seem to ask anyone around,' asked Emily.

'Why are you asking me all these questions?'

'I'll be honest with you, Bridget, we're all a little worried about you. You never seem to want to do anything but stay in your room. I mean, you're fifteen, you should be enjoying yourself with friends. The only time we see you is at mealtimes, and then you go straight back to your room. Is something worrying you that you'd like to talk about?'

'No, is that it? Can you leave me alone now,' Bridget snapped.

'I want to get to the bottom of what's making you hide yourself away so much, Bridget. Is it something to do with our mother?'

'I don't want to talk anymore, just go, will you,' said Bridget, replacing her headphones.

Emily was so frustrated with her younger sister that she felt like tearing the headphones off her, instead, she left and returned downstairs.

By this time, Alan had returned home from his office. 'Hi, Dad,' said Emily.

'Hi Em, Gwen's just told me the good news. Congratulations,' he said cheerily.

'Thanks dad, yes, I still can't quite believe my luck,' said Emily.

'It'll be Fleet Street next,' he said.

'That's my aim, but we'll see.'

'How did you get on with Bridget?' asked Gwen.

'Not too well, I'm afraid. She wouldn't open up to me at all.'

'Well, it's probably just because she's a teenager,' said Alan.

'I'm not so sure,' said Emily, 'she's always had this misguided loyalty towards Rhona. I think she might blame me for her mother vanishing the way she did.'

'Well, you can't blame yourself for that; you saved her from a life of complete misery,' said Gwen. 'Maybe we *should* consider some kind of counselling for her.'

'Yes, perhaps you're right,' said Emily, thoughtfully.

'I'll look into it on Monday,' said Gwen, 'it couldn't do any harm, could it.'

'No, I guess not,' said Alan, 'professional help might be what's needed, they have their ways of getting people to open up.'

'Anyway, on a more cheerful note, Patricia's coming home for the weekend. With all the excitement about your job, I completely forgot to tell you. She's driving home tonight,' said Gwen.

'Oh, that's great, it'll be great to catch up,' said Emily.

Patricia arrived in time for their evening meal. She and Emily had much to talk about, not only Emily's new role, but of Patricia's course. Patricia's course was going well, and she thought it would only be another year if she was lucky enough to graduate. One thing marred the evening for Emily, the way Bridget did not eat at all, but frowned at her across the dining table.

That night, Emily dreamt of Rhona.

# *Chapter 21*

IT HAD BEEN A FEW months since Emily had begun working as a staff reporter at The Surbiton News. Although it was just a weekly local paper, she was enjoying the work, and despite her qualifications, she was grateful to have been offered the job at the age of twenty-one. It was more than she could have hoped for. She intended to keep her promise of staying on at the paper for at least a year.

Every morning, driving to the office, she would pass 124 Main Street, her old home in which she had spent so many years. Somehow, her eyes were always morbidly drawn to it. There had been no sign of any activity from the property developer since the sale had been completed, that is, not until this particular day. Now, the large hedge that once hid the property from prying eyes had been removed, and trucks and plant machinery had moved in to commence work on converting it into apartments. She found herself slowing down for a better look, but the driver in the car behind her tooted his car horn, so she quickly drove forward.

All of the reporters shared one large office space on the second floor, apart from Bill Mortimer, who had his own office. There were three reporters in total on the staff, and each was assigned different reporting jobs for the day to report on. The assignments could range from interviewing a district council official on some matter that would interest the public to a more heartwarming story, such as a local boy who had adopted and trained an injured jackdaw. It was all fairly mundane but a good experience.

Emily, like any other good reporter, would always try to find a new angle on any of the assignments given to her, no matter how dull the story first appeared. Very often, depending on the story, one of the photographers would accompany her. On this particular day, Bill had given her two jobs and had written them in her desk diary, the imminent retirement of a postmistress who had been in the job for forty years and the opening of a new supermarket by a local dignitary. There would normally be other items worthy of reporting that would arise throughout the day.

Emily hoped that she would one day be working for a national newspaper, reporting on important issues that the entire country would read about. However, she knew that was a long time ahead, if indeed she ever secured such a highly sought-after position, for now, though, she was content. After drinking a cup of coffee, she telephoned the ageing postmistress to arrange a suitable time to go and interview her and to take a couple of photographs. But her first job of the day was at the new supermarket, the grand opening was to be at 10am, so she set off with her photographer in good time.

On arrival, there was a small crowd that had gathered to see the opening and to be among the first to shop there. The dignitary cut the ribbon at the stroke of ten, and Emily's photographer caught the moment with his camera. Alongside him was the photographer from their rival newspaper, The Echo. Afterwards, it was Emily's turn and she briefly interviewed the large man who had officially opened the shop and also the shop manager, asking what his supermarket had to offer compared to others in the district. There was precious little material to give on this story, "Lower prices," answered the manager proudly.

Emily returned to the office, typed out her story and printed out two copies. It did not take long. She took a copy to Bill Mortimer's office and handed it to him. 'Any other jobs come in, Bill?' she asked hopefully.

'Nothing at the moment. It's a pretty slow day. Why don't you take an early lunch until it's time for your next job.'

'Okay Bill, but would it be okay if I gave the police a call first, to see if they have anything for us?'

'Did that about an hour ago. They had nothing then, but please, be my guest.'

Emily made a cup of coffee and phoned the local police headquarters. Bill, as usual, was correct, they had nothing newsworthy for them.

She finished her coffee, put on her jacket and left for lunch. She opened Bill's office door ajar before leaving. 'You were right – nothing. I'll have that early lunch now and I'll see you later, bye.'


As Emily drove to the office a few days later, approaching her old house, it soon became apparent that something was going on there. There were two marked police cars parked on the road outside the property, a police van, all with their blue lights still flashing. There was also another car that was unmarked. She imagined it might have been an accident involving one of the workers on the site. Peculiar, though, she thought, as there was no ambulance in attendance on-site at that time.

The journalist in her automatically kicked in, yet an impending feeling of dread also washed over her. She stopped as close to the house as possible and went to a nearby telephone kiosk. She dialled out the direct line to the editor.

'Hello, Bill? It's Emily. There's something going on at a house in Main Street, there's a large police presence there, and I'd like to take a closer look, if that's okay with you?'

'Any idea what's going on?' asked Bill.

'No, not yet, I've only just stopped. Haven't had a chance to ask, I thought I'd call you first.'

'Yes, well, carry on if you think it might be newsworthy,' he said, 'I'll leave you to judge that. I'll send a photographer down there just in case.'

'Okay, thanks, Bill, I'll try not to be too long.'

Emily made her way back to the house; the front of the property was cordoned off, and a police constable stood guard. 'Good morning, Emily Parker, Surbiton News,' she said, showing her press card, 'can you tell me what the incident is?'

'I'm afraid I'm not at liberty to discuss that, miss,' said the constable.

'Well, is there anyone that could?' she asked.

'Just one moment, miss,' he said, clicking the button on his radio handset. 'Sorry to bother you, sir,' he said to his sergeant, 'there's a young lady from the press here who would like to speak to someone. Can Detective Inspector Jones spare a minute?'

The constable's radio crackled to life. 'Wait one, I'll ask him,' said his sergeant.

A few awkward minutes passed until a man in a suit, complete with a raincoat and Wellington boots that were caked in mud, appeared from the rear of the property. He approached, stern-faced at the press intrusion.

'What can I do for you, young lady?'

Emily flashed her press card again. 'I just wondering if you could tell me what's going on here?'

'And how, may I ask, did you become aware there was an incident here in the first place?' he growled.

'As a matter of fact, I was just passing on my way to work. I travel this way every day,' said Emily.

'I see. All I can tell you at the moment is that the building contractors here, this morning, uncovered what appears to be a shallow grave, which we are currently investigating.'

'A grave?' Emily's heart skipped a beat.

'Now, if you don't mind, miss, I'm very busy,' said the Detective Inspector. He began to walk away.

Emily called to him. 'Would you let me have more information if I were to tell you that I used to live here?'

The man turned slowly to her. 'When was this?'

'Up until 1984,' she said.

The man rubbed his chin thoughtfully. 'It might do,' he said, 'what's your name again?'

'Emily Parker, but at that time, I was Emily Thorne. I'm adopted, you see,' she said.

'Thorne – that name rings a bell. Why would that be?'

'Probably because the authorities were looking for her. She was abusive to us kids, you see, and they wanted to prosecute, but she disappeared, seemingly without a trace.'

'Yes, I remember now, *Rhona* Thorne, wasn't it?'

'That's right.'

'And weren't we also trying to track down your stepfather?'

'Yes, he went missing suddenly, my mother told me he'd left her. I've got a bad feeling about this now, though,' said Emily.

'Hmm, well, we'll just have to wait and see, but I can tell you a body has been uncovered, and it is male. We will almost certainly need you to come to the mortuary to see if you can identify him. Later today, perhaps.'

'Yes, that should be okay,' said Emily.

'Very good, I'll call you at your office,' he said.

'Okay, thanks. Oh, and Detective Inspector, I would like very much to have an exclusive on this if possible?' Emily said.

The man smiled vaguely. 'Well, you're a cool character, aren't you. Don't worry, it looks like you will anyway, doesn't it.'

At that moment, the staff photographer turned up. 'Is there any chance of a quick photo of the site where the grave has been found?' asked Emily.

'Just a distant shot, that's all,' said the Inspector. He guided them to where they could take a photograph. The excavated area was surrounded by a white plastic shielding tent.

'Thank you, Inspector,' said Emily.

'I'll speak to you later when the body is ready for identification,' he said.

# *Chapter 22*

'WELL, DID YOU MANAGE TO FIND OUT ANYTHING?' asked Bill on Emily's return to the office.

'Yes, yes I did, look, would you mind if we talked about it privately in your office, Bill?'

He looked puzzled. 'No, of course not,' he said, beckoning her to follow him. 'Now then, what's this all about?'

'I spoke to Detective Inspector Jones at the scene. It seems as if workmen on the site have unearthed a body in a shallow grave. It looks suspicious.'

'That's great work, Emily, some excitement on our quiet little patch at last, so why the cloak and dagger stuff?'

Emily hesitated. 'It's just that I thought you should know that I used to live at the property, so you see, it could mean I'm personally involved. I thought you should know, that's all.'

'I see. Well – do you think the victim is known to you?'

'Could be, yes.'

'I see.'

'Oh, don't worry, it won't affect my work. I have a feeling it could be my stepfather; we weren't very close.'

'So what makes you think that?'

'I'm adopted, Bill. My name used to be Emily Thorne. My mother abused and neglected me and my brother and sister terribly as children; she's a horrid woman. Anyway, one day, my stepfather went, and she said he had left her. I hadn't really thought about it until now, but the discovery has made me think that perhaps it's him they've found.'

'Emily, I had no idea. Why didn't you say anything about it before? I would never have guessed you'd been abused. You're always so strong.'

'Well, it's not something one likes to talk about. But the story, will you run it?'

'Yes, of course, I'll run it, but are you sure you're up to continuing with it, or should I assign someone else to cover it?'

'Absolutely, I feel quite detached. Oh, but I should tell you, the police want me to go to the mortuary to possibly identify the body later today. Of course, it may be someone completely different. Either way, though, I'll have a good source of inside information.'

'Okay, if you're sure, then stick with it,' Bill said encouragingly.

'Thanks, Bill, that means a lot.'

'Try to get as much information as you can before tomorrow when we go to press,' said Bill, 'I won't give you any more jobs today. Just concentrate on this for now, okay?'

'Yes, okay, Bill. Hopefully, I'll find out more this afternoon.'

Emily returned to her desk and began to type out a rough draft of the story so far, she would pause from time to time, wondering about whose body it really was that had been discovered. How would she feel if it transpired to be Peter? Although they were not close as such, he was not a bad man, just weak perhaps, and he *had* finally found the courage to help her when her mother locked her in the cupboard.

She was certain she would feel some sadness, but more than that, she would feel ashamed to have a mother who was a cold-blooded murderer. She thought again about where Rhona might be at this moment and what she might be doing? If the body was that of Peter, the hunt for Rhona would begin in earnest, and hopefully, she would brought to justice.

Yet, there was something else that played on Emily's mind. If Rhona *was* found, Emily would be irrefutably connected to her, and how, she wondered, would that affect her life and career? She was so glad she had taken the name Parker. Perhaps that would go some way to protect her. She eventually dismissed the thoughts from her mind and concentrated on writing the story. A few hours later, a call was put through to her. It was Detective Inspector Jones.

'Hello, Miss Parker? Detective Inspector Jones here. We're ready for you at the mortuary now. Are you free to come down and identify the body?

'Yes, Inspector, I could be there in fifteen minutes if that's okay?'

'Good. Would you like me to send a car for you?'

'That won't be necessary, thank you, I'll make my own way there.'

'Alright, Miss, we'll see you shortly then.'

'Okay, Inspector, goodbye.'

Emily popped her head into Bill's office. 'I'm going to the mortuary now, Bill, and of course, I'll try to pick up any further information while I'm there.'

'Okay, Emily, take care. I hope it's not too traumatic for you.'

'I'll be fine. Oh, would it be alright if I took a photographer with me?'

'Yes, that's fine, take James, he was with you earlier, so he'll know the story.'

'Thanks, I'll see you a little later then.'

A short while after, Emily and her photographer arrived at the mortuary. 'You'd better wait in the car, James. Maybe you can get a shot of the detective when I come out.'

'Sure,' said the young photographer, 'but what are we doing at the morgue anyway?' he asked curiously.

'It's a long story; I'll explain one day,' said Emily, 'I shouldn't be too long.'

The Detective Inspector was inside the waiting area. 'Hello Emily, you don't mind if I call you Emily, do you?'

'No, not at all,' she said.

'Well, I'm afraid this is going to be pretty grim for you. I'm not even sure you'll be able to make a positive identification; the body is very badly decomposed, you see. Are you sure you want to go through with it?'

'Yes – I'm sure,' she said.

'Well, if you're ready then, let's go in.'

Emily took a deep breath and entered the mortuary with the detective. What was obviously a body lay covered in a surgical sheet on the pathologist's examination table. There was a pungent odour of disinfectant and the stench of death in the room. They approached the body until Emily stood over it, all the time, the detective's hand comfortingly on her shoulder.

'Are you ready, Miss?' asked the pathologist.

Emily simply nodded. The sheet was pulled back, revealing just the head. She flinched at first, averting her eyes for a moment. She had never seen a corpse before, let alone one that was in a state of decomposition. She somehow found the strength to take another look.

'Well, Emily, is this your stepfather, do you think?' asked Jones.

Despite the condition of the body, Emily nodded. 'Yes, that's him.'

'Are you certain?' he asked.

'Absolutely certain,' said Emily.

'Okay, let's get you out of here,' said the detective gently.

'Yes, please,' said Emily.

She composed herself once out of the mortuary, although the stench of death still lingered in her nostrils. 'Do you know how he died yet?' she asked.

'Too early to say for sure, but the pathologist thinks it may have been a brain haemorrhage brought about by a blow to the head from a heavy object,' said Jones.

'So, my mother, my biological mother, that is, is a murderer?'

The question was rhetorical, but Jones answered anyway. 'It would seem possible, yes. Emily, now that you've formally identified the body, I'm afraid we'll need you to come in and make a statement.'

'Yes, of course.'

'Could you call in at the station tomorrow?' Jones asked.

'Tomorrow will be a busy day, we go to press tomorrow you see, and I've got a story to write. Could I call in tomorrow evening after work?'

'Yes, that'll be fine.'

'Oh, Inspector, can I ask a favour of you?'

'Yes, name it.'

'You're going to think I'm pretty cold-hearted, but could my photographer get a shot of you, and also, could you give me a few words on the case that I can print?'

He smiled wryly at Emily. 'You journalists! Yes – why not,' he said.

## *Chapter 23*

THE INFORMATION IMPARTED BY Detective Inspector Jones was nothing Emily did not already know. However, if she were to report on the incident, it was essential, the words came from him. Back at the office, she briefly consulted her notes and went into Bill's office. She also asked James to print the photographs he had taken as a priority.

'Take a seat, Emily,' said Bill, 'how did it go?'

'Well, I did manage to identify the body,' she said sombrely.

'So it *was* your stepfather, I presume.'

Emily nodded.

'I expect, given the circumstances, the police think it's a murder case?'

'Oh yes,' said Emily, 'and my mother is the prime suspect at the moment.'

'Are you okay? You can take the rest of the day off if you want to,' he said.

'No, I'm fine. Besides, I have a story to write.'

'This is your first scoop, Emily; I've decided to run the story on the front page.'

'Oh, great! she said.

'You deserve it,' said Bill, 'let me have the copy as soon as you've written it up.'

'I will, thanks Bill.' She returned to her desk to start work.

Although Rhona and Steven were married, Rhona had not used his name of Phillips, she had always used the name Thorne, from her first marriage, the name of the father of Emily, Simon and Bridget. Not through any sentimental reason, but simply because she felt it sounded better for her show business career, such as it was. This would make for a complex story, yet nothing Emily could handle. There would be no mention of Emily's family connection in the report.

She spent an hour or so writing and fine-tuning her report until she was finally satisfied, she took the final draft into Bill's office. He read it carefully as Emily sat waiting for his opinion. He made a few observations and amended a couple of words here and there, but nothing major.

'Yes, very good, Emily. I've noted a couple of changes; just type it out again, and we'll go to print with it. All in all, very well written.'

James knocked on Bill's office door at that moment.

'Come in.'

'Sorry to disturb you, but I have the photographs.'

Bill and Emily perused them. There was the picture he had taken at the scene showing the plastic sheet around the area where the body was and the one of DI Jones taken that afternoon.

'Yes, good. We'll use the photo of the crime scene on the front page, and the policeman picture can go on the inside page with your article, Emily.'

Emily rewrote the story and took it through to Bill. He quickly read through it. 'That's great, Emily, it's getting late, go home.'

'Yes, alright. You're sure you're happy with the story?'

'Absolutely, I'm proud of you. It was a good move on my part when I took you on. Now go on, go home and get some rest.'

It was 8pm by the time Emily reached home. There was such a lot to tell Gwen and Alan that she hardly knew where to begin. And as far as Simon, and particularly Bridget, were concerned, she felt it better not to mention the events at all.

'Hi mum,' said Emily, entering the living room. Gwen was watching the television.

'Hello dear, you're late, busy day?'

'Yes, you could say that,' Emily said, dropping onto a sofa. 'Where's dad?'

'He's taking a shower; the others are upstairs as well. We've already eaten, but your dinner is keeping warm in the oven when you're ready.'

'Thanks, Mum, maybe later; I'm not too hungry at the moment.'

'Of course, whenever suits you. By the way, I've managed to arrange a few sessions for Bridget with a counsellor; she starts them next week.'

'Oh, that's good,' said Emily.

'Are you okay? You seem a little distracted, love,' said Gwen.

'Sorry, it's been a long day,' Emily paused, 'as a matter of fact, I have something to tell you; I'm not sure where to begin.'

Gwen's body tightened; she sat upright in her chair. 'That sounds ominous,' she said.

'Oh, don't worry, mum, it's nothing that affects us, well, not as such,' said Emily.

'Well, what is it?'

'Okay, here goes, it's regarding Rhona and her second husband, Peter.'

'Go on,' said Gwen curiously.

'There's no easy way of saying this. His body has been found in a shallow grave at my old house; it seems he was murdered – probably by her.'

'Oh my God, that's truly awful. How did you find out? Are you okay?'

'Yes, I'm fine, really, I am. As it happened, I stumbled on it on my way to work this morning. The grounds of the house were crawling with police, and I stopped to investigate. Actually, I'm writing the story for the paper. You'll see it in tomorrow's edition. It's something of a scoop for me.'

'And do the police know about your connection?' asked Gwen.

'Oh yes, I told the detective in charge of the case. I had to go and identify the body this afternoon; actually, that was the worst part of it all. The body was badly decomposed; I can still smell death.'

'You poor thing, it must have been awful for you.'

'It wasn't pleasant, that's for sure. The funny thing is, I'm not that surprised; I always knew she was capable of anything,' said Emily.

'I know what you mean – but murder!'

'Yet looking on the bright side, as far as my career is concerned, it's a definite feather in my cap, I think.'

'Yes, I suppose it is,' said Gwen, 'I'll look forward to reading it.'

# *Chapter 24*

THE NEXT DAY, when Emily arrived at work, she picked up a copy of the paper in the reception. Her story dominated the front page with a picture of the crime scene and the headline: "Body Unearthed in Surbiton!" Below was a brief outline of the story with her name at the top. Emily couldn't help feeling a certain pride seeing the words "By Emily Parker." Her report continued on the inside page with the photograph of Detective Inspector Jones.

'Well, congratulations on your first big story,' Bill said as she entered the press room. The other reporters also congratulated her, albeit slightly enviously; they were all older than Emily, and some had worked at the paper for years without getting a story like this. None knew of her personal involvement in the case.

'Get yourself a coffee and come and see me in my office, will you,' said Bill.

'Yes, sure,' said Emily.

She entered his office with her mug of coffee. 'Take a seat,' said Bill, 'and don't look so worried. You've done a great job on this story so far.'

'Why do I think there's a "But" coming my way?' said Emily.

'There is no but. I was simply going to say that I want you to continue covering this story. For the time being, I'd like you on it full-time.'

'Thanks, Bill, that's fantastic.'

'Of course, now the story is out there, the other press, including the nationals, will be all over it as you can imagine, but the way I see it, you have the advantage over them. Find out anything you can. We need an angle to make our little paper stand out, so dig, and then dig some more. Is that alright with you?'

'Yes, of course it is. Thanks for this, Bill, I really appreciate it.'

'I've already informed the other staff. Now, there may be some slight resentment on their part, but I think you are strong enough to handle that. Oh, and I'm putting James at your disposal as well, just in case you need him. Okay, that's all, so let's see what you can come up with.'

Emily returned to her desk elated, thrilled at being given a free hand in covering the story. She finished her coffee and gathered her notebook, ready for the day ahead. What the day would bring and how it would end, she was not sure, but she knew how it would begin.

'Would it be possible to see Detective Inspector Jones?' she asked, standing at the front desk of the police station.

'I think he's out at the moment, Miss. Can I take a message for him?' said the desk sergeant.

'When is he expected back?' asked Emily.

'I'm sorry, I couldn't say, Miss. Could someone else help you, perhaps?'

'No, no, that's alright, I'll catch him later. Thanks anyway.'

'Very well, Miss.'

Emily had a good idea of where Jones might be. She drove to the crime scene. A constable still stood guard at the front of the property. She parked her car, put on a pair of Wellington boots, and approached him. 'Can I help you?' he asked quizzically.

'I'm looking for DI Jones, is he here?' she said, showing her press card.

'He is, but I think he's rather busy at the moment, miss,' he said.

'Well, could you tell him I'm here?' she said, showing her press card again, 'I think he might see me.'

The constable radioed his sergeant. 'Sarge, there's an Emily Parker of The Surbiton News here, says she would like to see the DI.'

Jones was standing next to the sergeant, and a forensic team inside the garden shed when the message came through. 'Tell him I'll be right there,' he said.

A couple of minutes later, Jones appeared at the front of the property. 'Good morning, Emily. What brings you here? How are you feeling today?'

'I'm fine. Just wondering if there have been any further developments, really?' said Emily.

'Well, it's early days; the investigation has hardly begun, as you can imagine.'

'Of course,' she said.

'Actually, there's a couple of things I need to ask you. Firstly, would you happen to have a photograph of your mother and Steven?'

'As a matter of fact, I think I may have one, yes,' said Emily.

'Marvellous! Could you dig it out and let me have it as soon as possible?'

'Yes, I can do that for you.'

'Good, and secondly, we'll need to take your fingerprints, just for elimination purposes you understand.'

'Okay, no problem.'

'Oh, and don't forget, I'll need to take a statement from you,' said the DI.

'Yes, I can come to the station whenever you like; my day is fairly free.'

'I should be finished here quite soon. Could you make it for 12 o'clock?'

'Yes, that should be fine. Can I ask what you're looking at here today?'

'The forensic team are dusting for prints on the garden tools in the shed, shovels, spades and so on. After that, we'll be closing it down as a crime scene so that the contractors can get back to work,' he replied.

'I see. Well, I'll go home now and dig out that photo you want, and I'll see you later.'

'Thanks, Emily,' he said, returning to his work.

'Hello Em, what are you doing at home at this time?' asked Gwen, sipping her mid-morning coffee in the kitchen.

'Hi, mum. The police want a photograph of Rhona, I think I have one somewhere. I didn't keep it for any sentimental reasons as you can imagine, I suppose I just thought it may prove useful one day, and it has. Here's the paper with my story in it,' she said, handing it to Gwen.

'Oh, thanks. Would you like a coffee?'

'Oh, thanks, I'd love one, I'll be down in a minute,' Emily said, rushing up to her room. She rummaged through her bedside drawers until she finally found the eight-by-six-inch black and white print. The picture was one that Rhona had professionally taken in her showgirl outfit; it was the only photograph Emily had of her. She looked at it with contempt.

'it's a very good article, Emily, I'm so proud of you,' said Gwen, as Emily sat next to her.

'Bill has given me the story full-time, or at least until there's nothing else to report. I have to go to the police station later to make a statement following my formal identification yesterday. He also wants my fingerprints.'

'I suppose they'll pull out all the stops to find Rhona now,' said Gwen.

'Sounds like it.'

'I'm not sure how I feel about that,' said Gwen thoughtfully.

'How do you mean?' asked Emily inquisitively.

'Oh, ignore me, I'm just being silly.'

'No, tell me, what's worrying you?'

'It's just that – oh, I know *you're* very strong, but it's Bridget that I'm worried about. It could affect her badly; she's not doing well even now, and I can't bear thinking of what it would do to her if she finds out her mother is a murderer.'

'We'll just have to try and protect her from it, mum, that's all we can do,' said Emily.

Emily returned to the office before going to her meeting with DI Jones. She went to the third floor, where the photographer's office and darkroom were. James was the only one in the office; he sat at his desk as she entered.

'Thank God, human life, I thought I'd go mad with boredom. Are we going somewhere?' he asked anxiously.

'I'm afraid not, not at the moment anyway. But I do have a little job for you, could you make some good quality copies from this photo?' she asked, handing him the picture of Rhona.

'Of course I can, is that it? Is that going to be the height of my exciting day?'

'I'm afraid so for now,' smiled Emily.

'Who is she anyway?' he asked.

'That is the suspected murderer, James!'

'How did you get hold of this? You seem to have a lot of information at your fingertips. What's going on?'

'Can you get these prints done in the next thirty minutes?' Emily said, avoiding the question.

'Yeah, I guess so.'

'Okay, bring them down when they're ready.'

'Yes, but you didn't answer my question.'

'No, that's right, James, I didn't.'

Once DI Jones had the photograph of Rhona, he told Emily there would now be a nationwide search to find Rhona and bring her to justice. There were still the outstanding charges of child neglect and abuse to be taken into account, he said. Emily had, as requested, given her fingerprints to eliminate her from the police investigation. Jones wanted the same from Simon and Bridget. The thought of Bridget having to go through that made Emily uncomfortable. She explained to DI Jones how Bridget had suffered long-term psychological problems caused by their harsh upbringing.

He was sympathetic but said it was necessary and explained it could be done with tact so as not to distress Bridget too much. Emily was not pleased but had little choice in the matter, it seemed.

# Chapter 25

*Three Days Later*

IT WAS AROUND 7PM when the phone rang. Alan answered.

'Good evening, sir. Is that Mr Parker?'

'Yes, speaking.'

'I'm sorry to disturb you, Mr Parker, it's Detective Inspector Jones of the local C.I.D. Is Emily there by any chance?'

'Yes, she's here, I'll get her for you,' said Alan.

Emily picked up the receiver. 'Hello, Detective Inspector, have you got some news?'

'Yes, I have, but not what you might be expecting. I'm afraid we've had no luck locating Rhona so far. But no, I'm afraid this is much more serious.'

'Why, what's happened?' asked Emily.

'We got a call from the site foreman at 124 Main Street about an hour ago. They had been excavating in a different location in the garden when they came across another suspicious-looking patch of ground.'

'Really? Okay, go on, Inspector.'

'We've got men digging up the area as we speak if we do find something, or should I say someone. Would you have any idea who it might be?'

'This is incredible, it can't be happening. No, I have no idea,' said Emily.

'Hmm, that's a shame,' he said.

'Well, could I come down to take a look? It may help if I'm there,' she said.

'I suppose it couldn't do any harm, but only through your personal involvement. This time, leave your journalist's hat at home, alright?'

'Alright, Inspector,' I'll be there in fifteen minutes,' she said and hung up.

Emily returned to the living room. 'Could I have a word in the kitchen?' she asked Gwen and Alan.

'What is it?' asked a concerned Gwen.

Emily hesitated before speaking. 'That was the detective in charge of the case. It seems there might be another body in the garden of my old house. I'm going down there now.'

'But who?' asked Alan.

'They haven't yet got a body, but they suspect there will be one.'

'Good grief,' said Gwen, 'what on earth is going on?'

'I'll see you later. I must go,' Emily said, grabbing a coat from the hallway.

Emily drove off as they watched through the kitchen window. 'What an evil bitch that Rhona is,' said Gwen, 'I wonder who it is this time? It's amazing really that the kids ever survived her wickedness, isn't it?' she said, leaning her head on Alan's shoulder.

'Yes, it certainly is,' said Alan.

A short while later, Emily pulled up outside the house. DI Jones was out on the pavement, taking a break and smoking a cigarette. She got out of her car and joined him.

He took the pack of cigarettes from his coat pocket. 'Cigarette?' he said, flashing the open pack to Emily.

'I don't really smoke,' she hesitated for a moment, 'but on this occasion, I think I will, thanks,' she said, taking one from the pack. She hesitated again before eventually placing the cigarette between her lips. Jones lit it for her. She took a draw on the cigarette, never really inhaling she blew the smoke straight out of her mouth.

'I can't believe this is happening,' she said, 'who can it be this time?'

'Yes, quite, that's what we need to find out,' said Jones, 'it's a bad business, especially for you.' He threw his cigarette butt on the pavement and stubbed it out with his shoe. 'Come on, follow me; it doesn't look like you're enjoying that very much anyway,' he said with a chuckle. As they walked through the mud to the rear garden, Jones said, 'You do realise I'm breaking some rules here, allowing you onto a possible crime scene?'

'Yes, and I appreciate it, but I do hope you won't get into trouble,' she said.

'No, of course not, I'm the officer in charge. I have certain discretionary powers; just don't touch anything, that's all.'

Emily acknowledged with a nod.

They reached the area where the digging was taking place, bright lights shining down on the area in question, and a forensic team stood by.

'How are you doing men?' asked Jones.

'I think we've finally hit something,' said one of the overalled policemen. 'It looks like some kind of rolled-up rug.'

The hole was much deeper than the one where Emily's stepfather was found. The earth had been far more compacted. It appeared to have been there for some considerable time. It took four police officers to carefully drag the sodden, earth-encrusted rug from the cavity. Suddenly, a memory flooded back to Emily, to that one occasion when Patricia and Tom came to her house, and the younger children pointed out a strange outline in the frosty ground. At the time, she dismissed it as nothing of any consequence, and she related this to DI Jones as they stood watching.

'What year would this have been?' he asked Emily.

'It would have been 1984, I guess,' said Emily.

Once brought to the surface, the forensic team went to work unravelling the rug. 'You stand back for a while, Emily,' said the DI as he moved in for a closer look. This time, there was no identifiable body, only the skeletal remains of what appeared to be a male. He returned to Emily. 'Well, there's no point in you hanging around now. There isn't a body for you to identify,' he said.

'Well, what is it then?' she asked.

'Well, yes, it was once a body, but only a skeleton now. Must have been here for quite a while,' he said, 'the only way we're going to identify this person is through dental records by the look of things. So you see, you may as well go home now, Emily.'

'I wonder who it could be? Anyway, I'm going to have to write something on this; but only in a personal capacity, you do understand, don't you?' Emily said, 'I have to follow up on the first body that was found.'

'Yes, I know you do. We all have our jobs to do, I suppose.'

'Will you keep me posted on any developments regarding the identity?' she asked.

'Yes, of course I will. It may take some time, though, so try to be patient young lady.'

Emily half smiled. 'I'll try.'

# Chapter 26

A WEEK AFTER HER article on the first body that was recovered from the building site, Emily's follow-up report was published, though there was very little information at that stage. Nevertheless, she wrote a compelling article that would capture the imagination of readers, but that was not all; it also gained the attention of national newspapers and television news channels. It was to be expected, though Emily was worried that perhaps she would lose her exclusive rights to the inside information on the case. Moreover, would her personal involvement be finally revealed?

Two weeks later, when there was no more information forthcoming, the national press lost interest, at least for the time being, yet it was then that one Monday morning, Emily received a call from DI Jones at her office.

His voice took on a sombre tone. 'Morning Emily.'

'Good morning, Inspector. Have you got some news for me?'

'Yes,' he said, 'could you possibly come down to the station this morning?'

'Uh, yes, of course,' she said eagerly.

'Okay, if you could come at around 10.30 then?'

'Is everything okay, Inspector? You sound different.'

'I'll see you at 10.30 then,' he said, avoiding the question, then hanging up.

Emily found his behaviour odd, yet she was keen to find out what information he had gained on the case. She told Bill where she was going and headed down to the police station at 10 o'clock. Not knowing why exactly, she was apprehensive about the meeting on this occasion. Jones was waiting for her at the front desk when she arrived punctually.

'Hello Emily, come up to my office,' he said, his voice still solemn.

She followed him upstairs to his office, neither of them speaking. The silence was palpable from Jones.

'Take a seat, Emily,' he said.

'There's something wrong, isn't there?' she said. Jones swivelled in his chair for a moment before speaking. 'As you know, we were checking on dental records for the second body. It's a slow process, but we now have the results, and they're conclusive, I'm afraid.'

Emily shifted uncomfortably in her chair. 'And?' she asked.

'Well, um, there's no easy way of saying this, I'm afraid the results show that the remains we found were that of, uh, were that of Roger Thorne.'

It took a few moments for the information to sink in. 'Roger Thorne – my father?' she said quietly.

'I'm afraid so. I'm so very sorry, Emily,' he said.

'And there's no mistake?' she asked.

'I'm afraid not.'

'How did he die, and when?' asked Emily, fighting back tears. She felt numb.

'He had a massive trauma to his skull, much the same as your stepfather. According to the pathologist, he wouldn't have known much. We think he died about fifteen years ago; we can't be exact, I'm afraid,' said Jones.

'I think you can make that more like thirteen years. I think I was about eight years old when my mother told me he had left.'

'So that would make it 1979, is that correct?' asked the inspector.

'Yes, about then,' said Emily. 'I'm assuming you're no closer to finding Rhona?'

'No, I'm sorry to say, we've drawn a blank on that so far. Rest assured though, when we do, you'll be the first to know,' he said.

'Thank you, I appreciate that. My father, murdered!'

'You must be devastated, Emily. I'm so sorry to give you such bad news,' said Jones.

'I am, I hardly knew him, but I never expected to feel this way, said Emily.

'No, it must be a shock. Well, thank you for coming in, Emily, I thought it best to tell you in person, and once again, I'm very sorry.'

She stood up and went to the office door. She turned to Jones and said, 'You know, I was hoping that one day I would find him, get to know him a little.'

Jones simply nodded.

On her return to the office, Emily knocked on Bill's door. 'Come,' he shouted. She entered.

'Oh, Emily, how did you get on? Any further developments?'

'Would you mind if I sat down?' she asked.

Bill looked at her with concern. 'No, please, sit down. Is something wrong?'

'Well, it's about the skeletal remains they found the other day. It turns out that – ' A tear fell as she sobbed, 'It turns out that it was – that it was my father, my biological father, that is.'

'Oh, my dear girl, I'm so sorry, I don't know what to say,' said Bill, getting up from his desk to comfort her.

'It never once crossed my mind; I suppose it should have, really,' she said, wiping her eyes. 'That's truly awful, Emily, I can't begin to understand how you must be feeling. You shouldn't be here; you should go home and take as long as you like.'

'But what about the story? I have to –'

'I think under the circumstances, I should take you off the assignment,' said Bill.

'No! Please don't do that, Bill, I beg you. I can handle it,' she protested.

'You're too closely involved now,' said Bill.

'I can do this, pleased don't take it away from me.'

Bill's face distorted as he dragged his hand across his face in frustration. 'Oh Emily, Emily, what am I going to do with you?'

'You know it makes sense, Bill. I'm the only one with inside information on this story.'

'I hope I'm not going to regret this. Alright, if you really think you can handle it, you can stay on it,' he said.

'Thank you, Bill, you *won't* regret it.'

'Alright, but for now, I want you to go home and take it easy for the rest of the day; you've had a nasty shock, and you need to grieve,' said Bill.

'But I'm okay now, really.'

'It's not up for debate, Emily – go home!'

Emily reluctantly obeyed and drove home. She had learnt that the editor's word was law, and besides which, she respected his judgement.

When she arrived home, the house was empty, Alan was at work, the kids were at school, and Emily remembered Gwen saying she was going to meet a friend to do some shopping and have lunch. It gave her some private time to reflect on the morning's bombshell. She hardly remembered her father, but the news had hit her harder than she imagined, and she wept.

Simon and Bridget would not remember their father at all; they would have been so young at the time; nevertheless, it would be a difficult task to tell them he had died all those years ago at the hand of their mother.

Around mid-afternoon, Gwen arrived home, and she found Emily curled up asleep on the sofa, Gwen tried not to disturb her, yet she woke anyway.

'Hello love, are you okay? You're not feeling ill, are you?' asked Gwen.

Emily stretched her arms and raised herself slowly from the sofa to a sitting position. 'No, I'm fine, just a little tired, that's all.'

'You're home early again. Has something happened at work?'

'Bill ordered me to come home, I'm afraid I received some bad news about the second body.'

Gwen sat next to her with a concerned look. 'What is it, love?' she asked gently.

'It seems the remains they found were –'

'Your father. Is that it, Emily?'

Emily nodded.

'Oh, my poor girl, how awful for you. I'm so sorry.'

Emily blew her nose; she had no more tears left. 'I should have guessed, mum.'

'You weren't to know, Emily. I have to say, though, it doesn't completely surprise me.'

'Looks like I've got two burials to arrange now, doesn't it?' said Emily.

'We'll help with that, don't worry. I take it they haven't tracked down Rhona yet?'

'No, they've drawn a blank so far, but it's made me determined that if the police can't find her – I will!'

# *Chapter 27*

SIMON HAD ALWAYS REMAINED strong, rather like Emily. Yet when Emily broke the news to him about their father, it hit him like a sledgehammer. She had not expected it to go that way. Gwen, Alan and Emily decided firmly against telling Bridget; they all agreed it would be harmful to her already fragile state of mind. There would be nothing to gain and everything to lose.

The next day, Emily returned to her office, eager to write an update on the story in readiness for the next edition of the paper. Bill was already in his office when she arrived. She knocked on his door.

'Come in.'

'Morning Bill,' said Emily.

'Good morning, Emily. What are you doing here? There was no need to rush back, you know. Anyway, you're here now. How are you feeling today?'

'I'm fine,' she said with a smile.

'I passed the crime scene on my way in and saw a small gathering of reporters outside,' Bill said.

'Yes, I saw them myself too. But they won't get a story standing there. The police have all but wrapped it up; they have all the evidence they're going to get from there. Anyway, I just thought I'd let you know that I'm here,' said Emily.

'There was a brief piece on the story on local radio this morning as well. Did you hear it?' said Bill.

'No, what did they have to say?' asked Emily.

'Not a great deal, just the basics. It seems your Detective Inspector Jones is keeping you well and truly in the loop, though, doesn't it?'

'Hardly surprising, really, seeing as the murderer is my mother.'

'Well, I can't deny, it's good for the paper, not so good for you though. The thing is, how long before we lose our monopoly on the story?'

'Yes, I know what you mean. I'll just have to give it my best shot while I can, I suppose,' said Emily thoughtfully.

'I've no doubt you will,' said Bill.

'Anyway, I'll get back to work and make a start on the latest.'

'Okay, let me see it as soon as you can,' said Bill.

'Yes, of course. And Bill, I think you can release James for other tasks now, I don't think I'll be needing any more photographs again for a while.'

'Okay, I'll let him know.'

A while later, as Emily worked on her piece for the next edition, James entered the press room where she was working. He stood over her desk as she typed. Without looking up, she instinctively knew it was James as he stood in silence. 'Hello, James,' she said, continuing to type.

He finally spoke. He was clearly upset. 'Bill tells me you don't need me on the case anymore.'

Emily broke off from her keyboard and looked up at him. 'Sorry, James, what did you say?'

'You don't need me any longer, is that right?'

'Yes, James, that's right. At least not for the time being. What's the problem?'

'I, well, I – '

'There's just nothing to take photographs of at the moment. I would have thought you'd be glad. You clearly don't like me very much,' said Emily.

'It's not that I don't like you. You never seem to take me into your confidence, that's all. And I think there's something funny going on as well.'

'There's nothing funny going on, I can assure you, James. But if you have a grievance, go and see Bill. Look, if I need a photographer again, I'll be sure to ask for you, okay?'

'I suppose so,' he said.

'Good! Can I get back to my work now?' she asked. He turned on his heels and left her.

She had been somewhat aloof with James and couldn't help feeling bad. She was not being evasive or obtuse by choice; if it had been any other assignment she was working on, she would have been open and honest with him. But this was not just an ordinary assignment, but personal, and one she felt ashamed to be so closely involved in. It did, nevertheless, appear that she had made an enemy of James.

# *Chapter 28*

THE INTERNMENT OF EMILY'S FATHER'S remains took place at St. Peters Church two weeks after release from the police. It was a simple graveside service attended only by Emily, Simon, Gwen and Alan. DI Jones also attended out of respect. There were no other known relatives.

They went home immediately after the brief internment; Jones took a short time away from his investigation to join them. 'Take a seat, Detective Inspector,' said Gwen.

'Oh, thank you, but I can't stay long, Mrs Parker.'

'Well, at least have a sandwich, I have probably made too many.'

'Lovely, thank you,' he said, taking one of the neatly triangled sandwiches.

'So, we gather from Emily you're not having much luck in tracing Rhona?' said Alan.

'No, I'm afraid we've had no luck so far, Mr Parker, but we're still on the case full-time. We're bound to find her eventually,' said Jones in a quietly confident manner.

'I hope so,' said Gwen, 'Emily and Simon need proper closure on this.'

'I realise that we're doing all we can,' said Jones.

'Oh, yes, of course you are, I didn't mean – '

'I know you didn't. I think we all need to see this case solved as soon as possible. It's all very strange; she seemed to simply disappear without a trace when she knew she was wanted for child abuse, and with the two bodies buried in her garden, it would have been all the more urgent for her to get away as soon as she could.'

'Yes, of course, we understand the difficulties you're facing,' said Alan.

'Anyway, thanks for the tea and sandwich. I really should be getting back to the station now, though.'

'Oh, haven't you got time for another sandwich, Inspector?' asked Gwen.

'Thank you, but I really must be going. I'll be speaking to you soon, Emily. And once again, I'm very sorry for your loss. I'll see myself out. It was nice meeting you all, I only wish it had been under different circumstances.'

'Yes, quite so,' said Alan, 'goodbye Inspector.'

'Come on,' said Emily, 'I'll show you out.'

'I'm not sure when I'll be in contact again,' Jones said as they reached the front door, 'but I promise I'll let you know of any developments straight away.'

'I know you will,' she said, 'doesn't look like that will be any time soon though, does it?'

'Hmm, no, the way things are going, I'm afraid you're right.'

'I know you're doing your best. Well, goodbye, inspector.'

'Goodbye then, Emily.'

Emily returned to work the next day. And as there was no further progress on the case, for the time-being, she returned to the routine work of reporting on local issues and events. It was, it seemed, yesterday's news and was no longer a priority unless there were significant developments.

Her phone rang as she worked at her desk. It was an internal call. It was James at the other end as she answered. 'Have you got a moment,' James said, 'There's something I need to show you. Can you come up?'

It sounded rather mysterious; it piqued her interest enough for her to say, 'Yes, I'll be right up.'

She entered the photographic department office; James was quite alone. 'Thanks for coming,' he said. He was holding a large brown envelope.

'So, what is it you want to show me?' she asked curiously.

James drew a couple of large prints from the envelope and threw them onto a worktop. 'Take a look,' he said, unsmiling.

Emily moved closer and picked up the photographs.

'They're of you, Emily.'

'What's the meaning of this? How dare you intrude on my private life?' Emily said angrily, looking at the pictures of her and her family at the graveside of her father. 'You had no right.'

'It was my day off yesterday; I had every right. I knew there was something not right. You were getting too much information on the murders that even the daily's weren't getting.'

'What do you want from me? And why do you hate me so much?'

'I don't hate you. I just wanted you to know that I'm on to you. These pictures could be an excellent earner for me if I were to sell them to a national paper. Who was he, your father perhaps? Either way, you're definitely related, and dare I say it, probably to the murderer as well.'

'Sell them for all I care,' said Emily.

James smiled. 'I already have, as a matter of fact. The Daily Express were very interested. I'm sorry, Emily, but I couldn't let a chance like this pass me by. Who knows, it might even get me a job in Fleet Street, away from this tin-pot little rag.'

'I see. Well, I hope your thirty pieces of silver make you very happy,' Emily said with a resigned calmness. She then left him and went straight down to Bill's office. She entered his office after knocking once on the door.

'Hello Emily, what can I do for you?' he said.

'There's something I think you should know,' she said, standing in front of his desk.

'I'm not sure I like the sound of that. You'd better take a seat.' He waited for her to sit and continued, 'So what is it you have to tell me?'

'Well, it seems certain that you're going to get a call from The Express and maybe some other of the national's about me.'

'What? *Why?*' he asked quizzically.

'It would appear that someone has told them of my connection to the murder case, I just thought I should warn you so you're prepared.'

'Who was it that spilt the beans?'

'It doesn't really matter who does it,' Emily said.

'It certainly does. Was it one of our own?'

'I really don't want to say.'

'I'm sorry, Emily, but if you know, I demand you tell me right now.' He was clearly angry at the thought of disloyalty among his staff.

Emily had never seen him so angry, his face red with rage. 'I don't think any harm was meant, so – '

'Spit it out, Emily. Tell me who it was,' he raged.

'It wasn't ever my intention of getting anyone into trouble. It was James,' she said reluctantly.

'Right! You can get back to work now, Emily, I'll deal with this.' With that, he immediately got up from his chair and made his way upstairs while Emily did as she was told and returned to her desk.

A short while later, James appeared with Bill, who was about to escort him from the building. He scowled at Emily as he passed by her desk. 'I hope you're pleased with yourself,' he said.

'You left me with little choice,' Emily said sympathetically. It was clear that Bill had sacked him on the spot.

A couple of other reporters looked on, puzzled at the scene.

After a consultation with Emily, Bill decided that now was the time to enlighten the other members of staff about Emily's personal involvement in the murder story. All were very understanding and sympathetic towards Emily. Not only that, they were full of admiration with regard to her professionalism under such difficult circumstances.

Later that day, Bill received a phone call from the editor of The Daily Express. After a few niceties and professional courtesies, the woman asked if she could speak to Emily. Bill placed her on hold while he spoke to Emily. 'You were right, it seems, Emily, I have the chief editor of The Express on the line. She'd like to speak with you. You don't have to. The choice is yours entirely,' he said.

'Well, I'd hoped to keep my family out of the news, but I don't think I can avoid it any longer. Yes, Bill, I'll speak to her.'

## *Chapter 29*

THE CONVERSATION WAS NOT as expected—Jean Wright was extremely amiable, and Emily liked her immediately. There were few questions about Emily's personal connection to the case, admiration for her writing skill, general fortitude and ability to professionally report on something that had directly affected her.

They spoke for about an hour, Emily becoming increasingly conscious that she had an article still to finish. Then it came. 'Well, I've kept you long enough, I think. Shall we get down to the nitty-gritty?' asked the woman.

'In what way exactly?' asked Emily.

'As I said, I've read the reports you wrote in your little paper. You have excellent qualifications, and it's obvious that your editor holds you in high esteem. I'm impressed by your skill as a writer and general demeanour, so how would you like to work on a national newspaper?'

Emily gasped inwardly. 'You're serious? You're offering me a job?'

'I am. What do you think?'

'I can't believe it.'

'Is that a yes?' asked Jean Wright.

'Well, there is a slight snag, I told my boss I would stay on as long as possible, he did, after all, give me my first break.'

'Loyalty! I like that in a person. But I'm sure he will understand that this is an opportunity you can't pass up. Surely Fleet Street must be your aim? Anyway, I'll give you a day to think about it – don't disappoint me, Emily.'

'Thank you so much.'

'Call me tomorrow.'

'I will, goodbye, and thank you again.'

Emily's heart was racing, her mind in overdrive as she went into Bill's office. She stood silently as he finished tapping on his keyboard. 'Won't keep you a moment, Emily,' he tapped again briefly and looked up at her. 'So, how did you get on with your phone call?

She could barely contain herself, fidgety with excitement. 'She's offered me a job, Bill.'

'Ahh,' was his initial reaction. It was not what he had expected. 'A job, eh? On The Express?'

'Yes.'

'You said yes, I presume?'

'No, I said I'd think about it, after all, I owe you so much, I'm not sure accepting would be the right thing to do.'

'Don't be silly,, girl, you must accept. You'd be an idiot not to,' he said sincerely.

'But I promised you I would stay on here for at least a year, and –'

'That was before. This changes everything. I'll be sad to lose you, but you must say yes, people can wait a lifetime for such a chance and still not get it.'

'Are you sure, Bill? I'd miss you too, you know.'

'I'm absolutely positive, and let me be the first to congratulate you,' he said, hugging her.

'Thank you, Bill, that means so much to me. I will, of course, stay on until you have a replacement.'

'Nonsense, we can manage. You start work with your new employee as soon as they want you to.'

'Bill, you're an angel,' said Emily, kissing him on his cheek. She returned to her desk to complete her article. Once that was done, she went home to give Gwen and Alan the good news. Later, she telephoned Patricia at her university.

'That's amazing, Em, congratulations,' said Patricia.

'Thanks, Pat, I still can't quite believe it. Anyway, how are things in Bristol? How's the world of medicine?'

'Good, thanks, only another year to go – hopefully.'

'You'll make a brilliant doctor,' said Emily.

'Let's hope so. When will you start your new job anyway?'

'Oh, I don't know yet. I have to phone the editor tomorrow.'

'Well, good luck, Em, I'm really sorry, I have to go, somebody's waiting to use the phone. Goodbye, Em, speak soon.'

As Emily got into bed that night, she couldn't help feeling a little guilty at letting down Bill, even though he was enthusiastic about her accepting the job. She also reflected on how James's plan had backfired on him. Bill had lost two employees today, she thought, one sacked and one head-hunted. Yet through the slight feeling of guilt, the overwhelming feeling she had was one of elation. It was like a dream come true. She slept soundly that night.

The next day at the office, with a combined feeling of excitement and nervousness, Emily prepared herself for the phone call she would be making to Jean Wright. It was around 10 o'clock when Emily picked up the phone and dialled out the number. 'Good morning. Miss Wright?'

'Yes, speaking. Is that Emily?'

'Yes, it is.'

'Thought I recognised the voice. Well, have you reached a decision, Emily?'

'I have, yes, and I would very much like to accept your generous offer,' said Emily.

'That's excellent news; you've made the right decision,' said Jean, 'I take it you've spoken to your boss.'

'Yes, I have. He's over the moon for me. He said I can start with you as soon as you want me.'

'That's great news. Could you come into the office to make the arrangements and meet your new colleagues? Once we've done that, I can see no reason why you couldn't start work a week on Monday. How does that sound?'

'Sounds great,' said Emily.

'Could you make it into the office today, say around 1pm?'

'I have an assignment this morning, but yes, I'm sure I could make it.'

'Good, I'll see you then. I'm looking forward to meeting you in person.'

After clearing it with Bill, she later drove to an art-deco-style railway station in Surbiton and hopped on a train for the thirty-minute journey into central London. She took a deep breath before entering the large glass-fronted building of The Daily Express. A very cheerful young woman like herself greeted her as she approached the reception desk.

Emily told her she had an appointment with the editor, Jean Wright, at 1pm she was ten minutes early, and the young woman asked her to take a seat and offered her a coffee. Emily accepted the offer.

At 1pm precisely, Jean Wright appeared from an elevator and recognised Emily from the photographs that James had sent. She greeted Emily warmly and escorted her into the elevator, which would take them to the press office. It was in stark contrast to the small, sleepy office of The Surbiton News. The large open-space office positively buzzed with activity. It was the kind of place where she had always dreamt of working. She never, in her wildest dreams, imagined that she would be living the dream so early in her career.

She immediately liked Jean Wright and the other staff journalists she had been introduced to. Without exception, they were all older than herself, yet it did not seem to matter.

'Well, Emily, what do you think?' asked Jean.

'It's wonderful, I can't wait to start,' Emily said with a large smile.

'Good, I'm glad you think so. You say your boss will let you start a week on Monday?'

'That's right.'

'Excellent! We'll see you then. Report to me at 8.30, we tend to start early here. You'll be working for a big grown-up paper now, Emily.'

# Chapter 30

*Five Years Later*

EMILY WAS TWENTY-SIX, almost twenty-seven, and after five years working at the Express, she had proved herself, through hard work and determination, to be a journalist who was finding an angle on a story where it appeared there was none. By this time, she found it more convenient to live in London and, therefore, bought and moved into a small yet comfortable flat in Peckham.

She did, however, go home to see her family as often as she could. Patricia was a qualified doctor by now and working at the St Helier General Hospital in Croydon. They met frequently to catch up on events. Simon was not academic, and although he had not achieved many academic qualifications, he now worked as an office clerk. Bridget's anxiety had held her back enormously; she now worked in a supermarket stacking shelves. She remained shy and very withdrawn despite the love and affection shown by Gwen and Alan.

Emily had kept in touch with DI Jones since she had left the local newspaper in 1991, yet after all this time, the police were no closer to finding Rhona. It was now a cold case. Despite her busy life, it was something that was never far from Emily's mind. How could her mother escape justice for so long? Emily speculated.

Five years before, when Emily was working for The Surbiton News, The Express had also covered the story, albeit with little to go on. Once the story went cold, however, interest faded, and the story was largely forgotten. That was, until one warm day in June 1996, an email appeared in Jean Wright's inbox. The sender, for now, remained anonymous but claimed the whereabouts of Rhona were known to them. The person also inquired if there would be a financial reward for the information.

Jean did not reply but went immediately to the editor-in-chief, John Day, for advice on how to proceed. However, she already knew the answer regarding a reward for the information. The paper was firmly against giving money for "hot tips" from the public.

'Well, what do you think, John?' asked Jean.

'Jean, it'd make a great story, but you know we can't pay this person, whoever they are. I don't think we have any choice but to pass the information to the police.'

'I agree,' she said, 'I just thought I'd run it past you.'

'What about Emily? Will you tell her about this?' John asked.

'I think she has a right to know, don't you?'

'Absolutely. Well, I'll leave it with you then.'

'Thanks, John,' said Jean. She then returned to her office.

Through the glass of her office, which looked out over the busy press office, she could see Emily busily tapping at her keyboard. She was writing a short piece on the riots that had taken place in Trafalgar Square involving English football hooligans after a defeat by a German international team.

Firstly, Jean contacted the police in Surbiton and informed them of the email she had received; she simultaneously forwarded it to them, marking it for the attention of Detective Inspector Jones. Secondly, she replied to the sender of the email, politely pointing out that it was against policy for respected newspapers such as The Daily

Express to pay for stories. She guessed she would not hear more from the sender again.

Jean rang Emily's extension number and could see her break off from her work to answer. 'Morning, Emily, could you come to my office for a moment?' she said.

'Good morning, yes, of course, I'll be right there,' said Emily. She clicked "save" on her computer and made her way to Jean's office. Jean's face was serious.

'Take a seat, Emily.'

'Is there anything wrong?' asked Emily.

'Something came up earlier this morning. I just thought you should know about it,' said Jean in a straightforward manner.

'Oh?'

Jean had a printout of the email at hand and passed it over her desk to Emily. 'Oh my God,' Emily said, stunned at what she was reading. 'Are we going to pay?'

Jean shook her head. 'You know the rules, Emily. We can't do that. You know very well we can't. No, what I've done is pass it on to the DI who was dealing with the case. You know him well, don't you?'

'Yes, I do, DI Jones.'

'Well, let's just wait and see what he makes of it, shall we?'

'I suppose so. It's a shame, though. If true, it would be a great story. Can't we somehow get around it?'

'No, Emily, we can't. That'll be all. You can get back to your work now,' Jean said, a little exasperated.

'Okay, sorry,' said Emily, about to leave the office. She turned to Jean again. 'What if I paid for the information myself?'

'No! Absolutely not,' barked Jean. 'I only told you out of courtesy, now just forget it, okay.'

Emily said no more but returned to her desk, feeling rebuked. It was not simply the story that interested her, but the thought of bringing Rhona to justice once and for all. It appeared, though, to be out of her hands. She continued writing her piece with a heavy heart. She worked on other stories to be ready for the next edition, working late, as all the staff did. By the end of the working day, Jean stopped by Emily's desk.

'Don't forget our conversation this morning, will you. Just be patient and don't do anything foolish that could jeopardise your career, okay?' Jean said, this time more gently. 'Coming to The Punch for a drink?'

'Uh, yes, alright, just for a short while, I'm quite tired today, so I won't stay long,' said Emily.

The Punch Tavern was one of the most popular with Fleet Street journalists, and this night was no exception. It was almost shoulder to shoulder-with journalists from just about every mainstream newspaper. Emily recognised most of them.

Finally, having had two glasses of wine which had been foisted on her by colleagues, Emily made her excuses and left. Usually, she would enjoy a couple of drinks with Jean and her colleagues, but tonight, she had a headache and was in no mood for socialising. She hopped on the tube at Temple and started her journey home to Peckham.

She collapsed into her comfortable armchair and pondered the morning's events. Emily respected Jean and knew the advice she had given was sound, sensible and logical. Emily had no intention of risking the career she had always longed for; she knew it would be foolhardy in the extreme, yet she felt she had to find out more about the anonymous tip-off.

Her headache was getting worse. She made herself some herbal tea and took a couple of painkillers before taking her mobile phone from her handbag.

Emily and DI Jones had now known one another for some years, Emily felt at ease and comfortable enough to use a nickname some of his colleagues used.

'Is that you, Jonesy?' she asked as he answered the call. It was quite late; the detective sounded as if he had been asleep.

'Huh, yes, who's that?' he said grouchily.

'It's Emily Parker.'

'Emily, what on earth do you want at this time of night? Oh, hold on, let me guess, it's about that damned email, isn't it?'

'I'm sorry it's so late, but yes, it is about that.'

'You just won't let this go, will you?'

'Have you got any leads on who might have sent it?' asked Emily.

'Give me a chance, for goodness sake; it's only been a matter of hours since your editor called me. Besides, I do have other ongoing cases, you know.'

'I realise that I'm sorry.'

'Look, Emily, go to bed and leave this to the police, will you? You know, it could turn out to be nothing more than a hoax.'

'Will you let me know if anything comes to light? This is me asking, not the journalist.'

'Yes, yes, I'll let you know. Look, it's late, I've had a busy day and I'm tired. Goodnight, Emily,' he said, abruptly terminating the call on his mobile. He rolled over in an attempt to find sleep again.

## *Chapter 31*

HAVING THE WEEKEND OFF, Emily drove to Surbiton to visit her parents, she had already let them know she was coming and was told that Patricia was also coming home on the same day. It was a beautifully warm day. Alan suggested they go out for a pub lunch as a family, the idea was welcomed by all. The Grove was a popular pub in Surbiton, so he phoned ahead to book a table for seven people at 2pm.

Bridget was twenty years old now, and although, through counselling, she was more stable, she was still very quiet and reserved. Over lunch, she did not engage in conversation freely. There was much talk of Patricia and Emily's work by the proud parents. Emily was acutely aware of her sister and brother's lack of what one would call a proper career.

'So, how are my little sister and brother doing?' she asked cheerily.

'Okay, I suppose,' said Simon, 'I hate my job, though I'm not cut out for office work.'

'Oh, well, why don't you look for something else, or maybe try to get some sort of qualification?' asked Emily, 'You always enjoyed cookery lessons at school, so why not train to be a chef?'

'Maybe,' he said.

'What about you, Bridget? How are things with you?'

Bridget shrugged, 'same old – same old,' she said, picking at her food.

'Well, it's lovely to see you both anyway,' said Emily.

Halfway through the meal, Emily's mobile rang. She took it from her handbag and saw that it was DI Jones calling her.

'Excuse me for a moment,' she said. She answered the call, making her way to the pub's courtyard.

'Hi Emily,' said Jones.

'Hi, how are you? I'm sorry about the other night. I didn't realise how late it was. Anyway, have you got some news for me?'

'Perhaps—although don't get too excited, it's very vague at this stage,' he said.

'Go on,' Emily said, with much interest.

'Well, as I said, the information we have is vague at best. We replied to the email, stating it was a police matter and that he should disclose any information he may have about her whereabouts to us directly. Otherwise, it might be seen as an obstruction of justice. Anyway, we waited and waited, but nothing. That is, not until today. The station called me a short time ago. It would seem that your mother is in Columbia. Of course, it may be that this person is mistaken – it may not be your mother at all.'

'Columbia? But it could be true, couldn't it?' Emily said, an air of excitement in her voice.

'It could be, yes, we just don't know. If I get any more information, I'll keep you in the loop, but don't go getting any silly ideas, okay?'

'Of course not, thanks, Jonesy.'

'Don't mention it. Enjoy the rest of your day.'

Emily's body shook with anticipation, there was a lead at last, however vague and improbable. She composed herself and returned to the others.

'Work?' inquired Gwen.

'Uh, yes, nothing important,' Emily said, avoiding the subject in the company of Bridget.

It was not until later, when Emily drove with Patricia back to their home, that she told Patricia about the phone call she had received and the background behind it.

'I hope you're not thinking of going after her,' said Patricia.

'I might be,' Emily said.

'You can't. She's dangerous, and so, for that matter, is Columbia. You mustn't do it,' pleaded Patricia.

'Let's see what action the police take first, shall we? I won't rush into anything, I promise.'

'Perhaps you should talk to mum and dad about it,' Patricia said.

'No, please don't mention it to them, not just yet. I don't want them to worry unnecessarily.'

'Okay, well, if you're sure.'

'I am,' said Emily.

The following Monday, DI Jones and his Sergeant were busy at their desks following up leads on a spate of burglaries in the area. The thieves had been clever enough not to leave fingerprints on the affected properties, but they had a small number of suspects in mind. One in particular gained his interest, a convicted burglar who had recently been released from prison. The man in question was a career criminal, and Jones was convinced he was their man. He and his Sergeant decided to pay the man a visit at his home. As they drove to the man's address, Jones's mobile rang. It was the technical department at police headquarters. It appeared that, through the wonders of modern technology, they had managed to identify where the email address was located in Columbia with some accuracy.

'Okay, thanks for the info, I'll be back at headquarters soon. You can fill me in on the details then,' said Jones.

They found the man at home. 'Mr Jefferies?' said DI Jones.

The man, though burly in stature, answered nervously, 'Yes,' he said, 'what do you want?' He knew by experience that they were police officers.

They took him back to headquarters for questioning while they obtained a search warrant. It took a couple of hours for a team of uniformed officers to search and report back that they had found the goods reported stolen, and the man was duly charged.

Upon the case being successfully completed, Jones went to the technical department, where they explained how they had traced the email address to an Englishman who lived in Columbia. The email address originated from a small city called Cartagena, a port on the Columbian Caribbean coast.

'Well done,' said Jones, 'but it's still not enough for us to go swanning off halfway around the world. It'd be like searching for a needle in a haystack. We need more to go on than that.'

'I'm sorry, sir, but that's the best we can do,' said the technician.

'Oh well, thanks for trying anyway. Good work!'

'Thank you, sir.'

'Anyway, I'll inform the Chief Constable of your findings, it's him that'll have the last say.' With that, Jones returned to his office and dialled the Chief's extension. 'Good afternoon, sir. Do you think you could spare me a few minutes of your time?' he asked the Chief Constable.

'Yes, DI Jones, I think I can do that, come up.'

Jones dashed up the stairs and knocked on the door. 'Come in!'

'Hello, sir.' The Chief gestured for him to take a seat.

'What can I do for you, Detective Inspector?'

'Well, sir, it's regarding the cold case of Rhona Thorne. Do you remember the case?'

'Yes, of course, I remember it well. Why, do you have some new information?'

'Well, yes and no, we've had a tip-off from someone in Columbia, of all places, who states he has seen her there. She may be living there. I just don't know. Anyway, our technical department has managed to locate the email address of the informant to a city called, Cartagena in Columbia.'

'And is that all you have?'

Jones chuckled. 'Yes, I'm afraid so, sir.'

'Well, there's not a lot we can do about that, is there. The chances of finding her are a million to one, I'd say, wouldn't you?'

'My thoughts exactly, I just thought it best to bring it to your attention, sir,' said Jones resignedly.

'Yes, of course, you're quite right, but I really don't think we can realistically spend time and money on such a long shot.'

'Very good, sir. Thanks for seeing me anyway.' There was a hint of disappointment in his voice, even though the decision from the Chief was expected. Jones returned to his office and a mountain of paperwork.

# Chapter 32

AFTER A BUSY DAY, DI Jones drove home.

The warmth of the day lingered into the evening. As he passed 124 Main Street, it looked like a very different house to one where bodies had been discovered all those years ago. It was no longer a grey, gloomy place of misery but a bright and comfortable looking house, the masonry painted white and the building converted into luxury apartments.

Each time he passed, he could not help thinking about Emily and her siblings and the misery they went through in the place. In fact, he and his colleagues who had been involved in the case called it the house of gloom.

On arrival at his home address, Jones's wife, Alice, was preparing the evening meal. He kissed her gently on the cheek and poured them both a glass of wine. 'Busy day, love? She asked.

'As usual,' he said, 'mainly paperwork, although we did wrap up that case of those burglaries in the area.'

'Oh, that's good darling, so we can sleep easily then?'

'Yes, he's already behind lock and key,' he said reassuringly.

'Dinner won't be long, you look tired, love, why don't you go through to the living room for a while?'

'Yes, good idea, darling, I think I will.'

He took off his suit jacket, fell heavily onto the sofa, kicked off his shoes and laid back. His eyes became heavy, he dozed, yet he was restless and after just a few minutes, he woke fully. Reaching for his mobile, he called Emily's number.

'Emily? It's Jones here.'

'Oh, Hi, how are you?' she said.

'I thought I should give you a call. I'm afraid it's not entirely good news.'

'Hold on a moment,' she said. Emily went into the kitchen, out of earshot from the rest of the family. 'Sorry, carry on,' she said.

'Well, our technical department has traced which city in Columbia the source email came from –'

'Well, that's good news, isn't it?' Emily said.

'I'm afraid not. I've spoken to the Chief Constable about the case. I'm sorry to say he won't allow us to pursue the lead. It would be too costly and there's no guarantee we would find her. We just don't have enough to go on.'

'Oh, I see.'

'I'm sorry, Emily. Just thought you should know, that's all,' said Jones.

'Just out of interest, where is it that the email originated from?' she asked.

'It's a city called Cartagena in the North of Columbia. Look, I'm sure the case will be reviewed at some stage, so don't worry too much. And who knows, we may yet gain some more details of her precise location.'

Emily jotted down the name of the place in Columbia on a scrap of paper. 'Okay, thanks for letting me know and being so honest,' she said, a little too calmly for Jones's liking.

'You know Emily, I'm only telling you this as a courtesy. Please don't do anything silly, like taking the law into your own hands. You'd never find her anyway,' said Jones.

'Don't worry, I won't.'

'Okay, that's alright then. Bye, for now, I'll let you know if anything changes.'

'Bye, take care,' Emily said, ending the call.

'Anything important?' asked Gwen as Emily returned to the living room.

'No, just work,' said Emily evasively. Patricia looked furtively at her. Emily caught the glimpse, suspecting Patricia knew otherwise.

A couple of hours went by, and Emily was restless and eager to get back to her flat. 'Well, I'd better be going. Thanks for a lovely lunch and everything,' she said.

'Oh, can't you stay a little longer?' asked Gwen, 'Patricia's staying the night before she goes back on duty tomorrow; I had hoped you would too.'

'I'd love to, but actually, I did arrange to meet someone this evening,' lied Emily.

'That's okay, I didn't realise,' said Gwen.

'Anyway, I'll see you all soon. And Simon, think about what I said about looking up some courses. Bridget, you take care now. Okay, bye, I love you all.'

Patricia smiled surreptitiously. She thought the manner in which Emily said goodbye seemed so final somehow. She went to the car with Emily. 'I know what you're planning, Emily, but as your sister, I'm asking you not to do it.'

Emily said nothing but kissed Patricia on the cheek, smiled, and drove home.

Once in her flat, she made herself a coffee and sat at her Toshiba notebook, eventually connecting to the internet. She searched for all the available information on Cartagena, its exact location in Columbia, and the population, which was around one million. She learned also that there were approximately four or five thousand English people who lived permanently in Cartagena. Not too many, she thought. She also looked for available flights, which were fairly frequent from Heathrow.

It was business as usual at the Express on Monday morning. Emily and the other journalists were briefed by the editor on the assignments allocated to them for the day. Emily went about her work as usual, and although not with her normal enthusiasm, due to her mind being preoccupied, she could not wait to have the chance to speak to Jean at the end of the day.

Emily knocked on Jean's door and, opening it ajar poked her head around. 'Hi, have you got a moment, Jean?'

'Yes, come in and take a seat.'

Emily remained standing. 'That's okay, I won't keep you. I was just wondering what annual leave I am due at the moment?'

'One moment, I'll take a look. Thinking of a holiday, are we?' asked Jean.

'Well, yes, I could certainly use a holiday, but only if it's okay with you.'

Jean pulled up Emily's records. 'Yes, it looks like you could take up to three weeks at the moment.'

'Oh, great, could I book it at your convenience then, please?' asked Emily.

'I don't see why not. When would you like to take it?'

'As soon as possible, if that's alright.'

'Yes, I'm sure we'll cope. You could start your leave from next Monday if that suits you?'

'Next Monday? Yes, that'd be great, thanks Jean.'

'Going anywhere nice?' asked Jean.

'Not sure yet, but somewhere hot.'

'Well, enjoy!'

Emily worked late that evening. She deliberately waited until her boss had gone home, and then, when the coast was clear, she searched Jean's office for the email sent from the source in Columbia. She eventually found a hard copy buried among various papers on the desk. After quickly making a photocopy, she replaced it where she had found it.

Later that evening, Emily booked her travel arrangements and hotel for her flight the following Monday evening. She had already made many photocopies of her mother's photograph, although she was aware that Rhona's appearance could have changed somewhat. It was going to be the most difficult of tasks. Finding Rhona was probably unrealistic, yet it was something she had to do, even if she ultimately failed. The prospect of failure, however, did not sit well with her. The word 'failure' was not in her vocabulary. But would this be the one thing that finally defeated her?

## *Chapter 33*

THE WEEK WENT BY QUICKLY, and Emily soon found herself on her flight, ultimately bound for Columbia. There would be a stopover in Mexico before a connecting flight took her to Cartagena, a total of sixteen hours of flying time. She had told her family she was going on holiday, not to Columbia, but to Spain, in order not to worry them. Patricia knew differently and tried her best to talk Emily out of such a risky trip, but her plea had fallen on deaf ears.

Emily mostly slept during the flight from Mexico to Cartagena, despite having drank two cups of coffee in Mexico's Benito Juárez airport while waiting to board her connecting flight. Before she knew it, the aircraft was coming into land. After going through passport control and collecting her suitcase, she soon found herself on the bus that would take her to Cartagena.

The bus took only twenty minutes to reach her hotel in the old part of the city. She was struck by its charm; the buildings were old and brightly coloured. It was a very hot day, and it was a relief to enter the relatively cool hotel reception where she checked in. She spoke a little Spanish which would prove helpful during the coming days.

Having found her room on the second floor of the hotel, Emily unpacked and freshened up, and yet, despite being exhausted from the long flight, she went down to the reception and asked the receptionist if they had a map she could use.

'Uh, Disculpe mapa de Cartagena, por favor,'

'Si Señorita,' said the young woman, handing her a detailed map of the city.'

'Gracias,' said Emily. She put on her straw sun hat and sunglasses and headed out to orientate herself. It was 2pm in Cartagena, and after walking around the old city, she found a Taberna and sat outside in the shade until a waiter appeared and took her order of fresh orange juice with lots of ice.

When the good-looking young man returned with a very long glass of orange juice, she asked, 'Do you speak English by any chance?'

'Yes, Señorita, I speak English very well.'

'Thank goodness for that, I'm afraid my Spanish isn't too good. I was wondering if you knew of any English bars or clubs in the city?' she asked.

He shrugged a little, his face expressing uncertainty. 'There may be a couple, senorita, but I'm not sure where they would be. I don't know of any around here, sorry senorita.'

'That's okay, thank you anyway,' Emily said. 'From the little I've seen of it, you have a very beautiful city,' she added.

'Oh yes, Señorita, but a little word of warning, beware of, how do you say, uh, pickpockets,' said the waiter.

'Thank you for the warning, I'll keep that in mind,' she said.

'What is your name, senorita? He asked.

'Emily Parker, and yours?'

'Emily. That's a nice name senorita, I am Sebastián.'

'I'm pleased to meet you, Sebastián,' said Emily.

'You know, Emily, I would be pleased to show you around during my time off,' he said.

'You would? That sounds great, but you really don't have to do that.'

'I have a day off tomorrow. I could meet you at your hotel. Where are you staying?'

'At The Casona del Colegio Hotel. Do you know it? Asked Emily.

'Yes, Emily, I know it well. Shall I meet you tomorrow morning, at, say, 10 o'clock?'

'Uh, yes, okay, if you're sure? That would be fantastic.'

'Good, I'll see you tomorrow then. Would you like another orange juice?'

'No, thank you. I'm going back to my hotel—I've had a long flight, I'm fatigued.'

Emily did not wake up until 6pm. She felt suitably refreshed, showered and changed her clothes, choosing some light linen trousers, a blouse and a matching jacket. Dinner started at 7pm, she was quite hungry by this time and went to the comfortable dining area of the hotel. The restaurant was full of tourists staying at the hotel, a few she recognised from the bus journey from the airport earlier that day.

The hotel served the traditional national dish of Bandeja Paisa after the soup. It was a hefty meal consisting of three types of meat, rice, eggs, plantains, avocado and red beans, but Emily, eating at the table set for one, found it delicious. Looking around the restaurant, she noticed she was not the only person eating alone. A fair-haired man, ruggedly handsome in appearance and perhaps a little older than herself, she guessed, ate at another table for one. Their eyes met briefly across the room; he smiled at her.

After dinner, Emily went through to the lounge bar for a drink, took a seat and ordered a cold beer. A large ceiling fan slowly whirled around above her. A number of other guests of the hotel had the same idea, too tired after their long journey to go exploring, instead, settling for a relaxing drink in the hotel. At the same time, gentle Spanish guitar music played quietly in the background.

As she sipped at her beer, the man from the restaurant appeared in the bar. He went to the bar itself, ordered a beer and sat on a high bar stool. Emily could feel him watching her and glanced at him. Their eyes met once again across the room, and he raised his glass to her with a disarming smile. A little coyly, she reciprocated. He hopped off his bar stool and made for where she sat. She felt her cheeks flushing as he approached.

'Hi, would you mind if I joined you?' he asked, in what was clearly an American accent.

'Uh, I suppose not,' said Emily. Did she sound aloof and standoffish? She did not mean to. She was instantly attracted to him.

'You're English, aren't you? I'm Harry Craig.'

'Emily Parker,' she said, extending her hand. 'And you're clearly American.'

'Yeah, I'm pleased to meet you, Emily Parker. Travelling alone?'

'Yes, and yourself?' she asked.

'Oh yeah,' he said. 'So what brings you to Columbia, Emily Parker?'

'The usual, a holiday. What about you?'

'The same, Columbia's my second home, I adore it. I have to say, though, it can be a pretty dangerous place for a woman to be visiting alone.'

'Oh, I don't know, the people seem quite friendly so far,' she said.

'Don't let that fool you, Emily. Did you arrive today?'

'Uh huh, yes.'

'Well, you have a lot to learn then,' he said, 'you can't let your guard down for a moment in Columbia, believe me. How long are you staying for anyway?'

'I'm not sure yet, possibly up to three weeks, it depends.'

'On what?' he asked.

'Oh, nothing, it doesn't matter,' Emily said cautiously while taking a drink of her beer.

'Let me get you another drink, a traditional Columbian drink.'

'I don't know, I'm very tired,' she said.

'Oh come on, the evening's young, just one more drink?' he said persuasively.

'Okay, just one more, then I really must get some rest.'

'Good, I won't be long; don't go away,' he said, making his way to the bar.

Emily found him charming and self-confident if a bit of brash. He returned after a few minutes with the drinks.

'There we go,' he said, 'you'll like this.'

'What is it anyway?' Emily asked.

'Aquardiente,' he said, 'it means fiery water. You'll love it!'

'It sounds rather potent to me, Harry,' said Emily.

'Try it, Salud!' he said, taking a large swallow himself. It did not affect him in the slightest.

Emily took a small sip and swallowed. It made her gasp. 'Yes, I think fiery water is a very apt name for it,' she said.

'You'll get used to it after a few mouthfuls.'

'Anyway, what do you do for a living, Emily?'

'I'm a journalist, and what do you do? I get the impression you travel a lot.'

'I own a private investigation firm, but yes, I'm quite lucky enough to be able to leave it up to my team a good deal of the time and spend my time travelling. So, you're a journalist, that must be exciting work,' he said.

'It is, but probably not as interesting as your work, I suspect. What sort of things do you investigate?' asked Emily with interest.

'Oh, mainly commercial work, you know. All quite boring, really.'

'Missing persons?' Emily asked.

'Sometimes, yes. Why do you ask?'

'Just interested,' she said. Emily needed to get to know him better before she told him her story. But there was no doubt in her mind he could prove to be invaluable. She took one more mouthful of the drink. He was right. One did get used to it.

'It's been nice meeting you, Harry. I really must go to bed now, though, I have a busy day sightseeing tomorrow.'

'Maybe I could join you if that's alright?'

'I'd say yes, but I already have a guide. I'm meeting him in the lobby tomorrow morning,' she said reluctantly.

'Oh, I see. Someone local?'

'Yes, a waiter from a nearby Taberna offered his services.'

'Well, maybe another time then. Take care, won't you?'

'I will. Goodnight, Harry, I'm sure I'll see you around.'

'You can count on it. Goodnight Emily.'

*Chapter 34*

EMILY FELT REFRESHED AFTER a good night's sleep; after breakfast, she was ready to meet with Sebastián in the hotel lobby. Sebastián was running late for their meeting. It was almost 10.30am when he entered the hotel rather breathlessly.

He found Emily seated in the lobby. 'I'm very sorry, senorita, I got held up,' he said.

'That's okay, it doesn't matter. Thank you for coming,' Emily said gratefully. 'Where are we going to start? As I said, I'm specifically looking for any English-speaking bars or clubs.'

'We'll see,' he said, 'I cannot promise anything, senorita, but I'll try my best.'

They left the hotel, and the heat of the morning, in comparison to the cool hotel lobby, hit Emily harder than she imagined it would.

Unbeknownst to Emily, Harry Craig had been observing the meeting from behind a marble pillar in the lobby. He followed them at a safe distance. The two started in the old town where she was staying, but as Sebastián had said the day before, there did not appear to be any English-speaking bars in the area. They walked for what seemed to Emily miles in the searing heat as they approached the newer and less attractive part of the city. All the time, Harry trailed them unnoticed.

Harry could see Emily removing her hat temporarily and vigorously fanning herself with it. 'It's no good, Sebastián, I need to stop for a drink and find some shade,' she said. He agreed.

There were Taberna's every few yards along the busy streets. Emily sat down under a parasol at one of them and waited for someone to serve them. Harry chose another Taberna just a couple of hundred yards away, ordered a beer and waited, hoping not to be spotted by Emily. But he was good at his job. He pulled his Panama down a little, safely observing them at all times.

He knew that the locals, especially young men, would not volunteer themselves to give guided tours unless there was something to be gained. He was suspicious by nature; his job had done that to him, and this was no exception. Besides, he liked Emily.

After thirty minutes, Emily felt like continuing. So far, they had found nothing, but perhaps in this part of town, something might turn up, she thought. After a while, it became clear to Emily that her guide was becoming tired of the fruitless job, yet she asked if they could continue a little longer if she paid him thirty dollars. He gladly accepted the offer and led her to a side street.

'There may be something along here, senorita,' he said. It looked as likely as anywhere they had visited, there were certainly some clubs to be found, but were any English? The street soon became a dead-end and slum-like. 'Sorry senorita, but I think this is where we part company. If you can afford to pay me thirty dollars, I'm sure you can afford more. I have a family to feed, so I'll ask you to give me all your money now.'

Emily, for once, felt real fear, she was alone in a dead-end street with a crook. For a moment, she was too shocked to do anything. He took a knife from his shorts, flicked it open and held it, pointing towards her throat.

'Will this convince you, senorita?' he said, menacingly.

At that moment, he saw a figure walking slowly and deliberately towards them down the shadowy street. The man oozed confidence—it unnerved Sebastián. 'What do you want, Señor? Just keep away.'

Emily arched her neck, still with the switchblade, almost in contact with her throat. The man was closer now. 'Is that you, Harry?'

'Yes, it's me, Emily.'

Harry got closer. 'Drop the blade. Otherwise, I may have to kill you.'

'I'm warning you, don't come any closer. It's me that has the blade.'

Just a few feet away now, Harry grabbed the man as Emily kicked him on his shin. A struggle ensued, Sebastián still clutching the knife as Harry tried to wrest it from his grip. For a moment when, during the scuffle, the blade was pointing directly at Harry's chest. Harry managed to turn the blade towards Sebastián and, using all his strength, thrust it into the man's chest. It went directly into his heart. He slumped lifelessly to the floor.

'Come on, let's get out of here,' said Harry.

'Shouldn't we report this to the police?' asked Emily, still in shock.

'No! Come on, hurry.'

They did not run but walked out of the street calmly as if nothing had happened. They walked away from the immediate area and caught a cab back to the hotel.

They sat down in the cool bar. Emily's shirt stuck to her, as did Harry's. He ordered them both a beer. 'You saved my life,' said Emily, but how did you know? You followed me all day, didn't you? Why?

He shrugged. 'I just had a bad feeling when you told me you were being guided by a complete stranger. I know what the local people can be like in these parts. You can't trust them all, so yeah, I followed you.'

'It's just as well you did; I might have been dead now if it wasn't for you. I don't know how to thank you. But what about the police?'

'Believe me, Emily, we wouldn't get a fair trial here. They look after their own, it doesn't matter that we were the ones being attacked, they wouldn't listen.'

'Somehow, I believe you,' said Emily.

'Just don't go down any back-alleys like that anymore, at least not without me. What were you doing down there anyway?'

'It's a long story, Harry,' she said thoughtfully.

'Well, I've got plenty of time.'

Emily was not quite ready to tell Harry her life story, but told him why she was in Columbia. 'I haven't seen my mother in years, and I believe she's living here in Cartagena,' she said.

'I see, which is the reason you showed interest in whether I investigated missing persons last night, I take it?'

Emily nodded. 'Yes. You don't miss anything, do you?' she said.

'That's my job. Besides, I find you interesting,' said Harry.

'No, I'm not interested at all,' she said modestly.

'I think you are,' he replied. 'And I'd like to help if you'd let me.'

'You're very kind, Harry, but you've done enough already in saving my life. I can't ask you to do any more than you already have.'

'What if I said I want to? Cartagena is a big place; you'll need help if you're going to find her. Do you have anything at all to go on?'

'No, not much, only an email from an unknown source saying that my mother was believed to be living here, that's it, I'm afraid,' said Emily.

'Do you have the email with you?' he asked, taking a large swallow of his beer.

'It's in my room.'

'I'd like to look at it, if I may?' he asked.

'I don't know, Harry. I'm not sure. It's rather a personal matter,' said Emily.

'Why do I get the feeling there's something you're not telling me?' asked Harry.

'I barely know you, Harry. There are things in my past I'm not exactly proud of sharing, said Emily.

'Do you really want to find your mother? Because if you do, you're going to need all the help you can get,' he said, spelling out the reality of the situation.

Emily knew he was right. 'What if I paid you in your capacity as a private investigator?' she asked.

'You're a stubborn woman,' he said with a smile, 'let's just call it a favour for a friend, shall we?'

'You seem to be a good man, Harry. What do you want to know?'

'Tell me more about your mother for a start. Why would she choose to live here, of all places? How long is it since you saw her last?'

'I last saw her in 1984. I was quite young then, of course. And as far as why she's living here, that is, if the information is correct, I imagine she wanted to get as far away from England as possible,' said Emily.

'Why would she want to do that?' asked Harry curiously.

Emily took a deep breath. 'Hmm, where do I start? Let me put it this way, I'm not looking for a cosy reunion with her, she was a beast to me and my brother and sister. Not only that, but – '

'But what? Take your time, Emily.'

'There's no easy way of saying it I suppose. The fact is, Harry, she's a murderer. She murdered my father and stepfather. I'm here to bring her to justice, and that's all. I really shouldn't be burdening you with all this, Emily said.'

'Don't be silly. I'm so sorry about your father, but let me tell you, if she is here, we'll find her,' said Harry, sympathetically.

'I'm not so sure anymore.'

'Trust me, we will,' he said.

# Chapter 35

IN THE PRIVACY OF EMILY'S HOTEL ROOM, they discussed the whole sorry affair of her mother in detail. Emily explained how her mother had been a club singer almost all her life and how she hoped, despite Rhona being older now, that she was still performing in a club somewhere in Cartagena.

'What about the police in England? Aren't they doing anything?' asked Harry.

'They've tried their best, but they simply don't have the resources to track her down. It's a cold-case now.

'I see.'

'I realise it's a long shot, the possibility of finding an English club here,' said Emily, 'but it's all I've got to go on. She lived for showbusiness to the point where nothing else, including us kids, mattered.'

'Well, we can ask around, but let's start with the email you received. Can I see it?' asked Harry.

'Yes, I'll get it, it's in my case.' She took the printout from her case and handed it to Harry. 'It wasn't actually sent to me; it was sent directly to my editor. As you can see, the sender was looking for a financial reward from the paper.'

'Okay, well, I can get on to my people to see if they can make contact with the sender,' said Harry.

'I'd be willing to pay whoever it turns out to be from for more information,' said Emily eagerly.

'Let's just see what happens first. Meanwhile, I'll ask around about any English clubs that may exist in the area.'

'I can't thank you enough for what you're doing, Harry. I still feel guilty, though. You're supposed to be on holiday.'

'It's my pleasure, believe me. I'd probably get bored anyway. Being in a good company is far more preferable.'

Emily blushed a little at the compliment.

'Would you mind if I asked the restaurant manager to arrange it so we have a table for two for the rest of our stay here?' asked Harry, 'it doesn't make sense that we sit at separate tables.'

'I'd like that,' said Emily.

'Good, I'll see to it. Now, I suggest we keep our heads down for the rest of the day and stay in the hotel after what happened earlier.'

'I agree,' she said emphatically.

'Look, Emily, I'm going to my room for a short while, I need to contact my people in New York about the email. Let's see what they turn up, shall we? I won't be long. Shall we meet down in the bar in, say, twenty minutes?'

'Yes, fine, I'll freshen up a little and see you down there,' she said.

After a quick shower and change of clothes, Emily heard a knock on the door. She froze for a moment before leaning against the door and asking: 'Who is it?'

'It's Harry.'

She opened the door with a deep sigh of relief. 'Thank God, I thought it was the police,' she said.

'Sorry, I didn't mean to scare you, I finished my phone call earlier than I expected. Just thought we might as well go down to the bar together. Don't be so jumpy, it'll be alright,' said Harry reassuringly, 'nobody saw us in that alleyway, I'm sure of it.'

'I can't help it. I'm sorry, it's not like me to be so nervous.'

'There's no need to be nervous. Emily, you did nothing wrong – just remember that.'

'I'm worried for you, Harry, I got you into this mess. I don't think I could live with myself if you were arrested,' said Emily.

'Nobody's going to be arrested, don't worry,' Harry said in his calm, reassuring manner. 'Come on, let's have that drink.'

As they drank their beers, Harry wanted to know more about Emily's upbringing and her mother. With Harry's easy-going nature, Emily opened up. 'What can I say, Harry? She was, and probably still is, a cruel, heartless woman. I suppose you could call her a psychopath. She left me for days on end, sometimes longer, to look after my younger brother and sister with hardly any food to live on.

She wouldn't allow us to have any friends at the house, and besides going to school, we weren't allowed out. She once locked me in a cupboard under the stairs for a whole day just for disobeying her. Her cruelty eventually caught up with her, though, thanks to my now adoptive parents. She fled soon after that. Several years later, when the house was sold, the property developers discovered the bodies of my stepfather and father buried in the garden. I've never seen or heard from her since the moment she fled. And that's about it in a nutshell.'

'That's awful, Emily. She really does sound like a dreadful woman. It must have been what made you into the strong person you are today because I can tell you are strong. I like that,' said Harry.

'Oh, I don't know about that,' said Emily, 'I was scared to death when you knocked on my door just now.'

'It's only natural. You had a nasty shock today,' he said, gently placing his hand around her shoulders. Emily smiled cautiously at him, simultaneously taking a sip of her beer.

An hour later, after two beers, they decided to go to their rooms for a well-deserved siesta before dinner. They left the bar and began walking to the elevator in the lobby. To both their dismay, two uniformed police officers approached the receptionist's desk. They both turned their faces away as they approached the elevator, pushed the button and waited for it to arrive, it seemed to take forever.

Harry strained to listen to what they were saying; their tone was serious, and they appeared to be showing the receptionist a photograph. The receptionist picked up her phone and dialled a number just as the elevator arrived and the door opened. 'Get in and go to your room,' Harry said.

'I'm not leaving you. What the hell are you doing?' said Emily.

Harry virtually pushed her into the elevator and pressed the button for their floor. He moved closer to the reception and stood out of sight behind one of the pillars, listening all the time as he lit a cigarette. After a few minutes, a second elevator opened and out came an elderly couple who went to join the police at the desk. He could tell they were American. He strained to listen to the conversation, and much to his relief, he established that they had been robbed by a pickpocket earlier that day. The police showed them a photo of a known pickpocket in the area and asked if it was the person who had robbed them.

Harry breathed a sigh of relief and went to the elevator once again. He knocked on Emily's door, and she opened it immediately. She could tell by his mischievous smile that everything was alright. She flung her arms around him and kissed him. 'Oh God, Harry, I thought for sure you would be arrested.'

'No honey, just one of the guests that had been pickpocketed.'

'What a relief,' Emily said, releasing her grip on Harry.

'You don't have to stop, you know,' said Harry.

Emily moved closer to him again. Harry clutched her arms tightly and drew her closer. They kissed; it was a long, lingering kiss. They were late for dinner.

# Chapter 36

THE FOLLOWING MORNING, Emily and Harry were having a convivial breakfast together in the hotel restaurant. Harry's cell phone rang unobtrusively as they were drinking their coffee. 'It's my office,' he said, looking at the incoming call display, 'I'll just take it. It could be about your mystery emailer.

'Yes, of course, carry on,' said Emily.

'Good morning, Harry, it's John.'

'Good morning, John. Have you got something for me?' asked Harry.

'I may have,' said Harry's colleague. 'I contacted the guy by email as you asked and told him there may be a small reward if he could give us more information on this Thorne woman.'

'And?'

'Well, he replied and said he was willing to help in return for a thousand dollars. I said I'd get back to him. What do you want me to say to him?'

'Tell him we accept, and ask him where should we meet?' said Harry.

Emily listened to the conversation, albeit only from Harry's side, yet she could tell it might possibly be good news.

'Get back to me as soon as you get a reply,' said Harry.

'That sounded promising,' said Emily when the call had ended.

'Yeah, it could well be, honey. My associate has made contact with your guy with the email. We just need to arrange a place to meet. John will let me know as soon as he hears something – hopefully sometime today,' said Harry.

'That's great news, Harry, thanks.'

'You're welcome, Emily, but there's a way to go yet. We don't even know whether this guy is the real deal or not.'

'Well, let's hope he is,' said Emily eagerly.

'Yeah, but have you thought about what you are going to do if we *do* find your mother?'

'I suppose I'll just have to cross that bridge when I come to it. My purpose for being here is simple: I need to confront her about why she did the things she did to us— and to get her back to the UK to face justice for murdering my father,' Emily said solemnly.

'That might not be so easy; it could be that she has citizenship here if she's lived here for a good few years. Had you thought of that?'

'Hmm, no, as a matter of fact, I hadn't. It didn't cross my mind,' said Emily, a little embarrassed not to have considered the possibility.

'I wouldn't worry too much about it at this stage. It may not be the case anyway,' said Harry in an attempt to lift her spirit.

'I hope not,' she said. 'So, what do we do now?'

'We wait to hear back from John. But that doesn't stop us from seeing some of the sights,' Harry said cheerfully.

Emily smiled. 'Yes, why not.'

'Good, we'll have one more cup of coffee, then take a walk around the old town. Sound good?'

'Yes, that sounds great,' said Emily.

Neither had fully explored the old town since arriving in Cartagena. It was quite beautiful with old colourful buildings, churches and many tabernas. The beach, with white sand and palm trees, was a short walk from the town. They stayed there for an hour, enjoying its beauty and listening to the gentle lapping of the waves of the azure waters. Emily's light skin began to darken under the sun's rays. Harry had sported a deep olive tan from the moment they first met.

They took a gentle stroll back to town and found a wonderful Taberna, where they enjoyed lunch and much-needed refreshments. Emily reverted to orange juice while Harry stuck with his ice-cold beer.

'I meant to ask you if you have a photograph of your mother?' said Harry.

'Just one, that's all. Actually, I have a copy in my handbag.' She took the folded photocopy from her bag and laid it down on the table before him. 'It's a very old photo, of course, taken some years ago.'

'She looks quite glamorous,' Harry said.

'It's a showbusiness photograph. How she looks now, of course, I've no idea,' said Emily.

'How old would she be now?' asked Harry.

'I suppose she'd be about sixty years old now. Do you know something, Harry? I don't even know when her birthday is. Isn't that awful?' she said.

'It's not your fault, Emily.'

The waiter came to their table and glanced at the picture.

'– Conozco a esa mujer,' said the waiter as he cleared their plates from the table.

'You do? I mean, ¿Lo haces?' said Harry to the waiter.

'What did he say? I didn't understand a word,' asked Emily.

'It's the darndest thing. He said he knows her.' He turned to the waiter again. 'Do you speak any English?' he asked.

'A little, señor.'

'Where have you seen this woman?'

The man indicated by pointing his finger downwards. 'Here Señor.'

'When was this?' asked Emily.

'Uh, hace tres meses,' said the man, reverting to Spanish.

'Three months ago, Emily, he said three months ago,' Harry said.

'Ask him what she was doing here?' said Emily.

Harry asked the man the question in Spanish.

'He says she was working here as a singer,' said Harry. '¿Volverá? Will she be coming back?' he asked the waiter. The waiter simply shrugged and went about his business.

'We've made a small breakthrough, Emily.'

'Well, at least we know she's here in Cartagena,' said Emily, 'thank goodness you asked to see her photograph.'

'I think Lady Luck is on our side, Emily. We now know she's still singing, and there are plenty of tabernas around here that cater to English and American tourists.'

'Let's hope so,' said Emily.

'I'm certain of it. Shall we try the same trick at another place before going back to the hotel?' asked Harry.

'Yes, why not? It's worth trying.'

They visited two more tabernas, in fact. Harry even showed the photograph to the waiters and began asking questions. Unfortunately, they were not so lucky on either occasion—no one recognised Rhona. They returned to the hotel.

Emily was exhausted. It had been a long day, and she felt the beginnings of a headache after enduring the heat and tremendous humidity.

'I think I'll go to my room for a lie-down. I'll see you at dinner,' she said.

'Of course, I might just do the same thing,' he said.

They parted company outside Emily's room. She went inside, closed the blinds, kicked off her shoes and fell onto the bed. After just minutes, she was asleep. Harry had the same idea. He also closed his blinds and intended to get some rest before dinner, threw himself on the bed, landing on his back. His hands cradled his head as he thought about Emily and reflected on the events of the past two days. Eventually, his eyes slowly closing, he found sleep.

He was woken just thirty minutes later at the sound of his cell phone ringing. Harry sat bolt upright and picked up the phone from his bedside table. 'Hi Harry, it's John, just to let you know that the guy eventually replied to my second email. He claims he can tell you where to find this Rhona Thorne character, and he's willing to meet you at The Clock Pub in Bourbon St. Cartagena tomorrow evening at 8pm.'

'Okay, John, thanks. How will I know him?'

'He told me he'd be sitting outside, smoking a cigar and reading a newspaper. That's all I've got.'

'Got it,' said Harry, jotting down the details on a piece of hotel notepaper.

'Be careful, Harry, I'm not sure I like the sound of this,' said John.

'Don't worry, John, I'll be fine.'

'One other thing, Harry, he wants the cash up front, and that's exactly why I don't like it. We know nothing about this guy.'

'Just let me worry about that, John,' said Harry.

'Okay, Harry, you're the boss,' said John, reluctantly.

'I'll let you know how I get on. How are things there?'

'Busy as usual,' said John.

'Well, I guess I'll be back at the office fairly soon. Any problems, you know where I am. See you, John.'

Harry was already seated at the table for two in the hotel restaurant when Emily arrived. He stood up to greet her, his face beaming, Emily looked striking in a long dress. He kissed her cheek before she sat.

'How do you feel now?' asked Harry, 'you look stunning.'

Emily looked a little embarrassed. 'Thank you,' she said, 'yes, I feel much better now.'

'Are you hungry?' Harry asked.

'Yes, I'm famished,' she said.

'Good, so am I. Shall we order a bottle of wine to start with?'

'Yes, good idea, why not,' said Emily.

The waiter arrived at their table to take their orders. They both chose the Sancocho, a traditional stew and a bottle of Cabernet Sauvignon.

'Have you heard anything from your friend?' asked Emily.

'No, not yet,' Harry said, coolly keeping the truth from her.

'Oh, that's a worry,' she said.

'Don't worry, I'm sure we'll hear something soon. The guy's probably playing it cool, that's all.' He raised his wine glass. 'Cheers,' he said.

'I'm sorry, Harry, I'm just being impatient, aren't I?'

'Well, we've only been here a couple of days. There's plenty of time. In the meantime, we should try to enjoy ourselves a little,' said Harry in his calm, reassuring manner.

'Yes, you're quite right,' said Emily, smiling at him.

'That's the spirit,' Harry said. 'Did you bring a swimming costume with you?'

'Uh, no, I hadn't planned on it being a holiday, so I didn't bring one. Why?'

'Well, we can get you one. I thought we might go back to the beach tomorrow and have a swim. What do you think?'

'I suppose we could, but –'

'But nothing, it'll take your mind off things for a while. It'll be good for you,' he said.

'Okay, Harry, you're on,' said Emily.

'That's my girl,' he said.

*Chapter 37*

IT WAS YET ANOTHER GLORIOUS DAY. In Cartagena, it was hot and humid all year round. Straight after breakfast, Emily and Harry went shopping for a swimming costume, and then they headed for the beach. They swam, Harry rather more expertly than Emily. She got quite worried when he dived underwater for what seemed an eternity, eventually bobbing to the surface next to her in the clear, azure Caribbean water.

Emily lay on her front on the beach, her hands cradling her head, while Harry sat facing her. He seemed mesmerised, gazing into her eyes. Was he falling for her? He wondered. He had always enjoyed a single life, but then he had never met anyone like Emily before. He was not only deeply attracted to her; she also fascinated him.

'So, what made you become a journalist?' Harry asked, rubbing suntan lotion onto her back.

'It's what I always wanted to do as far back as I can remember,' she replied. 'I never dreamt that I'd ever work for one of the big newspapers, though. Of course, I don't think it would have happened without the support of my adoptive parents,' she added.

'I think you would have made it, whatever happened in your life,' he said. 'You're a very resourceful woman, strong and determined.'

'I don't know about that; my real mother, Rhona, would have done everything in her power to hold me back,' said Emily.

'Well, your early life has certainly made you into the strong person you are today. I have no doubt about that,' said Harry.

'It certainly didn't help my sister,' Emily said, 'she's damaged, I'm afraid, and I'm not sure she will ever recover.'

'I'm sorry, Emily, I had no idea. Maybe if all of this works out, it will bring some sort of closure.'

'I'm not so sure,' said Emily.

'What about your current life? Is there someone waiting for you when you return to England?'

'You mean a man?'

'Yeah, that's exactly what I mean,' said Harry.

'No, there's no one,' said Emily, with a smile.

'That's good,' he said.

'How about you? Is there anyone special in your life?' she asked.

'There wasn't, at least not until now.'

'There's a slight problem, of course,' said Emily, 'you live in the States. I live in England.'

'I don't see any problem. I promise you there's nothing we couldn't overcome,' said Harry, self-assuredly.

'Don't make promises you can't keep, Harry,' she said, a hint of sadness in her voice.

'I'd never do that to you,' he said. He leaned over and gently kissed her lips.

'No, I don't think you would, Harry,' Emily said, returning the kiss.

'You know I'm falling for you, don't you?' said Harry.

'Ditto!' she whispered softly in his ear. 'But then we've only known each other a couple of days, it's quite ridiculous.'

Harry kissed her again. 'Two days or not, I don't need any longer. Another swim before we head back?' he said.

'Yes, why not,' said Emily.

It was 6.30pm when they returned to the hotel. Harry picked up a copy of the local newspaper from the lobby.

'Would you mind if we had dinner a little later tonight?' asked Harry as they approached Emily's room, 'I thought we could eat out somewhere for a change, say 9 o'clock. Would that be okay?'

'Uh, yes, that'd be fine,' she said.

'Great, I'll call for you. See you later, honey,' he said, kissing her on the cheek.

It was 7.45pm when Emily, having showered and washed her hair, clad in a bath towel, searched the wardrobe for something to wear for dinner. She looked idly out of the window when she heard a car pulling up outside. It was a cab. A few moments later, she saw Harry get inside. Her heart sank. Where was he going without her? Was he harbouring secrets from her after all?

It was just after 8 o'clock when Harry asked the cab to stop a couple of hundred yards away from The Clock Pub. He walked very slowly the rest of the way; it was a tranquil part of town and as he approached, he could see the bar was not bustling with people. Sure enough, as he got closer, he could see a man in a grubby Panama hat and an equally grubby white suit, reading a newspaper, a British newspaper, and smoking a large cigar. Harry stopped and lit a cigarette. The man lowered his newspaper and looked around for a moment, then continued reading.

'Good evening,' said Harry, standing over the man. The man slowly lowered his newspaper but said nothing.

'I believe you may have some information that's of interest to me?' Harry said bluntly.

The man took a deep puff of his cigar and blew out a large cloud of smoke into the night air. 'Please, take a seat,' he said casually. By his accent, his voice was gravelly, but he was clearly English. 'I may have; did you bring the money?'

'Do I look stupid to you?' said Harry. He took a seat at the table. 'I'm here to check you out, nothing more, Mr?'

'My name isn't important. And if you haven't got the money, I don't think we have anything to say to one another,' said the man, raising himself.

'I just want to know how you know Rhona Thorne and where I can find her? If I'm satisfied, I'll pay you half now and the other half when I've seen her for myself. Otherwise, there's no deal. Take it or leave it. It's up to you,' said Harry.

The man sat down again. He looked at Harry thoughtfully, rubbing the stubble on his chin. 'Let me see the money,' he said.

Harry took five hundred dollars from his jacket and showed the man. At that moment, a waiter came outside to take Harry's drink order. He quickly put the cash back in his pocket. 'Just a small beer, por favor.' The waiter returned to the bar inside to get the beer.

'Well, you've seen the money. Are you going to give me the information or not?' asked Harry sternly.

'And how do I know you will pay the other half?' asked the man.

'You'll just have to trust me, won't you? The same way that I'll have to trust you, and I have more to lose than you, wouldn't you say?'

The man considered Harry for a moment, staring directly into his eyes as he puffed on his cigar. 'You know what,' he said, 'I am going to trust you. You look honest enough to me.'

'Okay, so where can I find Rhona Thorne?' asked Harry.

The man coughed. 'The money?'

Harry smirked, took the cash from his jacket again and slid it across the table, yet keeping his hand on it. 'The information?' he said.

'You'll find her at The Café Havana on Calle 30. She works there most Tuesdays. When will I get the other half of the money?'

'I suggest you be at The Café Havana next Tuesday evening. Let's say 9.30, shall we? If she's there, you'll get paid,' said Harry.

'I'll be there,' said the man, 'but we must keep it discreet.'

'And you'd better hope that Rhona Thorne is there as well,' said Harry.

At that moment, Harry's beer arrived at the table. He glanced at his watch. It was 8.30. he paid the waiter and hailed a cab to take him back to the hotel. It only took ten minutes to reach the hotel, by which time, Emily was getting worried.

Harry knocked on her door, and she opened it immediately. 'Where the heck have you been? I saw you getting into a taxi cab, which got me worried. Why didn't you tell me you were going off somewhere?'

'Calm down, Emily.'

'I am calm, I'm perfectly calm, but I didn't know where you were going. Anything could have happened to you.'

'I'm sorry, I should have told you where I was going. I just didn't want to get your hopes up,' said Harry.

'So where *did* you go?' she asked.

'As it happens, I have some good news for you. I met with the mysterious email guy.'

'Without me?'

'I didn't have much information on him. I didn't want to put you at risk. It was all arranged by John this afternoon, and I met him at a bar. Anyway, I got what I went for. I now know where we'll find your mother, Emily.'

'You know where she is?' said Emily, she was completely stunned by the news.

'He told me we would find her at The Café Havana. She's there mostly on Tuesdays, apparently. I have no reason to think he's lying. I only paid him half of what he was asking for now.'

'You paid him? Then I must give you the money,' said Emily.

'No. You don't,' said Harry.

'It's only Saturday. So we have to wait a few more days then?'

'Not necessarily. We can still go along and check the place out before then,'

'Now, let's go out for dinner and enjoy ourselves. Oh, by the way, I have some other good news, I read in the paper that the police are treating the death of the guy who attacked you as gang-related, so we're in the clear.'

'Oh, thank God. I was really worried,' said Emily, 'I remember what you said about not necessarily getting an unbiased trial here. I had visions of us being arrested and thrown in jail to rot.'

'Well, at least you can stop worrying about that. Come on, let's go out, I'm starved.'

They stayed out late at a Taberna where lively music played, they danced along with local people and, for a while, forgot about everything, simply enjoying the moment.

# Chapter 38

THE NEXT MORNING, they had a late breakfast, and two hours later, at around 11am, while stopping at a café for a coffee, Emily took her mobile from her shoulder bag. 'Excuse me a moment, Harry. I think I should give my sister, Patricia, a call to let her know that I'm okay,' said Emily.

'Yes, of course, you really should,' said Harry.

She dialled the number; it rang for a whole minute before Patricia finally answered. She sounded tired. 'Pat, it's Emily, I'm sorry it's so early where you are; I just felt I should call you to let you know I'm okay.'

'That's okay, I've been on duty all night at the hospital, just about to go home. It's so good to hear from you. I've been worried about you. Are you okay? How is it going? Your search for Rhona, I mean.'

'Yes, I'm fine, and yes, it looks like we may be on to something. It would seem she's definitely here in Cartagena,' said Emily.

'*We?*' asked Patricia.

'Sorry?'

'You said *we* may be on to something,' said Patricia pointedly.

'Oh, yes,' Emily said, standing up and wandering away from the table where she and Harry sat. 'Well, to tell you the truth, Pat, I am getting some help from a really nice guy.'

'Really? You be careful, Emily,' said Patricia.

'It's okay, really, Pat. He's a really good man, he's an American on holiday. He also happens to be a private investigator. I'm not sure I would be getting anywhere without him.'

'Do I detect a possible romance?' asked Patricia.

'Oh Pat, really,' Emily paused, 'well, he seems quite a special man, I must admit.'

'I knew it. I could tell by your voice something had changed in you,' Patricia said.

'How is everyone at home?' asked Emily.

'They're all fine. So you think you and your friend may have tracked Rhona down then?'

'I'm hoping so, Pat. I'll let you know. Look, I'd better go. I'll see you soon, Bye Pat.'

'Bye then, take care.'

Emily returned to Harry at the table; he'd ordered some more coffee.

'How's your sister?' asked Harry.

'She's fine, thanks. She was just coming off duty, I think.'

'Oh, what does she do for s living?' he asked.

'She's a doctor at a hospital. Patricia is my adoptive sister.'

'Impressive! I've ordered some more coffee if that's okay. After that, I thought we could hire a scooter and take a tour of the countryside. What do you think?'

'Well, yes, sounds good. There's nothing else we can do at the moment anyway, is there?' said Emily.

'Not until this evening anyway, then we can pay the Café Havana a visit, just on the off-chance. You never know. We may get lucky,' said Harry.

'We might,' said Emily, sounding not quite so confident as Harry.

They finished their coffee and strolled down the bustling street to where Harry had previously seen an establishment that hired out scooters for the day.

'One or two?' Harry asked Emily.

'Definitely one. I wouldn't trust myself on one of these things,' she said.

'Okay, one it is,' said Harry. The formalities were dealt with. Harry paid the man, they mounted the machine and rode off with Emily holding tightly around Harry's middle. He rode fast, heading out of town towards the countryside, yet she always felt safe with him. They found themselves on the coastal road heading North. The road was rough and became narrower the further they travelled; palms and large tropical shrubs grew at the side of the road.

'Are you okay?' Harry said, raising his voice to be heard.

'Yes, fine,' shouted Emily joyfully.

A truck followed a few hundred yards behind them. Increasing in speed, the truck gained on them steadily but surely. Emily looked behind her as she heard the truck; it was almost on top of them.

'Harry!' she shouted.

'Yeah?'

'Look behind us.'

Harry craned his neck to see the truck. It appeared menacingly close; he twisted the throttle to gain speed, but the driver of the truck kept gaining on them. Eventually, the truck came alongside them, trying to force them into the jagged rock that followed the length of the road. Harry eased the throttle and braked hard so that the truck was now in front of them. He came to a dead stop on the road, skidding a little as he did so. The driver in front also stopped with the truck across the road, blocking their way.

Two rough-looking men jumped out of the truck and ran towards Harry and Emily before they could get away. They both held guns, which were now pointed at the couple.

Harry leaned towards Emily. 'Bandits,' he said.

'Oh, my God. What are we going to do, Harry?'

'Just try to stay calm,' he said as the two men moved closer. 'So, gentlemen, what can I do for you?' Harry asked in his inimitably cool fashion.

'Well, Señor, it seems you're paying a little too much interest in our employer,' said the man in surprisingly good English. Harry assumed he was the leader.

'I don't know what you're talking about,' said Harry.

'Oh, I think you do, Señor. Stop playing games.'

'Okay, are you talking about Rhona Thorne?'

'Now we're getting somewhere Señor, just stay away if you know what's good for you and the lovely Señorita.'

'And if I don't?' said Harry.

The man gestured with a wave of his gun and a menacing grin. 'Think about it, Señor. Stay away, okay!' he said sharply.

'I'll think about it,' Harry said.

'Oh, just one other thing before we leave,' said the man, 'I need your money, all of it!'

Harry knew he had no choice; he took out his money clip and handed him the cash. 'Three hundred dollars? Is that all of it?' said the leader.

'That's the lot,' said Harry.

'Sorry, Señorita, you too.'

Emily reluctantly pulled out two hundred dollars from her shoulder bag. She slammed it into his large hand. 'Low down thieving swine,' she said.

'Fiery! I like that in a woman. Well, we'll be leaving you now. Just think about what I said, Señor, and keep away. Consider this a warning.'

The two men drove off, leaving Emily shaken. 'I'm sorry, Harry, I should never have involved you in all of this. Anyway, this changes everything, I can't ask you to do any more. It's finished – over! It's becoming far too dangerous.'

'The hell it is,' said Harry, 'I'm not that easily scared off. We'll find a way, but I think from now on, I should go it alone. I don't want you put in danger.'

'I can't let you do that, Harry, I just can't,' said Emily.

'Look, I'm used to certain lowlifes. We're not giving up now. We've come too far.'

'If we do this, we do it together or not at all,' Emily insisted.

Harry sighed. 'Okay, we'll see,' he said. 'Let's get out of here, shall we?'

They got back on the scooter and went back the way they had come, eventually hitting the outskirts of the town once again. Harry stopped outside the Taberna where he'd previously been asking questions about Rhona.

'We stopped here the other day, do you remember? The waiter recognised your mother in the photograph,' said Harry.

'Yes, I remember.'

'Let's see if we can get any more information, shall we? Luckily, I always keep a secret stache of a few dollars in my shoe when travelling in these parts.'

'You think of everything, don't you?' said Emily.

'Well, as you found out, you have to in this country.'

They took a seat outside in a shady spot. The waiter soon came along to take their order. It was not the same waiter they had met before. Harry ordered two beers and the waiter disappeared inside.

'Have you got a copy of that photograph on you?' Harry asked Emily.

'Yes, I always carry it with me here.' She took it from her bag.

After a few moments, the waiter returned with their drinks.

'Perdona, do you speak English?' asked Harry.

The man shrugged. 'Not much, Señor.'

'Do you recognise this woman?' Harry asked, showing him the photograph.

The waiter understood what Harry was trying to convey but shook his head.

Harry mumbled, "That's a pity," under his breath. 'Could I speak with the manager – the director, por favor?'

'Sí.' He went inside again and shortly returned with a rotund man.

'Señor, what can I do for you?'

'Ah, good, you speak English. I was wondering if you recognise this woman? I saw one of your staff the other day, and he said she used to work here,' said Harry.

'Oh yes, that is Rhona.'

'Does she still work here?' Harry asked.

'I am sorry Señor, No. I have not seen her in quite a while. She used to play the guitar for our guests in the evening, but not anymore. Have you tried The Café Havana? They have entertainers sometimes.'

'Thank you,' said Harry, 'you've been most helpful, Señor.'

'You're welcome,' said the man, and then returned inside.

'Well, if nothing else, we possibly know that email man was telling the truth about Café Havana,' said Harry.

'Yes, it looks that way. But it's going to be dangerous. They know who we are now. Wait a minute, it's only just occurred to me. How did those men know who we are?' asked Emily rhetorically.

'That occurred to me as well, and the truth is, I just don't know,' said Harry.

'Unless our email man is a double-dealer. That's possible, isn't it?' said Emily.

'Yes, it's possible. I suppose I should try to find out. I'll pay another visit to the Clock Pub, where I met him.'

# Chapter 39

HARRY HAD LEFT EMILY at the hotel, and when he arrived just after 8pm, The Clock Pub was quiet. He had hoped that his contact was a regular at the bar, yet, for now, there was no sign of him. He took a seat at the same table outside as when they had previously met and ordered a whiskey. It was the same waiter as before. The waiter recognised Harry. He gave Harry a peculiar look. 'Welcome back, Señor,' he said before going to fetch Harry's drink.

Harry could see the waiter speaking to the man behind the bar, they both appeared to be in deep conversation and glanced out towards where Harry sat. The waiter returned with the glass of whiskey and placed it on the table. 'You clearly remember me, but do you remember the man I was with before?' asked Harry.

'Si Señor,' said the waiter, a little uneasy, Harry thought.

'Is he a regular customer?' enquired Harry.

The waiter simply nodded.

'Do you think he will be here tonight?'

'I could not say, Señor,' said the waiter, leaving Harry hurriedly. There was something odd about his behaviour, Harry thought. Harry took a drink of his whiskey and prepared to wait. He would give it a little longer, he thought. If the man did not appear after that, he would leave.

Harry felt uncomfortable; he was unsure why. He downed the whiskey in one large gulp after waiting for ten minutes, left enough cash to cover the bill and stood up to leave. At that moment, a police car screeched to a halt directly outside the bar. Two uniformed officers of the National Police jumped out of the car and came towards him.

'You need to come with us, Señor,' said one of the officers, grabbing Harry's arm.

'What the hell's going on?' asked Harry.

'Please, get in the car, Señor.'

The waiter and the man behind the bar stood outside and watched as Harry was bundled into the police car until it drove off into the night.

A few minutes later, the car arrived at the police station somewhere in town.

Harry was taken to a brightly lit room. 'Look, what's this all about?' he asked furiously.

'Sit down, Señor!' the officer said impatiently. Harry conformed and sat at the table; the two police officers sat opposite him. 'I'm Captain Sanchez, so let's start with your name, shall we?'

'Craig, Harry Craig. Look, I need to know what's going on,' he said.

'You're American?'

'Yeah, of course, I'm American, but –'

'What's the purpose of your visit to Cartagena?' asked one of the officers.

'What do *you* think? I'm on vacation, of course.'

'You know this man?' asked the captain, sliding a post-mortem photograph across the table of the man Harry was hoping to meet again that evening.

Harry was shocked but did not show it. 'We met the other night for a drink. I wouldn't say I know him, though. What happened to him?'

The Inspector looked suspiciously at Harry. 'He was murdered, Señor, and only a few yards away from the bar where you met him that evening. What do you have to say about that, Señor?'

'Are you trying to pin it on me just because I met him for a drink?' Harry asked.

'I see you are a private investigator,' said the officer, taking Harry's P.I. licence from his wallet.

'What's that got to do with anything?'

'The waiter at the bar saw you handing over an amount of cash to this man. Is that correct?'

'Did he also tell you that I was enquiring if he would be at the bar this evening? Why would I ask that if I'd killed the man?' said Harry, showing his annoyance.

'Why were you giving him a large amount of cash if that was the first time you had met Señor Craig? Why?'

'It was a private transaction connected with my work, that's all.'

'What sort of private transaction would that be?'

'I needed some information regarding a missing person. It's as simple as that,' said Harry, now are you going to charge me, or are you going to let me go about my vacation?'

'And do you always mix business with pleasure, Señor?'

'Not always, no. Can I go now? How was he killed anyway?'

'He was shot, once in the chest and once in the head,' said the officer, 'we have not found the weapon yet. I do not suppose you can help with that either, can you?'

'You're right, I can't! Except that it sounds like a professional job. Now, either charge me or let me go. I've done nothing, I know it, and you know it too,' said Harry.

'Which hotel are you staying at, Señor Craig?'

'I'm at the Casona del Colegio. You can find me there anytime you like.'

'Very well, we'll take you back to your hotel – for now! But I am afraid I will need your passport, Señor.'

'I don't carry it with me—it's at the hotel,' said Harry.

'Very well then.' The captain summoned a junior police officer and ordered him to take Harry back to his hotel and to collect his passport.

'Enjoy the rest of your evening, Señor Craig. I will be seeing you again, I am sure,' said the captain.

'Yeah, and I'll be seeing you to get my passport back. What was the victim's name?'

'Daniel Blake,' said the officer. 'Why do you ask?'

'Just curious,' said Harry.

'I suggest you keep your curiosity to yourself, Señor.'

'Goodnight,' said Harry, raising his hat to the officer.

A short while later, the police car pulled up outside the hotel. Harry was escorted to his room, where the policeman, as ordered, took his passport and left.

Emily had been pacing the floor in her room for what seemed a long time since Harry went out. He was out far longer than she had imagined he would be. She heard a knock on her door, and she opened it quickly. 'Harry, where on earth have you been all of this time? I was worried sick?'

'It's a long story, Emily, believe me,' he said. 'Let's go to the bar, I need a drink.'

'Okay, are you alright though?' asked Emily.

'Yeah, I'm fine. Just let's have that drink, and I'll tell you all about it.'

They ordered their drinks, Harry choosing a double whiskey and a beer.

'So, what happened? You look like you've been through hell. I was so worried about you,' said Emily, 'I didn't know what to think.'

'Well, everything is okay now, except that –'

'Except what?' interrupted Emily.

'Our email man is dead, or should I say, murdered. Daniel Blake was his name,' said Harry, taking a swig of his whiskey.

'Murdered? Who by?' asked Emily.

'Don't know. But that's why I was so long. It would appear that I'm a suspect. The waiter at the bar recognised me as having met Blake before. He was murdered the same night that I saw him, just yards from the bar, apparently shot. Anyway, tonight, the barman called the police, and I was taken away for questioning. They knew they had nothing on me, so they brought me back to the hotel. They took my passport, though, pending enquiries. So that was my evening, what about you?'

'I think I wore a hole in the carpet where I was pacing in my room. Oh God, what a mess. I wonder why he was killed? Do you think it's connected with us?' said Emily.

'I'm sure of it. I just don't know exactly how or why yet.'

'This whole thing is becoming silly now. What have we got ourselves into, Harry?'

'I don't know, but I'm determined to find out.'

They drank their beer in quiet reflection.

'You know, I've been thinking about Daniel Blake's murder. I wouldn't be at all surprised if his killer, or killers, were the same guys that ambushed us yesterday,' said Harry.'

'Harry, I understand what you're saying. It would be a huge coincidence if he'd been randomly murdered, but if you're right, how would they have known you'd spoken to Blake? What could the connection have been between Blake and Rhona? Not only that, but I've been wondering why she is so well protected?' said Emily.

'Yeah, all those questions had crossed my mind too,' said Harry.

# *Chapter 40*

THE NEXT DAY, AT BREAKFAST, Emily was concerned about Harry becoming so deeply involved in her problem. She was almost regretting having embarked on her mission, although she had no regrets about meeting Harry. He was lively, exuberant and adventurous, and she had to admit, she had never felt so alive.

'Harry,' she said, 'I know I've said this before, but I can't ask you to do any more. I think I should go it alone from here—I couldn't bear it if something happened to you.'

'Not a chance, honey, I'm in this until the end,' said Harry, forcefully.

'Maybe I should just forget about her,' said Emily.

'I don't like being beaten. Emily, we'll see this thing through. I'm going to the Café Havana tonight to check it out, and I'm going alone,' said Harry.

'No way,' said Emily, 'if you're going, I'm going, it's as simple as that.'

'No, it's too risky. Besides, it'll be less conspicuous if I go alone.'

'No deal, Harry, I'm going with you, and nobody is going to stop me, not even you, Harry.'

Harry drank his coffee. He was uneasy. 'And that's your final word, is it?' he asked.

'Yes, Harry, it is. We do this together or not at all.'

Harry shrugged, simply saying a reluctant "okay."

'Well, I'm glad that's sorted out,' said Emily.

Once they had finished breakfast, Harry asked, 'So what do you want to do until this evening?'

'Shall we just go for a walk?' asked Emily.

'Yeah, sure,' said Harry.

They left the restaurant and walked to the lobby. Inspector Sanchez sat at a table, pretending to read a newspaper. He got to his feet when he saw Harry and Emily leaving the restaurant, heading through the lobby and towards the street.

Harry spotted him. 'Captain Sanchez! This is an unexpected pleasure. What can I do for you?'

'I just dropped by, Señor Craig, to inform you that we still have no other suspects.'

'Emily, this is Inspector Sanchez,' said Harry.

'Good morning. You know, you're looking in the wrong place, Captain. Mr Craig is no murderer. What possible reason would he have anyway?' said Emily vehemently.

'I don't know yet, Señorita. And your name is?' asked the captain.

'Emily Parker. Do you know what time this murder took place, captain?'

'We believe it was around 9.30pm on the night in question.'

'Well, there you are then. Mr Craig was with me at that time in the hotel,' said Emily, 'in fact, a lot earlier. He returned to the hotel at about 9pm.'

'You did not tell me that, Señor.'

'You didn't ask,' said Harry.

The inspector appeared flustered. 'Just don't leave the country until I say you can, okay?'

'I'm not likely to do that, am I, Captain? You still have my passport, remember?'

The Inspector did not take kindly to being made a fool of, 'I'll be speaking to you again, Señor Craig,' he said, turning sharply on his heels and leaving the hotel.

'I don't think he likes you,' said Emily, laughing.

Harry smiled at her and said, 'I think you could be right.'

They strolled down the streets, the heat was blistering, the humidity high. They found shade in a beautiful old church, which the guide map said was the Sanctuary of Saint Peter Claver. They stayed in the coolness for some time, admiring the architecture and some of its fine paintings.

They sat for a while, then eventually braved the heat of the day once again. It seemed particularly hot. They found shade again at a taberna, where they both lingered over a long glass of fresh, ice-cold orange juice and tapas, simply watching the world go by.

Later, they returned to the hotel and went to their respective rooms, showered and changed clothes. The evening soon arrived, and they caught a cab outside the hotel to take them to The Café Havana. 'If there's any talking to be done, let me do it,' said Harry.

'I'm nervous, Harry, I wonder if she'll be there?'

'We'll soon find out, don't be disappointed if she isn't, there's always tomorrow. The object of tonight is to get familiarised with the place, after all, Blake said she worked Tuesday evenings, not Monday.'

The cab dropped them outside, Harry paid the driver, and they walked towards the entrance. The club sounded lively.

Emily stopped in her tracks as they got closer to the entrance. 'I'm not sure I can do this, Harry.'

'Take a deep breath, it'll be okay, I'm with you all the way,' said Harry.

Emily did as he suggested and took a very deep breath. 'I'm ready,' she said.

The place was crowded with what looked like a mixture of tourists and locals. A man in a glittering jacket was on the floor, singing a lively number in Spanish, though to Emily, he looked either English or American. They found one of the few tables at the back of the audience. The lighting was low, except for where the man performed— he was illuminated by bright stage lighting.

After a few minutes, one of the many waiters came to their table and took their drinks order. Where they sat was perfect; the lighting was low, so they could not be seen. The performer continued singing for some time until, eventually, he bowed to the audience and, departed the small stage and went to what Harry assumed was a dressing room backstage.

The lights dimmed on the stage for a short time, and then gradually lit up again, revealing a woman in a long black dress, seated with a Spanish guitar on her knee. The crowded audience fell silent. The woman, heavily built, with her dark hair tied up in a typical Spanish bun, began to strum a mournful tune on the guitar.

Could this woman be Rhona? Harry wondered. He looked over at Emily— her face was ashen, her mouth ajar, and she looked to be in a daze. 'Is that her?' he asked Emily.

'Huh,' was all she could say, transfixed on the woman.

'Is that Rhona,' he asked again.

'I think it is. Yes, it's her. I had no idea she played the guitar,' said Emily, still unable to take her eyes off Rhona.

'Emily, snap out of it!' said Harry.

'Yes, sorry, I suppose seeing her after all this time, it suddenly seems so real,' she said.

'But it's what you wanted, isn't it?' asked Harry.

'Yes, of course. How can such an evil woman play something so beautiful? Said Emily.'

Harry caught the attention of a waiter. 'Perdona, will the same performers be here tomorrow evening?'

'Si Señor.'

'Gracias, can I order two more of these, please?' said Harry, showing the waiter their glasses.

Harry's eyes darted around the place, looking for any way they could safely approach Rhona once she had finished her performance without being seen or accosted by the heavies in her employ. 'I'm going to take a look around the back of the building. I promise I won't be long. Will you be okay for a few minutes?'

'Yes, but please be careful and don't be long. Don't do anything silly, please,' pleaded Emily.

'I won't, I promise.'

Harry pushed past the crowded tables and made his way outside. He casually walked along the street until he found a backstreet that he hoped led to the rear of the place. It did, but from a distance at the dimly lit rear door, he could see a number of undesirable-looking characters lurking. There was also a car parked, the driver stood, leaning on it, as if waiting for someone. He would have been outnumbered certainly, and he guessed if they were Rhona's men, they would be carrying guns as well. He returned inside to Emily. Rhona still played her guitar.

'It's no good,' he said, 'the rear of the building is being covered by a number of heavies, and my guess is they're packing guns.'

'Well, that's it then, it's all over,' said Emily, 'we'll never be able to get near her.'

'I'll get you to see her somehow,' said Harry, 'don't ask me how, but I will. Although I should say that now we've traced her, perhaps you should inform the British police to get her taken home to face justice if possible.'

'Maybe you're right, but I still want to confront her myself,' said Emily.

'Don't worry, I'll think of something,' Harry said.

Emily seemed mesmerised by the beauty of the piece her mother played on her sad guitar, unable to take her eyes off her. Harry had to virtually drag her away, had a plan and was ready to leave.

'Come on, Emily, let's go. I want to get a cab; we're going to follow her when she leaves. If we can find out where she lives, we stand a chance of getting to her. We haven't a chance in hell of getting close to her here,' said Harry.

'But what about those people that are guarding her?' asked Emily as they made their way outside.

'That's why we need to follow them. I need to know exactly what we're up against,' said Harry.

# Chapter 41

ONCE OUTSIDE, HARRY HIRED A CAB. He told the driver to wait for a while. Twenty minutes passed until, eventually, the car he recognised as being the same one parked at the rear of the club pulled out onto the main road heading North.

'Follow him,' Harry said to the cab driver. The driver looked confused but did as Harry asked. 'Don't get too close,' he added.

Harry turned to Emily. 'Have you wondered why she is so heavily protected?' he asked.

'Yes, I have,' she said, 'but I can't think why. It's all very strange.'

'No, neither can I,' said Harry. I mean, I know she's wanted by the British police, but having round-the-clock armed protection seems completely over the top. There must be a reason, but what?'

The driver up front was becoming uneasy. He understood English and had overheard their conversation, especially the part about armed guards being in the car in front. 'I don't want any trouble, Señor,' he said nervously.

'Just keep your distance, and I promise there won't be,' said Harry. 'Have you have any idea where they might be heading? We seem to be a long way out of town,' said Harry.

'There's a villa overlooking the ocean a little further on—there's nothing else around here for miles, Señor.'

'How much further?'

'Only half a mile.'

'Good, when we get closer, park your car somewhere where it won't be noticed,' said Harry.

'Look, Señor, I'll take you there, but I'm not waiting. I have a family to think of.'

'I promise nothing will happen to you; I'll pay you fifty dollars on top of your fare to wait for me – deal?'

'Okay, but this is as far as I go,' he said, the car coming to a halt. Fifty dollars?' he asked, extending his hand to get paid the cash up-front.

Harry gave him the cash. 'And the lady will be waiting in the car as well, okay? Just in case you have any ideas of leaving us stranded.'

'Si Señor, whatever you say.'

'But I'm coming with you,' Emily protested.

'No, you're not, not this time. I need to move fast and stay undercover. This is just a reconnoitre. I need to know how I can get you to see Rhona safely. Now, be a good girl and stay behind, okay?'

Emily sighed deeply. 'Please be careful, Harry, don't take any chances.'

'I'm always careful. I'll see you soon,' he said, kissing her on the cheek. Harry then vanished into the night.

Harry reached the automatic gates, which led up a long driveway. He could make out lights inside the villa some five hundred yards away. The grounds were extensive, and the villa was impressive. He wondered how Rhona had gained so much wealth? Walls of seven feet tall appeared to surround the property, he wasted no time in scaling the wall, landing with a soft thud on the grass on the other side.

He picked himself up, brushed himself down, and walked cautiously in the direction of the villa, all the while observing the layout of the grounds while remaining vigilant. There appeared to be no one patrolling the area, so he sprinted straight to the building and peered through a window into a brightly lit room. Harry could clearly see Rhona—she was lying back on a sofa while one of her men poured her a drink and brought it over to her.

There were two men in the room, neither of which Harry recognised as the men who had ambushed Emily and himself the day before. How was Blake connected with this woman? He wondered. Had he previously been one of her flunkeys? Harry could not hear anything of the conversation that was taking place between Rhona and her men, but it appeared to be serious rather than light-hearted banter.

Suddenly, the grounds were flooded with light, and one of the men approached to open the French window. Harry shuffled himself into a recess of the outer wall and stood motionless. One of the men, a burly, moustached man who looked to be an unpleasant character, strolled outside and puffed on a cigarette for a couple of minutes. Harry could see the man had a scar that ran the length of his face.

The man eventually finished his cigarette and went back inside, leaving the doors open. Harry stealthily moved a little closer to the French windows to attempt to hear what was being said by the group and particularly, by Rhona herself. It was, however, impossible to make out anything with any clarity except that they seemed to be discussing business. But what business? It was clear she was involved in something illegal. Otherwise, why would she be so heavily protected?

Harry carefully moved his position and walked around the rear of the villa in order to familiarise himself with the complete layout. As he moved, he hugged the building where there were no garden floodlights. He found what appeared to be a kitchen and found no one there. He tried a window, but it was not locked. He also pushed the rear door, which was also unlocked, but he closed it again—this was no time for heroics. The men would, he thought, almost certainly be armed. It would not be easy to get Emily into the building at any time.

For now, Harry had seen enough. He needed to get back across the grounds without being seen. The only thing in his favour was that there were no vicious guard dogs roaming the property— something he had half expected. He glanced at his watch; he guessed he had been in the grounds for around twenty minutes and hoped the cab driver had not grown impatient and driven off with Emily.

Harry ran out of view from where Rhona and her men were in the spacious drawing room. He was about two hundred yards from the point where he had entered when he stumbled and fell onto the grass with a resounding thud. In the silence of the isolated grounds, the sound carried, and looking back, Harry could see both of Rhona's men rushing out, guns at the ready. They looked around, and as Harry rose to his feet, they could just make out his figure. He ran faster, trying not to stumble again, with the two men in hot pursuit.

Harry managed to reach the wall and clambered over it in one attempt. He ran to where the cab was parked and jumped in.

'Drive!' he ordered the cab driver. The driver did not hesitate and pulled away at speed, leaving a cloud of dust behind him.

'What happened?' asked Emily.

'I'm afraid I stumbled. They heard me and made chase, but I lost them. Don't worry, they wouldn't have been able to see my face, they didn't get close enough for that,' said Harry.

'Thank God you're alright. Did you see her?' asked Emily.

'Oh yes, I saw her alright, she was being waited on by one of her goons. I tried to get as close as I could to where they were. The French windows were open, but I'm afraid I couldn't make out what they were saying,' said Harry, catching his breath.

'Never mind, you're safe, that's the main thing,' Emily said.

'Yeah, but I wish I'd been able to get some idea what her angle is. She's obviously extremely well-off— you should see the place. One thing's for sure, though: she couldn't have made so much money by legal means. I just wish I knew what it was,' said Harry, frustrated.

'Does it really matter, Harry? I don't really care about what she is doing here. It's what she did back home that I want her to face justice for, nothing else.'

'I know,' said Harry, resignedly. 'Nevertheless, it might help us to know what we're up against, don't you think?'

'Let's not think about it right now; let's just get back to the hotel. I think you've been through enough this evening.'

'Yeah, you're probably right,' he said.

They reached the hotel at 11pm. 'I don't know about you, but I could use a drink right now,' said Harry.

'Yes, I think you deserve one,' said Emily.

They took a seat in the hotel bar and ordered their drinks. Most of the other guests had retired for the night; they were among the few people still there.

'So, what do we do now?' asked Emily, 'from what you've told me, it seems an impossible task for me to get to see Rhona.'

Harry was deep in thought. 'Harry?' said Emily.

'Yeah, sorry, I was miles away; what were you saying?'

'I was saying that it seems impossible for me to get to see Rhona now.'

'Yeah, I was thinking the same thing, but then I thought again.'

'What about?' asked Emily.

'Maybe we're approaching this all wrong,' he said, 'if we could just make contact with her somehow. We could simply say that her daughter wants to speak to her,' explained Harry.

'I don't know, Harry. I'm not sure that would work. Why would she want to speak to *me*?'

'I understand what you're saying, but honey, don't you think it's worth trying?'

'I'm tired, Harry, and I'm sure you must be as well. Can we talk about this tomorrow?' said Emily.

'Yeah, sure, you're quite right, it's late.'

'Come on, drink up, let's go to your room, I don't want to be alone tonight,' said Emily.

# *Chapter 42*

THE NEXT DAY, Harry persuaded Emily to return to The Café Havana during the afternoon to perhaps find out a telephone number for Rhona from the café's owner. They hoped that none of her men would be there at that time of the day. This time, they hired a scooter once again.

On their arrival at around 4pm, they found the café to be closed until 6pm. 'Stupid of me,' said Harry, 'I should have guessed that it's an evening-only joint.'

'Surely there must be someone around,' said Emily.

'Yes, there might be. I'll try the door,' said Harry. The door was firmly locked, so he banged loudly in the hope someone would answer them. There was no response at first, so he rapped on the door again in an urgent manner. He was in luck this time. A heavily built man unlocked the door, opening it wide. He stood in the doorway, his bulk almost filling it. He did not look in the best of moods.

'What do you want?' he said in a deep, gruff voice.

'Are you the manager?' asked Harry.

'He's busy,' said the man, beginning to close the door.

Harry bravely jammed his foot in the door. 'I'd like to speak to him, it's important,'

'How important?' growled the man.

'Very important!' said Harry.

'Wait there,' said the man, slamming the door shut.

Emily and Harry looked nervously at one another, and after a couple of minutes, the big man returned and opened the door once again. 'Come in,' he gestured with a flick of his head, 'you've got two minutes,' he said.

'Thanks,' said Harry as he and Emily stepped inside. The place looked very different in the dim lighting. They were escorted to a table where a well-dressed man sat.

'I'm a busy man. This had better be good,' said the man, lighting a cigar. 'Take a seat,' he added, while all the time, the heavily built man stood nearby.

Both Emily and Harry took a seat at his table facing the stage area of the club. 'So, what is so important is that you need to see me. I don't know you, do I?'

'No, you don't, my name is Craig, and this is Miss Parker, but don't worry, all my friend and I need is some information.'

'What sort of information?'

'Information on the woman we saw playing the guitar here last night,' said Harry.

The man's face changed instantly to one of concern. 'Why do you want information about her?' he said, vigorously stubbing out his cigar.

'Let me make something clear, we're not cops. We just want to speak to her, that's all.'

'You still haven't told me why,' said the man.

'You must have a phone number for her if she works here,' said Harry.

'You're beginning to try my patience,' said the man, 'I'll ask again. Why do you want information on her?'

'Okay, okay, well, if you must know, this lady here happens to be her daughter. She just wants to make a contact with her, even if it is just over the phone.'

'I see, I had no idea she had a daughter. But can you prove it?'

'I think you'll just have to take our word for it,' said Emily, 'I've come all the way from England to see her.'

'Hmm, do I take it you both had a slight encounter with some of her men the other day? Am I right?'

'That's right, what is it she's hiding?' asked Harry.

'I'm afraid your two minutes are up, now if you'll excuse me, I'm a very busy man. Miguel will show you out.'

'What, not even a phone number?' shouted Harry as they were escorted to the door.

'Have a good day,' said the man as the door closed in their faces. He immediately picked up the phone and called Rhona at her villa.

'Boss, it's Chico. I think you should know I've had a couple here asking questions about you. A young woman who says she is from England and an American guy. The girl claims to be your daughter. They also said they were at the club last night. What do you want me to do?'

'Did they tell you their names?'

'Yes, a Mister Craig and Miss Parker.'

'Leave this with me. I'll deal with it,' said Rhona brusquely.

'Okay, boss.'

'I'm sorry, Emily,' said Harry, 'I'd hoped for a better outcome than that.'

'It's not your fault, Harry. You did your best,' said Emily.

'Well, one thing's for sure, that manager is obviously protecting her as well. I can't figure any of this out, Emily.'

'Well, it seems I'm not going to be able to confront her as I'd hoped. I'll just have to accept that. I'll give the police in Britain a call when we get back to the hotel and leave it with them,' said Emily.

'Maybe that's not a bad idea, but don't give up on seeing her just yet. We'll come back to the club later if you like, said Harry.'

'Maybe this time, I should come alone. I'll be less conspicuous.'

'Not a chance,' said Harry.

They mounted the scooter and rode back to the hotel. Meanwhile, Rhona was giving orders to her men.

'I need you both to go into town and check something out for me. Check out as many hotels as you can in the old part of town. I want to know where Mister Craig and Miss Parker are staying. Report back to me as soon as you find out. Alright, jump to it!'

'What shall we do if we find them?' asked one of the men.

'Do nothing, at least not for now, just report back,' said Rhona.

The two men obeyed, getting into a Mercedes and driving to town. Once there, they parted company, each taking different hotels. There were several hotels in the old town, mostly used by tourists. One of the men, after trying others, ended up at the Casona del Colegio Hotel. He went confidently to the receptionist.

'Excuse me, Señorita, I'm supposed to be meeting my friends, and I can't remember which rooms they are in. Can you help me?'

'Their names?' asked the receptionist.

'Mr Craig and Miss Parker.'

'Yes, they are staying at the hotel,' said the receptionist, checking on her computer. I cannot give you their room numbers, I'm afraid, but would you like me to call them?'

'Oh no, that's okay,' he said, 'I'll come back in a short while.' He then left hurriedly. Once outside, he immediately rang Rhona on his cell phone. 'They're staying at the Casona del Colegio Hotel, boss,' he said.

'Room number?' asked Rhona.

'They wouldn't give me the room number, boss.'

'Alright, at least I know where they are. You'd better come back now,' she said.

'Will do, boss,' said the man, 'as soon as I've found Carlos.'

'Well, don't take too long,' Rhona said.

Emily was in Harry's room. She was about to phone DI Jones in Britain when Harry's room phone rang. 'Señor Craig, it's Maria in reception, I thought I should call you. Are you expecting to meet with a friend at the hotel?'

'A friend? No,' Harry said.

'Well, there was a man here just a few minutes ago enquiring about your room number. I thought I should let you know.'

'I take it you didn't tell him?'

'No, Señor Craig, it's against our policy.'

'Thank you for letting me know, Maria. Could you let me know if anyone else asks? About me or Miss Parker?'

'Yes, certainly.'

'Someone's been asking questions about us, Emily,' said Harry.

'I don't suppose we know who?' said Emily.

Harry shook his head. 'No doubt about it, though, we've certainly got their attention. You had better make that call to Britain.'

'Yes, I'll do it now.'

It was just after 2pm in Britain when DI Jones's mobile rang. 'DI Jones,' he said.

'Hi, it's Emily Parker. Can you hear me? The line isn't very good this end.'

'Yes, Emily, I can hear you fine. How are things?'

'Well, you're not going to believe this, but I've tracked down Rhona, where she lives, everything. She's here in Cartagena for the taking,' said Emily.

'You're in Cartagena? Have you actually spoken to her? Asked Jones.

'It's a little more complicated than that, I'm afraid. She's heavily guarded. Don't ask me why because I don't know myself yet, but she's obviously into something big here.'

'And there's no mistake? You're absolutely sure it's her?'

'Absolutely! Will you be coming out here to arrest her?' asked Emily.

'I don't know, Emily, I would need top clearance to do that. Are you there alone?'

'I have a friend, who without his help, I would never have got this far.'

'Look, I'll take this to the Chief Constable and get back to you. In the meantime, don't do anything stupid.'

'We've been warned off a couple of times already. It's beginning to get dangerous, I hope you can send someone, or better still, come yourself,' said Emily.

'Just hold fast. I'll get back to you by the end of the day,' said Jones.

'He's getting back to me, Harry,' said Emily, once the call had ended.

'Well, let's hope they come out and arrest her as soon as possible. In the meantime, I think we should lay low for a while. As you said, it's becoming far too dangerous, said Harry.

# *Chapter 43*

AMONG OTHER BUSINESS INTERESTS, Rhona owned The Café Havana, yet she still enjoyed the thrill of the stage lights being on her. It had never left her. However, she had given up singing and now only occasionally played the guitar at her club. She was a surprisingly talented Spanish guitar player, as Emily had discovered herself only the night before.

Now she prepared for the Tuesday evening performance, getting dressed in her personal room backstage. Rhona had amassed a good deal of money by marijuana farming and heroin manufacture in a factory within the grounds of her villa. She had a regular wholesale buyer for her goods. She never had to work hard; the money just kept rolling in on a regular basis.

When she absconded from England, she had emptied the joint account she held with her second husband, Peter, it was enough to start building an empire in a country such as Columbia. She had enjoyed life in Cartagena, the captive audience of her club, the only one for miles offering live entertainment. The regular income from that and her other business interests made for an extremely comfortable life.

Time had not softened her, though; she was still as selfish and ruthless as she had always been. Which was exactly why her boyfriend, Daniel Blake, had to die. He, like everyone in Rhona's circle, was watched constantly. Disloyalty was not tolerated. Like Peter before him, he increasingly found Rhona to be a bully and was planning to leave her, and when he was observed talking to a stranger, he had, in effect, sealed his own fate.

Now, Rhona faced yet another problem, her disobedient and troublesome daughter and the reason she had to flee the country in the first place. Yes, she had little doubt it was Emily, she remembered the name of the people that had taken her into their care as being Parker. Now, she had to find a way of dealing with Emily and her friend. Rhona speculated idly for a moment as to why Emily had travelled halfway around the world to find her. Was it curiosity? Retribution?

Her stage makeup finished, she picked up the phone in her dressing room and dialled the number for the hotel where Emily was staying. 'I'd like to speak to Miss Emily Parker. She's a guest at your hotel,' she said.

The receptionist dialled Emily's room number and then continued dealing with a guest. Emily was getting ready for dinner, struggling with a zip at the back of her dress. She eventually managed to pull up the zip and picked up the phone.

'Hello, is that you, Harry? Sorry, I was just getting dressed.'

'Hello Emily,' Rhona said, in a sinister tone of voice.

Emily recoiled and dropped the handset. She hesitated before picking it up from the bed where it had fallen.

She hesitated still further before speaking. 'Mother?' she said.

'Yes, this is mother,' said Rhona. 'I understand you would like to see me.'

'Yes, I would,' said Emily.

'Clever girl, tracking me down like this,' said Rhona, 'I'd love to hear how you did it.'

'Can we meet?' asked Emily nervously.

'I'll send a car for you at midnight. Look for a silver Mercedes outside the hotel.'

She paused again before answering, 'Alright, I'll be there.'

'Oh, and make sure you're alone. Whatever you have to say is between you and me, agreed?'

'Agreed,' said Emily. Rhona then hung up abruptly.

Emily was stunned and frightened. Was she being foolish to agree to such a meeting? Yet it seemed the best chance yet she had of confronting her mother about the treatment of her and the children all those years ago and, of course, the murder of her father. Would she also become a victim? And should she tell Harry about the conversation?

Harry called Emily's room at 7pm to escort her to the hotel restaurant for dinner. He detected an unease about her. 'Are you okay? You look a little pale,' he said.

'Yes, I'm fine,' said Emily curtly.

'You're clearly not. After all we've been through, I've never seen you so on edge.'

'Stop fussing, Harry. I said I'm fine, and I am. Let's just go to dinner, shall we?' she said.

He brushed aside her odd mood. 'Whatever you say,' he said.

The conversation at dinner was not as lively as it could have been. Emily was clearly distracted.

Harry looked at Emily thoughtfully. 'I guess it's too early to have heard anything from the police back in Britain, Huh?

'Yes, far too early. Things happen a little slower back home compared to the States,' she replied.

He continued to study her as she drank her wine in uncharacteristically large gulps. She refilled her glass.

'What?' she asked Harry irritably.

'Nothing, nothing at all,' he said.

'So why are you looking at me like that?'

'Like what?' he said, grinning.

'Now you're laughing at me,' said Emily.

'I promise, I'm not laughing at you. But you don't seem yourself. Are you keeping something from me?'

'No, of course not. But just for the record, if I were, it'd be to protect you, okay, but I'm not, so it's all academic.'

'Okay, okay, you win, Emily.'

'I'm sorry, Harry, I'm just a little tired and I have a headache. I think I'd like to call it a night if that's okay?'

'Yeah, absolutely. Come on, I'll take you back to your room.'

They reached Emily's room, and Harry kissed her cheek. 'Well, I hope you feel better. See you in the morning, goodnight honey.'

'Goodnight, Harry, I'm sorry I haven't been very good company.'

'Nonsense, you're always good company. Goodnight then.'

She closed her door. Harry's smile turned to one of concern. It was 9pm by then.

Harry went to his room but could not relax. He went downstairs again and ordered a beer in the bar, then another and another, until midnight finally arrived. The hotel was quiet at that time of night; the bar had closed and only a small number of guests were entering the hotel after spending time in the town. Finally, all had entered the elevator, heading for their rooms.

Harry heard the clattering of heels at pace going out of the hotel. He jumped to his feet and rushed to the lobby to see Emily making for the street. He shouted to her—she was at the doors by now. She turned and looked back at him briefly but did not stop. He gave chase, but it was too late; he saw her getting into the Mercedes, which sped off into the night. Where to, he didn't know.

Harry stood in the street, froze for a moment, wracked with a deep sense of panic. There were no cabs in the vicinity, and the panic in him grew with every passing second. He spotted a beaten-up pick-up truck that was parked on the opposite side of the street and ran over to it— the door was unlocked. Harry climbed inside, but there was no ignition key. He hurriedly tugged at some wires under the dashboard and, joining two of them together, managed to hotwire the vehicle with a spark. The engine roared to life, and he drove off in the direction Emily had gone.

He drove as fast as the truck could go. He could see in the rear-view mirror the owner of the truck standing in the street, waving his fists, but the only thing that concerned him was finding Emily. He quickly realised he was heading North on the road that led to Rhona's villa, which only served to increase his anxiety. Emily's behaviour at dinner was making sense now. Had she somehow made a contact with Rhona? he wondered. If so, then how?

It was some distance to Rhona's from the town. Harry glanced at the fuel gauge. It was low. He just hoped there was enough to get him there and to get him there in time before anything happened to Emily. If Emily *was* meeting with Rhona, then Harry, from what he had learned during the last few days, could not imagine the outcome to be a good one, and of course, whoever took Emily had the advantage of a fast car and a good head start.

*Chapter 44*

THE DRIVER, A MAN EMILY DID NOT recognise as one of the heavies she had encountered before, pressed a button on his remote control. The gates to the villa slowly opened and the car went up the long steep drive. Emily's heart pounded as the car got closer and closer to the gates of the villa. Now, she was finally going to see her mother after all this time, something she had long wanted. She realised now that she had no idea what to say to her. Perhaps it was simply nerves. Emily was unsure.

Harry had told her that the villa and grounds were impressive, yet Emily was still shocked to see it for herself as they approached the front of the building. The car stopped, the driver got out, took Emily's arm, and led her to the entrance of the villa. He tapped out a series of numbers on the security lock and they entered the spacious and ornate entrance hall. There were many doors leading off from the hall and a large, open staircase. The man opened one of the doors and told Emily to go into the room. He followed after her, closed the door and stood in front of it.

Emily stood perfectly still, unable to move. She saw Rhona standing with a glass of wine in one hand, a cigarette in the other, looking out of the open French windows, her back to Emily.

Rhona turned. 'Would you like a drink?' she asked Emily, her voice just as abrasive as Emily remembered. There was clearly no joy at seeing her daughter.

'No thanks,' said Emily.

'Please yourself,' Rhona said. 'So, what do you want? You've come a long way; you must want something. Is it money you want to keep quiet, or what?'

'It certainly isn't money I've come for,' said Emily.

'Then what?'

'An apology.'

Rhona laughed. 'You've come all this way for an apology? An apology for what? I don't believe you. There must be something more to it than that.'

'Not everyone is like you, mother. Your money doesn't interest me in the slightest.'

'Well, it's obvious you haven't changed. You always were so bloody perfect, weren't you?'

'I'm not perfect by any means, but you were cruel and wicked to us children. Aren't you in the least bit sorry for the way you treated us?'

'It seems a tough upbringing didn't do you much harm. Sorry, huh.'

'You couldn't be more wrong. It's haunted me all my life, the things you did, and as for Bridget, she's an extremely damaged young woman. She'll never be okay. Don't you feel *any* remorse?'

'You're beginning to bore me now,' said Rhona, feigning a yawn.

'Alright, how about the two murders you committed, in particular, my father? What have you got to say about that?'

'Very little. I'm afraid they both outlived their usefulness, and I needed the money. So, I suppose you plan on informing the police of my whereabouts. Correct?'

'They already know you live in Cartagena. Your time is coming to an end, Mother,' said Emily.

'You think so, do you? They won't even get close to me. The only reason *you're* here is because I chose it, otherwise you would never have got to me. And now, I'm tired of you, my dear. Diego, take her to the basement.'

The man took Emily roughly by the arm and led her away. 'What are you going to do to me?'

'We're going to keep you close for the time being,' shouted Rhona.

Diego, once reaching the basement, opened a door and threw Emily unceremoniously into the room. It was dark and humid. She wondered what they had planned for her; would she just be left to rot? Surely though, Harry would suspect where she was and inform the police, she hoped.

Harry had made slow progress. By the time he reached the vicinity of the villa, the truck had chugged to a halt, out of fuel a few hundred yards from the gates. Now, whatever happened, there was no way back to the hotel except for a very long walk. He abandoned the truck and made his way to the wall which he had climbed over the previous night.

Although it was very late, he could see lights emanating from the villa. There was no time to waste, immediately, he climbed over the wall and headed for the villa. As before, floodlights illuminated the grounds like a football pitch. This time, he didn't care, he thought he must reach Emily before anything bad happened, if it hadn't already.

As he got closer to the villa, he saw the Mercedes on the gravel drive directly outside the front entrance. This confirmed that Emily was there. Stealthily, he positioned himself just to the side of the French windows. He glanced cautiously into the drawing room and could see Rhona and just one man standing by her. They seemed to be in deep conversation. There was no sign of Emily in the room.

Harry did not hesitate, he instinctively grabbed a handful of gravel and threw it to the ground, then waited, hidden in a recess of the outer wall. Diego pulled out the gun from his shoulder holster and moved cautiously to the open French windows. He peered onto the grounds, his gun poised for action, then moved outside, his eyes darting from side to side.

Harry moved fast. He jumped the man as he reached the spot where he was hiding. There was a struggle; both men fell to the ground, rolling in the gravel. Diego was much the larger man, yet Harry was trained in self-defence and martial arts. The fight went on until Harry landed a blow to Diego's chin, dazing him for just enough time so that Harry could loosen the man's grip on the gun. He grabbed the gun and struck Diego's head with the haft of the gun, rendering him unconscious.

Harry slowly raised himself from the ground. Rhona had a gun of her own, though, and was now standing in the doorway, pointing it at Harry.

'Drop it!' she said sharply.

'Where's Emily?'

'She's alive, if that's what you mean? Now, drop the gun.'

Harry had little choice; he dropped the gun to the ground.

Rhona gestured with her gun. 'This way,' she said, leading him to the basement. She unlocked it and told him to go inside the room, pointing her gun at him at all times. 'There we are. You can rot with your little friend now,' she said cruelly. She slammed the door shut and returned to the drawing room, by which time Diego had partially recovered from the blow to his head.

'Where is he?' he asked Rhona.

'He's safely locked up with the girl, no thanks to you,' she said.

'Let me get my hands on him, I'll kill him,' said Diego.

'They'll die soon enough,' said Rhona, 'Now leave me, I need to think of how we're going to dispose of them.'

Harry and Emily embraced when they were reunited in the basement. 'Thank goodness you're okay,' said Harry.

'I'm glad you are too. How did you manage to get here?' asked Emily.

'When I saw you being driven away, I stole a truck, I guessed this was where you were being taken.'

'And now you're in danger as well. You shouldn't have come,' said Emily.

'How did you end up coming here anyway?' asked Harry curiously.

'Rhona somehow found out where I was staying. She called me at the hotel and said she'd send a car to pick me up. I'm sorry I was so secretive; I just didn't want to put you in danger.'

'Well, I guessed as much; that's why I stayed up after you went to your room, and here I am,' said Harry. 'Now we have to figure a way out of this hole we've got ourselves into, and fast.' Harry felt in his trouser pocket for his cigarettes and lighter, took one from the pack and lit it. 'Would you like one?' he said, offering the pack to Emily. She rarely smoked but took one. Harry lit it for her, then, with his lighter, searched the room for anything that might be useful.

The basement was almost empty, but searching every corner with what little light he had, Harry managed to find a few lengths of timber in a far recess of the room. Also, lifting his cigarette lighter higher, he noticed there was an opening to the ground floor. It was small, narrow and too high to reach, but he thought that Emily might just fit through if they could somehow get to it.

He pondered the situation for a moment. 'Do you think you get crawled through that window if I were to get you up there on my shoulders?' he asked.

'I don't know, but I'll try,' she said.

'Okay, let's give it a try,' said Harry.

'But what about you?' asked Emily.

'Never mind that right now. If you can get out, it'll help. Now, if you manage it, just run and hide as far away as you can.'

'I'm not happy about leaving you, Harry,' said Emily.

'I'll be fine, don't worry about me. Now, climb onto my back first of all,' he said, stooping down. 'That's it, now step onto my shoulders and steady yourself against the wall. I'm going to slowly stand up so you can reach the window, okay?'

He raised himself until he was upright, with Emily precariously balancing on his shoulders. 'Are you okay? Can you reach?' asked Harry.

'I'm almost there, but I'm not sure if I can pull myself through the opening,' said Emily anxiously.

'Do you need more height?' said Harry.

'A little, but I don't see how unless you're miraculously going to grow by a couple of feet.

'Okay, I'm going to grab your feet and push you up.' With all his strength, Harry took hold of her ankles from his shoulders and pushed Emily upwards. The strain on his arms was tremendous as he pushed and held her in position. 'Any good now?' he said, his voice strained.

'Yes, I'm there, I've opened the window, and I'm pulling myself through,' Emily said. There was a brief moment of silence as the pain left his arms, and Emily made her way outside. She poked her head back inside. 'I'm still not happy about this,' she whispered to him through the opening.

'Just run, but don't be seen or heard. Go on, run, now!' ordered Harry.

Emily did as she was told and ran towards some shrubs and hid while she caught her breath. She could hear Rhona's guitar coming from the villa, the piece was the same as the one she had played at the Café Havana. Emily was spellbound by its beauty. Yet behind that beauty, she was only too aware of the beast that played it. She began to run again, she had no idea where to go, she only remembered Harry telling her to get as far away as possible.

# *Chapter 45*

CAPTAIN SANCHEZ'S INVESTIGATION INTO the Blake murder was going nowhere. He had hit a brick wall without any clues or prime suspects, that is, apart from Harry Craig, yet he knew he had no evidence or even a motive for why Harry would murder Daniel Blake. He was working late into the night, catching up on paperwork and examining case files, especially the Blake case.

Sanchez was a diligent man who took his job seriously. He would not rest until a case was solved, this, at times, meant painstaking investigation, pouring over every shred of evidence, but this case was proving difficult. In the absence of any additional information, he decided he had no choice but to bring in Harry Craig for further questioning the next morning.

By 1am, he'd had enough for one day and decided it was time to go home to his bed. He left his office and went into the main reception. Before going home, he stopped by the desk. 'Anything going on tonight?' he asked, he asked the night officer.

'Not much, sir, a couple of thefts from tourists, pickpockets, I suppose, and a vehicle theft from outside The Casona del Colegio Hotel, and that is about it tonight so far.'

'Okay, goodnight then.' The captain, weary from a long day, headed to the door but turned to the officer again. 'Wait, did you say the Casona del Colegio?'

'Yes, sir.'

'Any witnesses?' asked the captain.

'Only the owner of the truck. He saw the vehicle being driven off, heading North.'

'Did he see who was driving?'

'No sir, it all happened too fast, apparently.'

'Have any officers tried to find the vehicle?'

'Not yet, sir.'

'Well, get on to it now, send a car,' the captain blasted.

'But sir?'

'Don't argue, man, send a car, North, now! I'm going to drive out there myself, too. It's just a hunch, but I may need backup.'

The junior officer looked confused but reached for the radio handset and ordered a car to proceed North in search of the vehicle.

Captain Sanchez went to his car, and he suddenly felt more awake. He drove off at speed, heading in a Northerly direction out of the town, and along the lonely coastal road. After travelling for a few miles, he became aware of a vehicle following behind and, as it got closer, realised it was the police car he had ordered.

They were now ten miles from Cartagena, and Sanchez wondered how much further they could travel. The road went on for miles beyond Rhona's villa. If he did not find the stolen truck soon, his colleagues might well think him mad for going to so much trouble over what seemed to be a fairly routine theft.

Soon, though, they reached the turn in the road which led to Rhona's driveway. Sanchez slammed on the brakes, noticing with his headlights track marks on the dusty road, he took the turning, the police car behind him followed. Much to his relief, Sanchez spotted the truck just before the gates of Rhona's villa. He got out of his car as did the other officers.

'It's abandoned captain, what now?' asked one of the officers.

'But why here?' said Sanchez, 'it makes no sense.'

'A joy-rider maybe?' said an officer.

Sanchez shook his head. 'No, why would they pull off the road in the middle of nowhere? Where would they go on foot from here? There's nothing around here for miles,' he paused for a moment, 'except this place, of course,' he said, pointing to the villa.

He looked for an intercom near the gates, but there was none, only a notice saying, "Private, Keep Out."

'Does anyone know who lives here?' asked Sanchez. The two officers shook their heads. 'Well, I think we should find out, don't you? Get over that wall, will you,' he said to the officers.

They both managed to scale the wall and end up on the ground. 'Now give me a minute,' said Sanchez, struggling to climb over. He was older than the others. In fact, he was approaching retirement. He finally climbed the wall and fell unceremonially to the other side.

'Okay, let's go up to the house,' he said, brushing away the grass from his uniform.

They walked up the grassy incline to the villa amid the glare of the floodlights. Only fifty yards from the main entrance, they were confronted by Diego, who, seeing their uniforms, concealed his gun. He greeted them with a smile. 'What can I do for you, officers?' he said.

'There is a vehicle abandoned outside this property; we believe it to be stolen. Are you aware of it? Has anyone approached you tonight?' asked Sanchez.

'No, Señor, no one has been here,' said Diego.

'Are you the property owner?' asked Sanchez.

'No, Señor, the owner is Rhona Thorne. You may know her as the owner of The Café Havana. I am her security officer.'

'I see, yes, I recognise the name. Would it be possible to speak with her?' asked Sanchez.

'I'm afraid she is in bed; it's very late after all.'

'Yes, of course. And you haven't seen anyone all night, you say?'

'No, Señor, as I already said, I've seen no one.'

'Okay, thank you for your time, goodnight.'

'I'll be sure to open the gates for you on your way out,' said Diego.

'Thank you,' said Sanchez.

As Sanchez and his officers walked away, Sanchez said, 'He's lying.'

'What makes you say that, sir?' asked one of the officers.

'A gut feeling, nothing more than that at the moment. Get on the radio to headquarters and get them to check the current status of a Harry Craig at the Casona del Colegio hotel, will you? Oh, and also, Emily Parker. I want to know if they're in their rooms right now.'

'Is this something to do with the Blake case,' asked one of the officers.

'It might be,' said Sanchez.

About twenty minutes passed as they stood waiting for news from the hotel. The police radio crackled to life. A voice began to speak. 'The hotel staff have tried phoning both of their rooms. They've even gone to their rooms. Personally, neither of them is there,' said the voice over the radio.

Sanchez checked his watch. 'It's 1.30am, I'm sure this place is where we will find them,' he said.

# Chapter 46

HARRY SAT ON THE FLOOR of the basement, smoking a cigarette, wondering where Emily was. Had she got away? Was she safe? Had she been captured? He had no way of knowing. He felt powerless to do anything.

Emily, meanwhile, had done as Harry said and ran as far away as possible from the villa. She found herself at the outer perimeter of the grounds and near the cliffs. Without any means of transport and having had her mobile phone taken from her, there was nothing she could do to get help. Emily wondered if Harry was safe and how long it would take before Diego and Rhona realised she had escaped and began looking for her. She considered for a moment, walking back to the town, but decided against it, as it would take at least an hour to get there on foot.

Emily could not bear to think of Harry being at the mercy of Rhona and her men, while she hid away in relative safety, and having thought about it, she decided to make her way back to the villa. It was, she considered, the right thing to do, even if she was in danger of being recaptured.

She had noticed a large timber building earlier within the grounds and thought there might be something inside that could help in rescuing Harry, a rope, anything. And as she approached the building, she noticed a faint glimmer of light from inside. Emily hesitated before going any closer. Would there be someone inside the building? She steeled herself after a few moments and reached the doors. She opened one of them carefully. It creaked slightly as she entered.

There was no one to be seen. There were rows of plants under plastic sheeting. The air was heavy with the smell of marijuana. She soon realised that Rhona was running a drug farm, which may have partly explained her need for such heavy protection, as well as the fact she was wanted for murder in Britain. Rhona was almost certainly responsible also for the murder of Blake, who had given the tip-off about her location earlier and subsequently given further details to Harry. The building seemed deserted of people. She explored, searching for something that might help her to rescue Harry.

Captain Sanchez's request for backup arrived. He told them to wait for further orders from him and to stay by the villa gates while, once again, he and his two officers scaled the wall and walked up the sweeping lawn that led to the villa.

'You think that Señor Craig and the lady are here, sir?' said one of the officers as they walked.

'I don't know what is going on yet, but yes, I'm convinced they are here,' said Captain Sanchez.

'Do you still think that Craig is involved in the Blake case?'

'Involved? Yes, but whether he is responsible or not, I'm not so sure,' said Sanchez.

They were a hundred yards from the villa when the door opened. Diego, once again had observed them walking up the well-manicured lawns and pre-empted them pulling the doorbell. 'You again, gentlemen. What can I do for you this time?' said Diego.

The captain was as diplomatic as he could be. 'Are you absolutely certain you've seen nobody tonight, Señor?' he asked.

'I told you, I've seen no one,' Diego said impatiently.

'Hmm, you see, the problem we have, Señor, is that there is nobody in the vicinity outside of these grounds, and we're miles from anywhere else,' said Sanchez.

'I still don't see –'

'Would you mind if we took a look inside?'

Rhona appeared from her bedroom dressed in a nightgown. She came down the large staircase that ended in the main entrance hall. 'What can I do for you, captain? I'm the owner.'

'Good morning. Señora Thorne, is that correct?'

'Yes, that's right. What seems to be the trouble?'

'Oh, nothing much, Señora. We've traced a stolen vehicle near your property, the thief could be dangerous, and we would like to check your property and grounds, if that's okay with you?'

'I don't see why not, captain,' said Rhona charmingly, 'if there's someone potentially dangerous on the loose, you need to catch him, don't you? Please, come in.'

'Thank you, Señora,' said Sanchez, entering the spacious hall with his men. 'Is it okay if I set my men to work checking your rooms?'

'Of course, carry on, but I don't think they'll find anyone, Diego is very good at his job,' said Rhona.

The captain looked at Diego with a low grin, 'Yes, I'm sure he is,' he said.

Captain Sanches gestured to his men to get to work. They obeyed and started their search of the rooms upstairs first. There were many rooms to check, but eventually, they reported back to Sanchez that they were all clear.

'Okay, well, try the downstairs rooms, and be sure to be thorough in your search,' he said.

'Can I get you something to drink, captain?' asked Rhona.

'No, thank you, Señora, we'll be done here soon.'

Emily was making her way back to the villa. She had found two sets of overalls in the marijuana farm, and had tied them together in the hope that Harry would be able to squeeze himself out of the narrow opening of the basement at the rear of the villa. She sprinted all the way back to the villa, worrying that some harm could happen to Harry at any time. She soon arrived and whispered to him through the opening.

'Harry, are you still there?'

'Emily, what are you doing here? I told you to get away,' he said.

'I know, but I came back for you. Do you think you can squeeze through?' she said, dropping one end of the overalls down to him.

'Clever girl, I'll certainly give it a go. Okay, pull me up.'

Harry clambered up the inside wall as Emily pulled hard. He reached the opening when he heard the basement door rattling. 'Get away, Emily, someone's coming.' He dropped to the floor once again. He wondered what was in store for him. Then, the rattling stopped as quickly as it had started.

One of Sanchez's officers reported back. 'There is one place we can't check, sir. The door is locked.'

'Show me,' said Sanchez.

The officer took him to the basement door. Harry, on the other side, heard the rattling again as Sanchez tried it. 'Where does this lead to? Can I have the key?'

He turned to Rhona, who had now taken the gun from her nightgown pocket and was pointing it at him and his officer. Diego also had his gun trained on them.

The second of Sanchez's officers appeared from one of the rooms, taking Rhona and Diego by surprise. The officer recognised what was happening and reacted fast by drawing his gun and firing. He drew Rhona's and Diego's fire and took a bullet in his shoulder; he dropped to the floor. It gave Sanchez enough time to draw his gun and fire at Diego. He found his target, Diego fell to the floor with a mortal wound to his chest. Rhona backed towards the main door, her gun pointed at Sanchez and his officer. She then ran off into the night.

'You stay here and shoot that lock off,' said Sanchez to his officer, 'I'm going after the woman.'

'Is there anyone in there?' shouted the officer.

There was what seemed a long pause, but eventually, Harry shouted back. 'Yes, Harry Craig, who's that?'

'The police Señor. Stand back from the door, I'm going to shoot the lock.' The officer released four shots around the lock and then tried the door. It opened, and Harry made his way out with his hands up.

'Señor, what is going on here exactly?' asked the officer.

'It's a long story. Have you found Emily? Is she safe?'

'Not yet, but we will. Excuse me a moment, I have to radio for an ambulance. My friend has been shot.'

'I have to go and find Emily,' said Harry.

'I would advise against it, Señor Craig, the woman, she has a gun.'

'I still have to go,' said Harry, grabbing Diego's gun and running out of the front doors. He could just make out Captain Sanchez in the distance. There was no sign of Emily or Rhona.

He followed in Sanchez's footsteps, realising he must be in pursuit of Rhona. But Emily was his main concern. He had to find her. He shouted her name several times, but there was no answer. Harry caught up with Sanchez. He had lost Rhona. She was too quick for him and knew the grounds.

'I've called my back up team on the radio, they're joining the search of the grounds,' said Sanchez.

'Maybe it would be better if we split up,' Harry said.

'Yes, good idea, but take great care. You can explain all of this to me later, Mr Craig,' said Sanchez.

'It'll be my pleasure. Does this mean I'll get my passport returned to me?' said Harry.

'I think we can safely say that, yes,' said Sanchez, with a smile.

'Okay, I'll go right if you take the left of the grounds,' Harry said.

Sanchez nodded. 'Okay.'

They went their separate ways, Harry heading, unaware to him, towards the cliffs. He kept shouting Emily's name, but there was still no answer. He kept going. Already, the morning light began to show itself, much to his relief. It would make finding Emily a little easier. If she was hiding, she was doing a good job, he thought.

He had almost reached the end of the extensive grounds of Rhona's villa. He shouted again. 'Emily! Where are you? It's Harry.'

He thought he heard his name being called; it was faint, yet he was certain it was Emily's voice. He kept moving, all the time calling her name. When she answered this time, he heard her voice more clearly calling out his name; he was getting closer, and she sounded scared.

# Chapter 47

'WHY DID YOU HAVE TO COME HERE?' Rhona asked Emily, pointing her gun at her.

'I told you before,' said Emily, 'I need to hear you say sorry for what you did to me, Bridget and Simon.'

'You've ruined everything. I had a good life here until you had to poke your nose in.'

'That's exactly what I'm saying. You are, and always were, selfish to the core. A psychopath and a murderer,' said Emily.

'So, what's one more murder?' Rhona said menacingly. 'Although, I suppose your death could be seen as an accident,' she added.

'I don't think so, do you?' said Emily.

'These cliffs are lethal; one false step, and it's a very long drop.'

'And you really think the police will believe that?' said Emily.

'They'll have to. There are no witnesses to say otherwise,' Rhona said confidently.

'You really are quite mad, aren't you?'

Rhona laughed. 'You think so? Keep moving back, Emily.'

With the gun pointed at her, Emily had no choice but to do as Rhona ordered. She walked slowly backwards, getting closer and closer to the cliff edge. 'Aren't you even curious about Bridget and Simon?'

'Stop talking and keep moving. You think you're so clever, using delaying tactics, but then you always were trouble, weren't you?'

'I was trouble? You abused and neglected us children for your own selfish needs. You murdered my father *and* my stepfather. How can you stand there and say that *I* was trouble? All I want from you right now is an apology.'

'Keep moving!' said Rhona, losing her patience.

Emily took no more than one step at a time; she was just a few feet away from the cliff's edge now, the earth and rock becoming more unstable underfoot.

'Good girl, just a little further. It won't be long now,' said Rhona.

Emily tripped on the uneven ground a little as she moved closer to the edge. 'You can't possibly hope to get away with this,' she said, looking behind her at the precarious cliff edge.

'We'll see. Goodbye Emily.'

'Rhona!' came a voice from behind. Rhona turned in shock to see Harry pointing a gun at her. She slowly moved closer to Emily, her arm outstretched in readiness to give Emily a final push. Harry did not hesitate a moment longer. He pulled the trigger. Rhona stumbled as the bullet hit her, but with her last breath, she pushed Emily over the cliff, then, losing her balance, fell over the cliff herself. Harry rushed to the edge. He could see Rhona's prostrate body on the rocks below, the sea waves lapping around her.

And much to his relief, he could see Emily clinging to the rocky edge just a few feet below him. 'Okay, I've got you,' said Harry, stretching his arms to reach her. He pulled her to safety at the top of the cliff, where she slumped to the ground, exhausted.

'I thought I'd lost you for a moment, Emily,' said Harry, 'I'm sorry I was so late.'

'Don't be silly, Harry, you saved my life.' Emily looked over the cliff down to the rocks below, her mother's arms and legs flailing around in the waves that washed around her.

'She's finally gone,' said Emily. 'She didn't have one word of regret, you know.'

Harry nodded sympathetically. 'People like that never do, Emily,' he said, 'are you okay?'

'A little sad, but yes, I'm alright.'

'Come on, let's get you away from here,' said Harry.

'I'm all for that,' said Emily, 'thank you, Harry, I'm certain I'd be dead now if it wasn't for you,' she said, kissing his cheek.

'Don't go getting all sentimental on me. Let's find Sanchez and get this mess over with and put this behind you once and for all,' he said.

'Yes, you're right,' said Emily, 'I suppose it's always been there in the back of my mind. Now, at last, I have some closure. I don't know how I'm going to tell my sister that my mother is dead. It won't be easy.'

'You'll find a way. And who knows, it may just bring closure for her as well,' said Harry comfortingly as the dawn broke.

'You're a good man, Harry Craig,' said Emily as they walked back to the villa.

'I know,' he joked.

Emily laughed. 'I'm going to miss you,' she said quietly.

'I'll miss you too, honey, more than you could know,' said Harry.

After a short while, they found Sanchez and his men heading towards them. 'We heard a gunshot, but we weren't sure where it came from,' said Sanchez, 'are you both okay? Where is Rhona Thorne?'

'She's back there, at the bottom of the cliffs,' said Harry, 'the shot came from me. She tried to kill Emily, but I got there just in time.'

'Okay, you two go back to the villa. Some of my officers are there. Have a drink. You both look like you could use one.

I'm going to take a look at the body. I will have to get it recovered by boat. We will, of course, have a lot of questions to ask you, but that can wait.'

'Thank you, captain, we'll see you later,' said Harry.

Police cars were in abundance when Emily and Harry reached the villa. There were also two ambulances in attendance. One of the crews was giving first-aid to the officer who had been shot in the shoulder while the other loaded the body of Diego into their vehicle. Emily's trousers were torn at the knees and blood-stained where she had fallen. One of the crew applied dressings.

'Can we get a drink?' Harry asked one of the police officers, 'Sanchez said it would be okay.'

'Help yourself,' said the officer. 'Was the woman found?' he added.

'Yes, I'm afraid she's dead,' said Harry.

They both sipped a large glass of brandy each and sat down on one of Rhona's sofas, both slumping back with relief that their ordeal was over. 'You know, despite everything that's happened, Harry, it's been fun,' said Emily, 'am I wrong to say that?'

'No, you're not wrong, I was thinking exactly the same thing,' Harry said reassuringly.

'I'd do it all again, you know, Harry,' said Emily.

'Me too, it's been quite an adventure,' said Harry.

An hour later, Captain Sanchez returned to the villa. He found the two asleep in each other's arms on the sofa. He rocked Harry's shoulder gently; he woke with a start. 'I think it's time we got you back to your hotel for some proper rest. I'll speak to you later in the day. It's been a long night for all of us.'

'That sounds good to me, captain,' said Harry as he gently woke Emily from her deep sleep.

'Come, I'll take you back in my car,' said Captain Sanchez.

DEATH FALL

*Chapter 48*

IT WAS 9AM WHEN SANCHEZ dropped them off at their hotel. They went straight to Emily's room, where they dropped onto the bed and fell asleep immediately. Emily woke after four hours to find Harry was no longer next to her. She called his room number, but there was no answer at first, so she tried again.

'Hello,' said Harry.

'Where were you? I was worried,' said Emily.

'I didn't want to wake you; I woke up and decided to come to my room for a shower and change of clothes. Do you feel better now you've had a rest?'

'Yes, thanks, much better. I'm sorry, Harry, I just panicked for some reason,' said Emily.

'It's okay, that's understandable after what you've been through. Look, I don't want to use the word celebrate, but do you feel like going out tonight for a good meal and a few drinks to mark the end of our adventure?'

'That sounds pretty final. Are you going home?'

'Well, my vacation is almost over. I'll have to return to my work soon,' he said sombrely.

'Oh, I see. In that case, yes, I'd like that,' said Emily, 'and yes, I suppose I should be leaving quite soon as well. After all, we both have our jobs to think about, don't we?'

'Yeah, I guess we do. Anyway, let's not think about that just yet. We'll go somewhere really special tonight,' said Harry, lightening the mood.

'Yes, that'd be nice,' said Emily.

Once she had hung up the phone, she fought back a tear. She felt low at the thought of not seeing Harry again once he returned to the States and her to England. It was too painful to contemplate. She took a shower in an effort to wash away the fear of losing him forever.

A short while later, Harry received a call from Captain Sanchez. 'Now we are all rested. Could you and Miss Parker come to the police headquarters to go through some formalities?'

'Yes, of course, what time?'

'Well, there's no time like the present, I'll send a car for you now, if that's alright?'

'Okay, I'll let Miss Parker know,' Harry said.

Fifteen minutes later, they found themselves in the back of a police car on their way to police headquarters. 'What you said earlier about going back to the States, will I see you again?' asked Emily.

'You can be sure of it,' said Harry, gently squeezing Emily's hand as the car came to a halt outside the police headquarters.

'Good afternoon, I hope you are suitably refreshed,' said Captain Sanchez, 'come into my office. There are a few loose ends to clear up. It should not take too long. The body of Rhona Thorne has been recovered, by the way. So, let us start at the beginning. What was your connection with her?'

'She was my mother,' said Emily, 'She was wanted for two murders in the U.K., my stepfather and my real father. I came here in the hope of getting her back home to face trial. You can check all of this with the British police.'

'I will,' said Sanchez. 'And what about Señor Blake's murder?'

'It's exactly as I told you, captain,' said Harry, 'he was the one that originally contacted Emily, or should I say, the newspaper she works for, giving information about Rhona's whereabouts. The trouble was, he didn't say exactly where in Cartagena. That's why I had to contact him.'

'And did he tell you?' asked Sanchez.

'Oh yes, he told me we would find her at the Café Havana, and as you know, he paid the price for giving me that information. I still don't know how he was connected to Rhona, though; I didn't get the chance to find out,' said Harry. 'As you know, I returned to meet him again and pay him for the information. By that time, of course, unknown to me, he was already dead.'

'It seems she had a great deal to lose from you trying to get to her,' said Sanchez, 'we found a drug factory on her grounds. She was farming marijuana and manufacturing heroin. She had quite an operation going on. I suppose if it had not been for you poking around, we may never have found it.'

'So what now, captain?' asked Harry.

I'll need official statements from you both. After that, you're free to go,' said Sanchez.

After writing their statements, Harry said, 'My passport?'

Sanchez grinned, took it from his desk and handed it to him. 'I believe these cell phones belong to you both as well. How much longer do you both plan on staying in Cartagena?' asked Sanchez.

'Another day, maybe,' said Harry.

'I suppose the same goes for me,' said Emily, 'there's nothing more to stay for.' She looked sadly at Harry as she spoke.

'No offence, but I won't be sorry to see you go. You've created a mountain of paperwork for me,' Sanchez joked.

'Nice meeting you, and thank you,' said Emily.

'Goodbye, it was good to meet you too. I'm sorry it did not work out better for you,' said Sanchez.

'Thanks, captain, Adiós,' Harry said, tipping his hat.

'Well, that's that then,' said Emily to Harry.

'Yeah, I guess it is,' he replied, 'it's been quite an adventure, hasn't it?'

Emily half smiled. 'Yes, you could say that. But now it's over,' she added sadly.

'Yeah, I know. But let's have a good time this evening, eh?'

'Yes, of course,' said Emily, attempting to hide her sadness.

They chose to walk back to the hotel, stopping for a drink along the way. Harry ordered a beer, and Emily an orange juice. 'You know, Emily, being with you and all we've been through, well, it's the best time I've ever had,' said Harry, clutching her hand across the table.

'Me too, I think everything may seem rather boring from now on,' Emily said.

'I know what you mean,' he said.

'Oh well, I suppose we both knew it had to come to an end sooner or later,' said Emily.

'Hmm, yeah, I guess so.'

'So, you told Captain Sanchez you'd be here one more day. That must mean you're leaving tomorrow, right?' asked Emily.

'I really should. I don't want to, but –'

'There's no need to explain,' said Emily, 'I understand. You have a business to run.'

'Emily, I –'

'Please, Harry, don't say any more. Let's just enjoy what time we have left.'

Harry hesitated for a moment, then said. 'Okay, honey, it's a deal.'

In the evening, they found a lively place to eat their last meal together, where there was dancing and a lot of joy. Neither spoke much all evening. They danced closely together.

Harry had booked an early flight the next morning, Emily's was not until the evening. He woke at 5am, his bag already packed, Emily rose with him, and after he'd had a shower and dressed, it was time for them to say goodbye.

'See you, Emily Parker,' said Harry.

'See you, Harry.'

As she watched down the street from her hotel room, she saw him approaching the taxi cab. He looked up sadly towards her and blew a kiss.

Emily returned the kiss; she wondered if she would see him again.

# *Chapter 49*

EMILY'S LONG FLIGHT LANDED in England at around 5pm the next day. She was exhausted both physically and mentally, the parting from Harry had been painful. All she wanted now was to get back to her flat in London and sleep.

The weather in London was in stark contrast to that of Cartagena. It was a dreary day with light rain, which only increased her depressed mood. Once in her flat, she made some tea, kicked off her shoes and laid back on her sofa, and after just a few sips of her tea, she fell asleep.

It was 8pm when she woke to her mobile phone ringing.

'Emily, it's Jones, I've been trying to reach you for days. How are you?'

'Hello, Jonesy, I'm sorry about that, I was going to call you later as a matter of fact.'

'Good news, I've got the go-ahead to fly out to Cartagena to arrest Rhona,' said DI Jones.

Emily paused before speaking. 'I'm afraid that won't be necessary, Jonesy.'

'What do you mean?'

Another pause. 'She's dead.'

'What? Dead? How?' asked a shocked Jones.

'It's a very long story. I'm back home now after a gruelling flight. Could I come to see you tomorrow and explain?'

'I suppose so, but how did she die?'

'Badly! She was shot and fell from a cliff as she was trying to kill me.'

'I'm so sorry, Emily,' said Jones.

'Don't be. It's over. That's all that matters,' said Emily.

'Well, I'd better let my superiors know that the trip is off first thing tomorrow. In a way, she escaped having to serve a lengthy prison sentence.'

'If it's any consolation,' said Emily, 'you probably wouldn't have been able to bring her back home to face justice. She was responsible for one murder that we know of in Cartagena. She would have been arrested for that if she hadn't died.'

'I see. Well, come in to see me tomorrow if you can. There's really no hurry now, is there?'

'I'll do that,' said Emily.

Emily made herself some more tea, settled back on the sofa again and called Patricia's number. 'Pat, it's Emily, are you at work?'

'No, I'm off duty. Where are you?'

'I'm home now, Pat, safe and sound,' said Emily.

'Thank God, I've been worried about you. What happened?'

Emily explained everything in detail.

'My God, you certainly had a lucky escape, Em. So that's it, it's over?' said Patricia.

'Yes, that's it.'

'Changing the subject slightly, what about your mystery man?'

'Harry? He had to fly back to New York for his business. I don't expect to see him again.'

'You sound sad, Em, I take it, it was rather more than a mere flirtation. Something tells me you fell in love.'

Emily fought against a tear. 'We both have our separate lives. As I said, I don't think I'll see him ever again. Such is life,' she said bravely.

'You do love him, don't you?' said Patricia perceptively.

'Yes, yes I do.'

'Call him and tell him how you feel,' said Patricia.

'He knows where I am. If he feels the same way, he'll call me; if not, he won't. Anyway, Pat, there's no point in crying over spilt milk. How are you?'

'I'm fine. Are you going to let mum and dad know that you're home and about where you've really been?'

'I'm going to see them tomorrow, I promise. I feel awful having deceived them, but I didn't want to worry them. I hope they understand.'

'I'm sure they will, the thing is, you're safe, that's all that will matter to them,' said Patricia.

'Yes, I'm sure you're right.'

'I'm off duty again tomorrow. I'll go around there and give you some moral support if you like? It'd be good to see you anyway.'

'That'd be nice,' said Emily, 'right now though, I need more sleep, I'll see you tomorrow, Pat.'

Emily went to bed early. She lay there for some time thinking about Harry and their adventure before finally finding sleep.

The next morning, Emily travelled to Surbiton police station to see DI Jones. He listened to her story with interest. 'It's not that I can't take your word for all of this, but I'll need to corroborate it with the Columbian police. You do understand, don't you, Emily?'

'Yes, of course, you'll need to speak to Captain Sanchez of the Cartagena police, I have his number,' said Emily.

'It's a fantastic story, Emily, so she was a big-time drug dealer as well, you say?'

'Oh yes, she was doing very well out of it too.'

'Does this Captain Sanchez speak English?' asked Jones.

'Yes, he speaks it very well. You won't have any problem there,' said Emily.

'Good, that should make life easier. Okay, Emily, thanks for coming in, I think that's all I need to know. Shame, I was looking forward to a trip to Columbia,' Jones said with a grin.

'I'll keep in touch from time to time, Jonesy,' said Emily.

'Yes, do. Goodbye, for now, Emily.'

After leaving the police station, Emily drove the short distance to her parents' house. She was not sure how she would break the news of where she had been for the past week, or what she had been doing in Columbia. She phoned Gwen ahead of her visit to say she was coming.

'Emily! How lovely to see you. Did you have a good holiday?' asked Gwen.

'Hi mum, it's good to see you too. Is Pat here?'

'Yes, she's in the sitting room. Come through and tell us all about your holiday. Look at you. You've certainly caught the sun.'

'Yes, I suppose I have. Oh, hello Pat.'

'Hi Em,' said Patricia.

'Well, sit down and tell us all about it. I think you said on the phone that you got back yesterday. Is that right?' asked Gwen.

'Yes, that's right. In fact, I still feel a little jet-lagged.'

'You don't get jet lag travelling from Spain, dear,' Gwen laughed.

'I know, and that, apart from wanting to see you all, is why I'm here. I have a confession to make to you,' said Emily awkwardly.

'A confession? What do you mean, a confession?' asked Gwen curiously.

'I wasn't in Spain. I've been to Columbia.'

'Columbia? What on earth for? Why didn't you tell me?'

'I didn't want to worry you, mum. I went in search of Rhona,' said Emily.

'I don't understand,' said Gwen.

'The Express had a tip-off about her. Some guy said he knew where she was, and that was Cartagena in Columbia. I needed to go and follow it up. It was wrong of me not to tell you, I know, I just thought it would be better if you didn't know.'

'Yes, Emily, it was wrong, just please don't lie to me again. Anyway, you're safe, that's the main thing. Did you find her?'

'Eventually, with some help. Anyway, the whole thing is over with now, Rhona's dead,' said Emily.

'How?' asked Gwen.

'She fell over a cliff after being shot by –'

'Oh my God, it sounds to me as if you were in real danger over there. Were you?'

'Let's just say I had someone to keep me safe,' said Emily

'She's being coy, mum, the truth is she met someone special,' said Patricia.

'Did you, Emily? How special? Is it serious?' asked Gwen.

'It's pointless talking about it, really it is,' said Emily.

# *Chapter 50*

EMILY RETURNED TO HER WORK sooner than she had originally expected.

Jean, her editor was surprised to see Emily turn up for work on the following Monday after her return to England.

'Emily, what are you doing here? You weren't due back for another two weeks?' asked Jean.

'I know, Jean. Could I possibly see you in your office for a moment?'

'Yes, of course you can. Is something wrong?'

'Where do I begin?' said Emily, 'Well, it's about the Rhona Thorne story.'

'Oh! Look, Emily, we've been over that already, I'm not able to send you to Columbia on a wild-goose chase. The editor-in-chief won't have it. Besides, it's far too dangerous,' said Jean.

'Actually, Jean, that's where I went during my leave, so it hasn't cost the paper a penny.'

'You've been there. You mean you had this planned all along?'

'Yes, I'm afraid so, but it was during my own time,' said Emily.

'That was very foolhardy of you. Anything could have happened. What *did* happen?'

'Quite a lot, Rhona's dead now. There's a story to be told in the paper if you want it?' said Emily.

'I'm sorry, Emily, was she dead when you arrived there? Did she die of natural causes?' asked Jean.

'No, it was a little more complicated than that. She was killed while trying to kill me.'

'God, what happened exactly? I told you it would be dangerous.'

'With your permission, I'd like to write the story for you to see. It would take too long to explain now. If you like it and want to go to print with it, that's fine. If you don't want the follow-up story, that's fine as well. What do you think?' said Emily.

'Well, yes, I think a follow-up story would be good. Yes, please go ahead. I can't wait to read it. I'm intrigued.'

'Okay, Jean, thanks, I'll start work on it straight away,' said Emily.

'Alright, bring it to me the minute it's done. And Emily, I'm glad you're back safely.'

'Thanks, Jean, me too.'

A few hours later, Emily had finished a rough draft of the story for her editor. She took it to Jean's office.

'There we are, Jean, see what you think, I'll leave it with you,' said Emily, placing the pages on Jean's desk.

'No, stay, take a seat,' said Jean, 'I'm going to read it now.'

Jean read each page in detail, occasionally looking over the rim of her glasses at Emily with a knowing smile. 'Wow, that's quite a story,' she said as she reached the end.

'I know you wouldn't want to print the whole story. I just found it easier to explain what really happened to you on paper,' said Emily.

'What a dreadful woman. It sounds to me like you're lucky to be here,' said Jean, 'and *Harry*? He sounds an interesting character.'

'Yes, he is. I wouldn't have made it without him, I'm certain of that,' said Emily. 'Anyway, that's the whole story.'

'And what a story! I'll need to cut some of it, of course, but yes, we have to print it,' said Jean. 'I'll take it to the editor-in-chief now.'

'Thanks, Jean.'

'Now, you were supposed to be on leave for three weeks. Do you really want to come back to work so soon?' asked Jean.

'Yes, I'd rather be at work, if that's okay?'

'If that's what you want, you can start back officially tomorrow, but for now go home. You've clearly been through a lot.'

'Well, if you're sure?' said Emily.

'Quite sure, all the jobs are already assigned to others today,' explained Jean.

'Okay, well, I'll see you tomorrow then,' said Emily.

When she left the building, Emily found that the morning gloom had made way for a brighter afternoon. It lifted Emily's mood a little as she had to put her story to paper. It'd had a therapeutic effect. Yet still, she could not erase Harry from her memory. But then, she thought, it was early days. The pain would eventually subside, and she would return to her normal everyday life, immersing herself in work.

She made her way home on the tube from Temple Underground. As always, it was very busy. At her Peckham flat, she made some tea and sat by a large window, looking languorously out at the busy street below. Was she somehow expecting Harry to appear? Was he thinking about her, as she was thinking about him? she wondered. She was convinced he would be too busy with his work to be doing that.

What they had found was very special. At least, that was what Emily thought. She truly believed Harry had felt the same way, but they lived and worked thousands of miles apart. Emily told herself to be realistic about any future together. It really was never going to happen, she thought, and yet it seemed she could think of little else. She pulled herself away from the window, made some more tea and lounged on the sofa. She looked at her mobile phone and Harry's number. She thought about calling his number but then dismissed the idea as foolish.

Three and a half thousand miles away, Harry was carrying out telephone inquiries for a big client of his company. He, too, thought about calling Emily but did not surrender to the temptation. Like Emily, he decided to give his work his undivided attention. That way, being so far away would not hurt quite so much, he thought.

Emily's abridged report made the newspaper the next day. From then on, it was back to her normal reporting assignments. Yet among the routine work schedule, she found time to visit her old editor, Bill Mortimer, at The Surbiton News for a chat about her experience and to, once again, thank him for giving her the first job she'd had in journalism.

'I read your story in The Express,' said Bill, 'of course, somehow I always knew you would find Rhona.'

'Did you?'

'Oh yes, you're very resourceful, you always were,' he said.

'Where I am is all down to you, Bill. I really can't thank you enough for what you did for me,' said Emily.

'Nonsense, I'm sure you would have still made it without my help.'

'I don't know about that. Anyway, I'd better be going. I'll see you around, Bill.'

After that, the weeks went by very slowly.

*Chapter 51*

A MONTH WENT BY since Emily's return to England. The newspaper was keeping her busy with many stories to cover. Not least the massacre in Dunblane, she and other reporters were sent there to cover the story, which, to say the least, was extremely traumatic for everyone concerned.

Then, there was the divorce of Prince Charles from Princess Diana, which was mainly covered by the royal correspondent. However, she did have some input into the story. The rest was routine work, but it kept her mind occupied and prevented her thoughts from straying back to Cartagena and her time with Harry. It was during the quiet times in her flat that she thought about him the most. It was at such times that she was very tempted to call him in New York, yet she always held back.

That week happened to be Emily's birthday. Gwen had arranged a family dinner for Friday evening to celebrate, while in the meantime, Jean had also arranged some surprise celebratory drinks in the office after work on Wednesday. So, when Emily had finished for the day and was about to go home, Jean and the others stood around her and sang the birthday song. All the staff received the same treatment on their birthdays, yet it still came as a shock to Emily. She stood, slightly embarrassed as they had sung.

'Thank you so much, everyone, what a lovely surprise,' said Emily.

'Come on, have a drink, birthday girl,' said Jean.

'Oh, lovely,' said Emily, 'I didn't expect this, being a relative newcomer.'

'Nonsense, you're a part of our family now,' said Jean.

'Thanks, Jean, that means a lot.'

'We got you a small gift. Hope you like it,' said Jean, presenting the package to Emily.

'You shouldn't have, really,' said Emily.

'It's only something small,' said Jean.

Emily unwrapped the gift to find it was a very nice pen. 'Oh, it's great, it really is. Thank you all so much,' said Emily.

'Cheers! Happy birthday, Emily,' said Jean, raising her glass. She then steered Emily away from the others. 'The pen is symbolic; I think you should seriously consider writing a book about your experiences.'

'Oh, I don't know about that, Jean.'

'I'm serious, I really think you should – during your own time, of course.'

'I don't think I'd know where to start *or* how to end it,' said Emily.

'Well, maybe the ending hasn't happened yet,' said Jean, 'excuse me a moment, my phone is ringing.'

Jean returned after a minute or so. 'Now, where were we?' she asked, 'oh yes, the ending for your book. Well, who knows, maybe the ending is close at hand.'

'What do you mean?' asked Emily.

At that moment, the lift door opened. All eyes turned, and the room went quiet. Emily's eyes turned away from Jean momentarily. She did a double take until she realised who it was standing outside the lift with a large bunch of flowers and a beaming smile.

'Harry?' Emily said quietly.

'Go to him,' Jean said.

Emily began walking across the press room, as did Harry, it soon became a dash into each other's arms. They embraced closely.

'Happy birthday, honey,' Harry said softly.

'You came,' said Emily, tears of joy in her eyes.

'Yeah, I came.'

'It's a long way to come just to wish me a happy birthday. How did you know anyway?'

'I made a contact with your boss, she told me. But I'm not here just to wish you a happy birthday, Emily. I came because I realised I couldn't live without you,' he said.

'Do you really mean that?'

'I've never been more certain of anything,' said Harry, kissing her gently.

'Maybe Jean was right about an ending,' Emily said.

'What?' asked Harry.

'Oh, nothing, Harry, it's not important.'


The End

9 781805 586937